A DEATH VALLEY CHRISTMAS

Look for these exciting Western series
from bestselling authors
William W. Johnstone and J.A. Johnstone:

The Mountain Man

Preacher: The First Mountain Man

Luke Jensen: Bounty Hunter

Those Jensen Boys!

The Jensen Brand

MacCallister

The Red Ryan Westerns

Perley Gates

Have Brides, Will Travel

Will Tanner, Deputy U.S. Marshal

Shotgun Johnny

The Chuckwagon Trail

The Jackals

The Slash and Pecos Westerns

The Texas Moonshiners

Stoneface Finnegan Westerns

Ben Savage: Saloon Ranger

The Buck Trammel Westerns

The Death and Texas Westerns

The Hunter Buchanon Westerns

A DEATH VALLEY CHRISTMAS

WILLIAM W. JOHNSTONE
and
J.A. JOHNSTONE

KENSINGTON
PUBLISHING CORP.

www.kensingtonbooks.com

KENSINGTON BOOKS are published by

Kensington Publishing Corp.
119 West 40th Street
New York, NY 10018

PUBLISHER'S NOTE
Following the death of William W. Johnstone, the Johnstone family is working with a carefully selected writer to organize and complete Mr. Johnstone's outlines and many unfinished manuscripts to create additional novels in all of his series like The Last Gunfighter, Mountain Man, and Eagles, among others. This novel was inspired by Mr. Johnstone's superb storytelling.

All Kensington titles, imprints, and distributed lines are available at special quantity discounts for bulk purchases for sales promotion, premiums, fund-raising, educational, or institutional use. Special book excerpts or customized printings can also be created to fit specific needs. For details, write or phone the office of the Kensington Special Sales Manager: Attn. Special Sales Department. Kensington Publishing Corp., 119 West 40th Street, New York, NY 10018. Phone: 1-800-221-2647.

Library of Congress Card Catalogue Number: 2021931072

The K logo is a trademark of Kensington Publishing Corp.

ISBN-13: 978-1-4967-3199-9
ISBN-10: 1-4967-3199-9
First Kensington Hardcover Edition: July 2021

10 9 8 7 6 5 4 3 2 1

Printed in the United States of America

A DEATH VALLEY CHRISTMAS

France, December 24, 1917

The raucous strains of a French Christmas carol filled the room as the group of a dozen pilots gathered around a wood-burning stove for warmth on this chilly night. The wine they were consuming—a little on the cheap and sour side, but not too bad—warmed them, as well.

No patrols over no-man's-land and enemy territory tonight, they had been told. As long as the Boche stayed on the ground, so would they.

That respite from death was enough of a reason to celebrate, even if tomorrow were not Christmas Day. Casualties had been high in this squadron. They were high in *all* the flying squadrons.

War, even that fought high in the clean, clear sky, was a dirty business.

On one side of the room, taking their ease in a pair of armchairs, with their legs stretched out in front of them, two men sat and nursed glasses of wine as they watched the ongoing hilarity of their comrades.

One was a compactly built man with a thin mustache. He wore the uniform of a major in the United States Army Air Service, part of the Allied Expeditionary Forces under the overall command of General John J. Pershing.

The other man was a lieutenant in the same service, younger, more rangily built than his companion, with dark hair and a friendly, open face.

The major reached down to the floor beside him and rubbed the ears of an unlikely creature to be found on a military aerodrome: a half-grown lion cub. A slightly larger second cub lay on the floor next to the lieutenant's chair.

"It's good to see the men enjoying themselves," the major said in a voice with a fairly heavy French accent. "A man should be able to forget about killing . . . and dying . . . at this time of year. At least for one night."

"Reckon that'll be up to the Huns," the lieutenant replied. His drawl marked him as a man of the American West.

Until recently, both of these men had been part of the already legendary Escadrille N-124, also known as the Lafayette Escadrille, the unit of the French air force manned by volunteer American pilots. The major had been born in France but had spent a lot of time in the United States, even joining the US Army at one point. He had never lost his accent, though.

The lieutenant, like most of the other pilots, had come over here to France partially because he thought it was the right thing to do—and partially out of a thirst for adventure.

Against the odds, both men had survived numerous combat missions against the German fliers and had shot down a number of enemy planes, enough for both of them to be considered aces. Along with the other American pilots, they had been transferred out of the French air force into an American unit a few months earlier, but the danger had continued. If anything, it had intensified. But they had brought with them their courage and skill—and the two lion cubs named Whiskey and Soda, the squadron's mascots.

The major sipped his wine again and said, "Tomorrow it will be back into Death Valley for us, eh, *mon ami*?"

"Probably," the lieutenant agreed. "I've heard rumors the Boche are planning a big push along this part of the line and are set to go any day now. The brass will want us scouting to see if we can pick up any signs of it." He smiled thinly. "And those fellas in their Flying Circus know that and will be waiting for us."

"Death Valley . . ." the major mused. "How many men have we lost there?"

"Six in the past month," the lieutenant answered bleakly. "I expect that's why they gave the name to that swath of no-man's-land."

The major looked over at him. "There's a place out West in America called Death Valley, isn't there? I've heard of it but never been there."

"Oh, sure," the lieutenant said, nodding. "It's in California. Hottest, driest place you ever saw. As bad as the Sahara, I'll bet, although I haven't been there. The Sahara, I mean. I've been to Death Valley. I even camped there with my dad and uncle and cousins. There's an old family story about the place."

"Really?" the major said. "Is it a good story?" He smiled. "Full of cowboys and shooting, like the other stories I've heard you tell?"

The lieutenant laughed. "Sure. My dad and my uncle were right in the middle of it, and it even happened at Christmastime, too."

The major downed the rest of his wine and reached for the bottle that sat on the small table between the armchairs.

"Well, then, let us hear the tale, Lieutenant. Unless you'd rather listen to more of that atrocious singing . . ."

"No, thanks." The lieutenant scratched the ears of the lion cub Whiskey and went on, "It didn't start in Death Valley. My dad and uncle were farther west, in Los Angeles . . ."

Chapter 1

"I'll take two cards," Chance Jensen said.

The man directly opposite him at the table smiled as he dealt the cards. "You must have the makings of a pretty good hand."

"We'll find out, won't we?"

Ace Jensen stood a few feet away, with his back to the bar and his elbows resting on the hardwood. The half-empty mug of beer he'd been nursing sat next to his right elbow.

From where he was, he couldn't see his brother's cards. Chance might have the makings of a good hand, as the other man had said—or he might be bluffing.

With Chance, anything was possible.

Ace and Chance were twins, but not identical. Ace was an inch taller, twenty pounds heavier, and had a rumpled thatch of dark hair under his pushed-back hat. Chance's hair was sand colored. He wore a flat-crowned brown hat that went well with his tan suit, white shirt, and brown ribbon tie. Ace preferred range clothes: jeans and a denim jacket over a faded red bib-front shirt.

Both brothers packed guns. Ace carried a Colt .45 on his right hip, in a well-worn holster. Chance had a Smith & Wesson in a cross-draw rig under his coat.

They had ridden into the California settlement of Los Angeles earlier today. It was a fast-growing community. The railroad had arrived a few years earlier and brought a lot of new businesses with it.

However, this saloon on the old plaza was a throwback to the days when Los Angeles was a sleepy little hamlet that served the needs of the cattle ranchers in the nearby hills and valleys. The bar wasn't crowded. Customers sat at about half the tables. The poker game in which Chance played was the only one going on.

In one corner, an elderly Mexican sat on a stool and strummed a guitar's strings as he played a quiet tune. A few young women in low-cut gowns drifted around the room, delivering drinks and visiting with the customers.

One of those saloon girls came up on Ace's right side and smiled at him.

"Hello, cowboy," she said. "You look like you could use a drink."

Ace tipped his head toward the beer mug beside his elbow. "Got one."

"Well, you could buy one for me," she suggested.

Ace considered that idea. She was a good-looking girl. Not short, not tall. Dark brown hair that spilled over her shoulders and a short distance down her back. Heart-shaped face. Painted cheeks, but Ace got the impression that they would be rosy even without the paint. Her brown eyes were almost as dark as her hair.

The gown she wore was tight enough and cut low enough to draw any healthy young man's interest. Ace was plenty healthy. He knew all he'd be buying for her was a glass of watered-down tea, but he didn't care. Saloon girls had to earn a living, too.

"Sure," he said. He straightened from his casual pose and turned toward her. "What's your name?"

She cocked her head a little to one side. "They call me Trixie."

"Maybe that's what they call you. I asked what your name is."

She caught her lower lip between straight white teeth and hesitated for a second before saying, "It's Myra. Myra Malone."

"Hello, Myra. I'm glad to meet you." He caught the bartender's eye, slid a coin across the hardwood, and nodded toward the girl. "My name's Ace."

"Maybe that's what they *call* you." Her smile seemed more genuine as her words poked at him.

Ace laughed. "Yeah, I reckon I had that coming. My real name is William Jensen, but I've been called Ace since farther back than I can remember. My brother's name is Benjamin, but he's called Chance. That's him at the poker table, in the brown hat."

"Ace and Chance," Myra repeated. "Your mother must have been a gambler."

"No, but a gambling man raised us. Our mother passed away when we were born. We're twins, although you wouldn't know it to look at us."

Myra's smile dropped off her face.

"Oh, I'm sorry," she said. "Not about you being twins, but about . . . I mean . . ."

"It's all right," Ace told her. "I know what you mean. I'm sorry we never got to know her, but you can't miss what you've never had."

"No, I suppose not."

The bartender put the drink he had poured for Myra on the bar in front of her. His hand swooped over the coin Ace had laid down and made it disappear. Myra picked up the glass and raised it to Ace, who lifted his beer mug in response.

"I'm glad to know you, Ace Jensen—" she began.

She stopped short as a man said in a loud voice, "You bluffed me with a hand like *that*?"

He sounded more surprised than angry.

Ace looked around. Whatever was going on, more than likely Chance was involved in it.

Sure enough, Chance had leaned forward in his chair to rake in the pot from the center of the table. It was a good-sized pile of coins and greenbacks. What looked like a folded piece of paper was mixed in with the money.

The man across the table from him stared at Chance for several seconds, then leaned back in his chair, shook his head, and laughed.

"Well played, young man," he said. "I figured you had at least three of a kind."

"I know," Chance said. "That's what I wanted you to think."

Over at the bar, Ace leaned closer to Myra and said, "Do you know the fella my brother bluffed out of that pot?"

"I do," she said, nodding. "His name is Tom Bellamy."

"He's not the sort who's going to get mad and pull a hideout gun or a knife because he got beat, is he?" Ace set his beer down as he asked the question. His hand moved to hover near the butt of the holstered Colt on his hip.

"I don't think so," Myra said. "If your brother bluffed him and beat him fair and square, I think Tom's more likely to admire that than to get mad."

The way she said the man's name made Ace feel that she was well-acquainted with him. That was a reasonable assumption, since both of them no doubt spent a lot of time in this saloon.

Chance sorted the greenbacks from the pile, squared them up and tapped them on the table to even them out.

Bellamy said, "You're going to give me a chance to win some of that back, aren't you?"

"My brother and I just got into town earlier and haven't had supper yet," Chance replied. He grinned. "There's enough here to buy us some mighty nice steaks."

"There's more than that."

"Yeah, I know." Chance tucked away the folded money inside his coat. He picked up the folded piece of paper. "When you threw this into the pot, you said it's the deed to a silver mine?"

Bellamy's lean, dark face grew solemn. "That's right. It's up in the Panamint Mountains, over on the western edge of Death Valley. Nothing you'd be interested in, kid."

"I don't know about that," Chance mused as he unfolded the deed and studied it. "I've never owned a silver mine."

Ace listened to this conversation with great interest. Chance was right. Neither of the Jensen brothers had ever owned much of anything other than the clothes on their backs, some good guns, and a pair of good horses.

That was all they needed, because they never stayed in one place for very long. They had been born with the urge to drift. It might wear off one of these days, but until it did, they didn't want anything tying them down.

On the other hand . . . *a silver mine* . . . It was hard to turn down an opportunity like that.

Bellamy spread his hands and shrugged.

"If you're sure," he said. "I still think it's only fair that you give me a chance to win back some of what I lost, though."

"Maybe another time."

Chance folded the deed and put it in his coat pocket with the money. He took off his hat and raked the coins into it. Then he stood up, nodded to the men sitting around the table, and said, "Good game, gentlemen. I enjoyed it."

"You should have," one of the men said. "You 'bout cleaned us all out."

"No hard feelin's, though," another man added. "You're good, kid."

"I had a good teacher," Chance said.

He didn't explain that he and Ace had grown up under the care and tutelage of Ennis "Doc" Monday, a professional gambler who had been in love with their mother and had promised her when she was on her deathbed that he would look after the boys. Doc wasn't their father, not by blood, but he had raised them.

Their real father was someone totally different.

Chance carried the hat over to the bar and set it on the hardwood. The coins inside it clinked.

"You reckon you could turn those into bills for me?" he asked the bartender.

"Sure, I suppose so," the man said. He started digging the coins out of the hat.

Chance turned to Myra and smiled. "Well, hello there. I see you've met my brother."

"That's right, Benjamin," she said.

He frowned at Ace. "You told her our real names?"

"I sort of had to," Ace said. "It was only fair." He didn't explain. Instead, he nodded toward the girl. "This is Miss Myra Malone, sometimes known as Trixie."

"Myra is a much prettier and classier name," Chance said as he took her hand. Ace thought for a second Chance was going to kiss the back of it, but he just clasped it instead. "And as such, it suits you much better."

From the corner of his eye, Ace watched the bartender count the coins and then take some greenbacks out of the till. He didn't have any reason to believe the man might try to cheat them, but it never hurt to be careful.

When they had their money, Chance said, "We were about to get some supper. How would you like to join us, Myra?"

She shook her head and sounded genuinely regretful as she said, "I can't. I have to work the rest of the evening. But I recommend that you go along the street a couple of blocks, turn right, and eat at Howell's Café. The food is good, and it's not terribly expensive."

Chance took his hat back from the bartender, put it on, and pinched the brim as he nodded to her. "Much obliged to you for the suggestion," he said. "Maybe we'll see you again."

"I'm here most of the time," she told them.

The brothers walked out of the saloon. The game had resumed at the table, but Tom Bellamy wasn't playing the next hand, Ace noted as they left. He had gotten up and appeared to be headed toward the bar. Myra looked like she was waiting for him.

None of his business what she did, Ace told himself.

"I like Los Angeles so far," Chance said. "Winning a silver mine and meeting a pretty girl in the same evening! What are the odds?"

"Yeah," Ace said. "I reckon this town is just full of luck."

Chapter 2

Howell's Café turned out to be a frame building with a homey atmosphere inside. Delicious aromas floated in the air. Ace and Chance sat at a table with a blue-checked tablecloth. A waitress with blond braids and dimpled, smiling cheeks came over to take their order.

"We'll have two thick steaks with all the trimmings," Chance told her. "And plenty of coffee."

"I'll tell the cook and then bring you your coffee," she promised.

The Jensen brothers took their hats off and set them aside on the table. Ace said, "Let's see the deed to that mine."

"You heard that conversation, did you?"

"I'm in the habit of keeping an eye—and an ear—on you."

Chance scoffed. "That's right. You have to look out for me, don't you, *big brother*? How many minutes older than me are you? Five?"

"That's enough to make me the responsible one."

Chance looked like he might dispute that. Then he shrugged and said, "It's not worth arguing about." He reached inside his coat, took out the folded paper, and tossed it in front of Ace. "I would have showed it to you, anyway."

Ace picked up the deed. He unfolded it and read everything on it, paying close attention to the description of the mine's location.

"Surprise Canyon," he said. "Ever heard of it?"

Chance shook his head. "No, and I hadn't heard of the Panamint Mountains, either. I'd heard of Death Valley but didn't know there were any mountains there. We've never managed to get over into those parts."

"That's one of the intriguing things about this silver mine, isn't it? It's an excuse to go somewhere we haven't been."

Chance leaned back in his chair and grinned. "Yeah, I thought about that. I also thought about the possibility of that mine making us rich. How would you like that, big brother?"

"I'm not sure I'd know what to do with a lot of money if we had it," Ace replied honestly.

"Oh, I'll bet we could figure it out."

They fell silent for a moment as the blond waitress returned with cups, saucers, and a coffeepot. She filled their cups, then said, "The cook's out now, killing a cow for you boys."

"Tell him to make it a good-sized one," Chance joshed back at her. He had never met a woman he couldn't flirt with. "We're growing lads, you know."

She eyed both of them with appreciation and said, "I'm sure you are." She turned and went back to the counter with a little extra added sway to her hips.

"So, about this mine," Ace said as he tapped the paper with his index finger. "The deed's registered in the land recorder's office in Panamint City. We'll have to figure out how to get there. I suppose when we do, whoever runs the place can tell us exactly where to find the mine." He frowned. "Do you know anything about mining for silver?"

Chance smiled, shook his head, and said, "Not a blessed thing."

"But you think it's going to make us rich."

"I think it *might*. That's what I'm hoping, anyway." Chance spread his hands. "How hard can it be? You dig the ore out of the mine and see if there's any silver in it."

Ace had a hunch the actual process would turn out to be a lot more difficult than that. But first things first, and that meant getting to Panamint City.

A short time later, the blonde returned with big platters filled with steaks, potatoes, greens, and huge fluffy biscuits. She fetched a gravy boat from the counter, added more coffee to their cups, and brought bowls of deep-dish apple pie to round out the meal.

As she was about to leave the table again, Ace asked her, "Do you happen to know how to get to Panamint City?"

"Well, a stagecoach runs between here and there a couple of times a week. You could take it."

Chance said, "There must be a good road, then, if the stage uses it."

"Well, there's a road," the waitress said. "I don't know how good it is. I've never traveled over there myself." She shook her head. "Goodness, it's hot enough here in Los Angeles. I've heard stories about Death Valley. It's hard to even imagine how hot it must be. I've heard some old desert rats say that it's the hottest place they've ever been. The hottest this side of Hades!"

"It's probably not that hot in the mountains that run around the valley, though," Ace said.

"Maybe not, but I'm still all right staying here." The young woman laughed. "I never lost anything in Death Valley!"

Neither had he and Chance, Ace thought, but the likelihood was that they were going there, anyway.

The food was good, as Myra had told them it would be. As they ate, Ace said, "What about Luke?"

"What about him?" Chance replied.

"Well, we wrote him that letter and said we might meet him here in Los Angeles for Christmas . . ."

"*You* wrote him a letter and told him that. Anyway, you sent it, what, six months ago and never heard one word back from him."

"More like five months, I'd say. Maybe a little longer."

Chance snorted. "Which doesn't really change a thing. Anyway, I like Luke, but spending Christmas with him versus claiming a silver mine that could make us tycoons . . . I'm not sure that's really much of a choice."

"He *is* our father," Ace pointed out.

"Yeah, and how many years did we get along just fine without knowing that?"

"He didn't know it, either. Even after we met him, he didn't have any more idea we're related than . . . well, than we did!"

Ace spoke the truth. They had been acquainted with Luke Jensen for several years, but other than having the same last name, they hadn't been aware of any connection. In their wanderings, they had met Smoke Jensen, the famous gunfighter and Luke's younger brother, first. They had even joked about the possibility of being related to somebody as well known as Smoke.

The idea that he was actually their uncle had never entered their heads.

Over time, they had gotten to know Smoke pretty well and had spent time at the Sugarloaf, his ranch in Colorado. They had met Luke, as well as Smoke's adopted younger brother, Matt Jensen; and Smoke's mentor, Preacher, the old mountain man. By then, Ace and Chance had been regarded as good friends and honorary members of the family and had always been welcome at the Sugarloaf, whether it was a holiday or not.

Then, almost a year earlier, at the previous Christmas gathering at Smoke's ranch, Doc Monday had shown up, and the truth had come out at last: Ace and Chance *were* members of the family. Back in the Missouri Ozarks, in the days when the Civil War was erupting to tear the country apart, a young Luke Jensen was in love with the local schoolteacher, Lottie Margrabe. Unknown to Luke, when he went off to enlist and fight the Yankees, Lottie was carrying his children—twin sons.

Life had taken a lot of tortuous twists and turns since then. For many years, Smoke had believed that Luke himself was dead, murdered through treachery during the last days of the war, over a shipment of Confederate gold.

For his part, Luke had used the last name Smith and avoided his family, as he had lived the dangerous life of a bounty hunter, a profession that many folks regarded as disreputable and shameful.

In recent years, some of that had changed. Luke had reunited with his family and had started using the name Jensen again. And then, as much of a surprise to him as it was to them, he'd discovered that he was a father and had a pair of tough, strapping, gun-handy sons. And like him, Ace and Chance had been born to wander, too. None of them were likely to settle down anytime soon.

Because of that, the idea of getting together to celebrate Christmas in Los Angeles this year had been a shot in the dark. With the holiday only three weeks away, Ace and Chance had planned to tarry here until after the first of the year.

But that was before they had found themselves the owners of a silver mine.

Well, legally, *Chance* was the mine's owner, Ace reminded himself, but the brothers had always shared most things. He figured the mine would be the same. Chance hadn't said anything to make him think otherwise.

Chance took a drink of his coffee and went on, "If you want to wait here until after Christmas, just in case Luke shows up, I don't suppose I'll argue with you. But I have to admit, I don't

much like the idea of letting that mine just sit there. Somebody else might move in and claim it. We might have a fight
on our hands."

"That's true," Ace admitted. He frowned in thought. "Why
do you reckon Bellamy is over here in Los Angeles, playing
poker in a saloon, if he's got a silver mine in the mountains?"

"I don't have any idea. Maybe he came to buy supplies and
left some fellas there to work the mine while he was gone. I
didn't think to ask him. I was more concerned with making
him think I had good cards in my hand, instead of no two alike
and the highest one the nine of hearts!"

"That's what you bluffed him with?"

"Yeah," Chance said with a smile.

"But . . . I was watching. You bet just about everything we
had on that hand."

Chance tapped his coat where he had cached the money
and the deed. "And it paid off, didn't it?"

"But if he hadn't folded—"

"We'd have done something else. That's the good thing about
living the way we do. Every day's a new adventure, isn't it?"

Ace nodded. "You're right about that."

"So . . . are we going to Death Valley?"

"I reckon we are."

Chance picked up his coffee cup, then raised it, as if he
were making a toast.

"To becoming silver tycoons."

"Silver tycoons," Ace repeated. He clinked his cup against
his brother's.

Chapter 3

Myra Malone looked across the table at Tom Bellamy and asked, "Are you broke, Tom?"

"Broke?" Bellamy repeated. He sounded like the very idea was ludicrous and more than a little offensive. "Of course I'm not broke. Only a fool throws his last cent into a pot."

"So . . . almost broke? Down to your last cent?"

"It's not that bad." Bellamy hesitated. "Not quite."

Myra sighed, leaned back in her chair, and shook her head. "I was counting on you, Tom," she said.

"And you still can," he assured her. "I'm going to get you out of here, never you fear about that, my lovely girl."

"Don't start talking flattery. It's nice to hear, but it doesn't mean anything."

Myra picked up the glass in front of her. It had about an inch of amber liquid in it, and unlike the tea she sipped when customers bought her drinks, this was the real thing. She swallowed about half of what was in the glass and felt the bracing warmth as it went down.

She and Bellamy sat at a table tucked away in a rear corner of the saloon's main room. The hour was late, and the place was half-empty now. The Mexican with the guitar still plucked idly at the strings. The tune he played was a mournful one. It fit Myra's current mood quite well.

She had known Tom Bellamy for a couple of months. She'd met him soon after he drifted into Los Angeles. He was a lean, dark-haired man, handsome in a slick way, and he wore his clothes well. Myra had caught his eye, and vice versa. They got along well. He was in his midthirties, a good fifteen years older than her, but she didn't care about that. As a good-looking girl who'd been on her own since she turned thirteen, she figured that by now she was considerably older than her years.

And seven years of doing whatever was necessary in order to survive was plenty. More than enough. So when he had suggested that she come with him when he left Los Angeles, so they could make a fresh start somewhere else, she had agreed without hesitation. He had even offered to marry her, if that was what she desired.

Myra hadn't made up her mind about that, but the idea of a fresh start was the best thing she'd ever heard.

The only problem was that Bellamy wanted a good stake first. He planned to build that up by gambling.

So the days had turned into weeks, and the weeks into a couple of months, and they were still here.

She set the whiskey glass on the table and said, "What's this about a silver mine? If you had something like that—"

He stopped her with a wave of his hand and a chuckle.

"Don't worry your pretty head about that," he told her. "That so-called silver mine is worthless! Another fellow and I worked that claim for months. Oh, we got some color out of it, all right. But never very much, and it wasn't high-grade ore. We didn't break even on the cost of supplies. And then what was there played out. I knew it was time to move on."

"What about your partner?"

"What about him? He talked like he might stay on, but if he wanted to be stubborn and break his back for nothing, that was his business and none of mine."

Myra frowned at him. "But you had the deed."

"Well . . . I decided to bring it with me. I thought I might, ah, get some other use out of it."

"Like using it in some sort of swindle," Myra said. "Or betting it in a poker game when you'd run out of cash."

"I wasn't out of money," Bellamy snapped. "I'm not out of money." He reached in his vest pocket and brought out a five-dollar gold piece. "But why throw in your last coin when you have something else you can use?"

With a snap of his thumb and forefinger, he spun the half eagle on the tabletop.

He sighed and added, "I really thought that kid had a good hand. I never would have believed he had the guts to run a bluff like that."

"Well, he did, and now we're right back where we started."

"I know. And I'm sorry. But my luck's bound to change, Myra. It has to." He rested his right hand on her left. "You still believe in me, don't you?"

She looked at him for a long moment, then sighed and nodded. She didn't have the heart not to. "I may be a damn fool," she said, "but I suppose I do. Just don't let me down too many more times, Tom."

He raised his hand, as if taking a pledge. "I give you my word, I won't. Pretty soon we'll have plenty of money, and we'll make new lives for ourselves, far from Los Angeles."

"City of Angels," she murmured.

If any angels of the guardian variety existed, they hadn't been following her around.

Ace and Chance paid a visit to the stage line office the next morning. Since the completion of the transcontinental railroad more than a decade earlier, the steel rails had branched out all over the country, but plenty of places still existed that they didn't reach. Stagecoaches still served the needs of settlements like Panamint City.

"Sure, we go there," the clerk in the office replied to Ace's question. "Next run is three days from now. You gents want to buy a couple of tickets?"

"Actually," Ace said, "we were hoping you'd let us take a look at any maps you have of the route."

The clerk sniffed. His affable attitude chilled. "So you don't want to buy tickets. You just want to know how to get there."

"That's about the size of it," Chance said.

"You see, we already have saddle mounts and a couple of packhorses," Ace said, hoping to soothe the clerk's ruffled feelings. "But we've never been to those parts and only have a vague idea of how to get there."

The clerk glared for a few seconds longer, then made a face and shrugged. "Oh, all right," he said. "The map's there on the wall. I can't very well stop you from taking a gander at it, can I?"

Considering that he was half a foot shorter than either brother and weighed maybe 120 pounds soaking wet, he couldn't.

Ace smiled, anyway, and said, "We're sure obliged to you."

He and Chance went over to the framed map that hung on the wall, and began studying it. The roads, railroads, and land-marks were all well marked. The stage line's routes were indicated in red, so they had no trouble following the one that led to the Panamint Mountains, on the western edge of Death Valley.

Ace reached inside his denim jacket and took out a piece of paper and a stub of pencil. He made several sketches and wrote a few notes regarding the route to Panamint City. He was confident that he and Chance could locate the settlement without much difficulty.

The clerk must have decided it wouldn't do any harm to be

friendly. Anyway, some conversation would pass the time and beat working. He asked, "What takes you fellas to the Pana-mints?"

"A silver mine," Chance replied. "I won the deed to it in a poker game last night."

Ace frowned. It would have been smarter to keep that information to themselves. Somebody might get the idea of waylaying them and stealing the deed.

"Oh, you're the one—" The clerk stopped his surprised exclamation in mid-sentence. "I mean, how about that? A silver mine, eh? Well, I wish you the best of luck with it."

Chance was still staring at the map on the wall. He nodded and said in a distracted voice, "Yeah, thanks."

After a few more minutes, he asked Ace, "Have you seen enough?"

"I think so. Shouldn't be a problem." Ace put away the crude map and notes he had made, and nodded to the clerk. "Thanks again."

"Oh, it's my pleasure, friend. My pleasure."

The smirk on the man's face made Ace's forehead crease even more as his frown deepened.

The Jensen brothers started to leave the office. Ace paused on the boardwalk outside and told Chance, "You go on to the general store, and we'll start putting together a load of supplies. I thought of one more thing I want to check on that map."

"Sure," Chance said. He strolled on while Ace turned back to the stage line office.

The clerk looked up from his desk in surprise when the door opened and Ace walked in again. "Forget something?" he asked.

"That's right." Ace walked over to the desk, leaned forward, and rested his fists on its top. "I forgot to ask you what's so funny about my brother winning the deed to a silver mine."

"Why . . . why, nothing, I guess—" the man began as he started to look nervous.

Ace's right hand shot across the desk, grabbed the front of the clerk's shirt under his bow tie, and twisted the cloth as he half lifted the man out of his chair.

"You started to say something," he snapped at the startled, frightened clerk. He didn't like pushing people around, but his gut told him this could be important. " 'You're the one,' you started to say to my brother. The one what?"

"Nothing! I . . . I . . . didn't mean anything by it! I just heard . . ." The man stopped again.

Ace suppressed the impulse to shake him like a terrier with a rat. "Heard what?" he said through clenched teeth.

"That the mine's worthless!" the clerk blurted out. "The man who lost it to your brother in that poker game . . . he told some girl in the saloon that the silver is all played out in it. The . . . the bartender overheard them talking, and he told somebody, and they told somebody else, and . . . and . . ."

"And the gossip got around to you, is that it?"

"Yeah, mister, but I don't know if it's true or not. Like you said, it's just gossip!"

That was enough to make the two of them laughingstocks in Los Angeles, though, Ace thought as he let go of the clerk's shirt and allowed him to sag back into his chair. Ace tugged the shirt back into place and then patted the man lightly on the chest.

"Sorry," he muttered.

"Look, I shouldn't have said anything. I was just a little annoyed because you wanted to study the map but weren't going to buy any tickets. These days, stage lines have a lot more trouble making it than they used to. The blasted railroads are everywhere!"

"Yeah, that's true, I reckon," Ace said. "I shouldn't have lost my temper. I just don't like the idea of anybody laughing at my brother."

"And I don't blame you," the clerk said. "Uh, what are you going to do now?"

Ace shook his head and said, "Try to figure out some way to tell Chance that we're going on a fool's errand."

Ace studied her intently, unsure whether to believe her or not. She *seemed* sincere . . . but girls who worked in saloons had to be skilled at lying. They spent a great deal of their time telling gents what they wanted to hear, whether it was true or not.

Recalling what the clerk at the stage line office had said, he asked, "What else did Bellamy tell you?"

She shook her head. "I don't know what you mean."

"Did he tell you that silver mine I won the deed for is worthless?" Chance demanded.

Myra's brown eyes widened. "What?" she said. "Worthless? No, he never told me anything like that."

"The bartender overheard him talking to you, and the story got around," Ace said.

"I don't know what some nosy bartender *thinks* he overheard," Myra replied with a trace of heat in her voice, "but Tom never said the mine was worthless." She paused, as if in thought. "He said it was more *trouble* than it was worth . . . to him." With a smile, she added, "I don't really know Tom all that well, but from what I do know about him, he's not that fond of hard work. Why do you think he was sitting in a saloon, playing poker?"

"So the mine *does* have silver in it?" Chance asked.

"How in the world would I know? I've never been to Death Valley and have no desire to go!"

Ace and Chance looked at each other. Chance shrugged and said, "Could have happened that way, I suppose."

"Maybe. Let's go somewhere and talk about this." Ace nodded to Myra. "We're obliged to you."

"I'm not sure how much help I've been, but for what it's worth, that's all I know," she said.

Ace wasn't convinced of that, but he had to admit she might be telling the truth. Something half overheard in a saloon could get garbled. Once the story had gone through half a dozen other versions as it was passed around, it might bear very little resemblance to what was said.

Chance pinched the brim of his hat to Myra, then walked out of the saloon with Ace.

"Why don't we go back to that café and get some coffee?" Chance said. "We can talk about it there."

"Sounds like a good idea," Ace agreed.

"What it comes down to," Chance said as he stretched his legs out and crossed them at the ankles, "is that we don't have any reason to stay here and no reason not to go have a look at that silver mine."

Ace drank some of the coffee and set his cup back on its saucer. "I'm not sure it's going to pan out," he cautioned. "I know what the girl told us, but do we believe her?"

"What does it matter? Listen, let's say he actually did tell her the mine is worthless. There are two possibilities, as I see it. One, he was mad because I bluffed him out of that pot, and claiming the mine is worthless was just sour grapes on his part. A way to save face, I guess you'd call it. Or it really is worthless, and he put one over on me . . . but I still won all his money." Chance spread his hands. "Either way, we haven't lost anything, have we?"

Ace pursed his lips, in thought. After a moment, he shook his head. "No, I reckon we haven't. The only problem is, Luke could still show up, and we will have missed him."

"And that would be a shame," Chance said. "But there's just as strong a possibility that he *won't* show up, in which case we would have waited here for nothing. In fact, given the way he moves around so much, I'd say there's an even better chance he won't be here. He probably never even got your letter."

"You're bound and determined to go, aren't you?"

Chance grinned. "We'll spend the holiday in the mountains. Shoot, it'll probably seem more like Christmas up there, where it's cool, instead of down here, where it's so hot and steamy."

"Yeah, the weather doesn't really feel much like the season in these parts, does it?" Ace said. "I reckon they don't have many white Christmases around here."

Chance sat up and said, "It's settled, then. We're going to Death Valley . . . or at least as far as the mountains on this side of it."

"Surprise Canyon," Ace murmured. "I wonder what's waiting for us there."

"Surprises," Chance said with a confident smile.

Myra picked up one of the pillows from the rat's nest of a bed that Bellamy had made of it and walloped him with it as he slept. He woke with a startled yell and lunged up from the tangled covers. His hand shot toward the pistol lying on the small bedside table.

Myra clamped her fingers around his wrist to stop him from grabbing the gun. An image flashed through her mind from a couple of years earlier as she recalled a violent incident at the house where she'd been working. She'd had to drive a dagger through the back of a man's hand and pin it to a table so she could get away from him before he hurt her.

Thankfully, she didn't have to go that far with Tom Bellamy. He looked up at her and blinked in confusion. Then his stare cleared as he recognized her and realized he wasn't in danger.

And yet, he might be, she thought. She let go of his wrist and straightened.

A whine edged into his voice as he said, "What'd you do that for? You shouldn't wake a man up that way. There's no telling what he'll do."

She said through clenched teeth, "You loose-lipped fool. It got back to those Jensen boys that your so-called silver mine is worthless. I happened to go downstairs just now, as they were asking the bartender where to find you."

Bellamy sat up with an alarmed expression on his face. "Are they looking for me?" he asked. "Maybe I'd better get out of town—"

"That's the worst thing you could do right now. I already told them you'd left town. Gone to San Francisco, I thought."

Bellamy relaxed a little. "That was smart of you. I've always said you're a very smart girl, Myra."

"I told you before, skip the flattery. You need to stay right here in my room. The Jensens know I work here but don't know where I live, so they're not likely to come looking for you." Her mouth quirked. "Anyway, I made it sound like you and I weren't close, so they don't have any reason to think I might be hiding you."

Bellamy leaned back against the headboard and ran his fingers through his tangled hair.

"What the devil time is it?" he asked. He squinted at the window. A little light came in around the curtain. "Is it the crack of dawn out there?"

"It's almost noon."

"Like I said—"

Myra turned away from the bed. "I have to get back to work," she said over her shoulder. "I just wanted to warn you to lie low until the Jensens have left town."

"Are you sure they're going to leave?"

Myra paused at the door and looked back at him. "I told them that the gossip they heard was wrong. That you never told me the mine was worthless. Chance wants to go to Panamint City and find out for himself, and I'm pretty sure his brother is going to play along with him. They'll be gone today or tomorrow, I think. Then it'll be safe for you to go back to . . . whatever it is you're going to do next."

"I've been thinking about that," he said with a note of excitement in his voice. "There are a number of different options. I just have to go over every one of them in my mind, think through all the different angles, and decide which of them holds the most potential." He pointed. "There's a bottle there on the dressing table. Maybe if you wouldn't mind handing it to me, my brain could function better with a little liquid lubrication—"

She let out an eloquent snort as she stepped out of the room and slammed the door behind her without fetching the whiskey for Bellamy. It wasn't her job to lubricate his brain.

Chapter 5

Myra Malone sent one of the swampers at the saloon around to the various livery stables to ask questions and find out where the Jensens kept their horses. The old drunk was happy to take on that task. He would have done almost anything to get a smile from the beautiful saloon girl.

When he reported back to Myra that he'd found the right livery stable, she set him to watching it.

"You keep an eye out for them," she said after describing the Jensen brothers. "If you see them . . . *especially* if they leave town . . . come tell me right away."

"I sure will, Miss Trixie," the swamper promised. "I don't have to work until later, and, uh, I don't really care about that noways. I'd rather help you."

He looked at her like a dog eager for a pat on the head. When she gave him a fond smile, if he'd had a tail, he would have wagged it.

She held up a silver dollar, as well, and said, "This will be yours when the job's done."

That wasn't enough money for a real binge, but it would be a good start. The swamper's head bobbed up and down. He hurried from the saloon to carry out her orders.

Ace and Chance Jensen picked up their supplies at the

store, loaded them onto the two packhorses, and left Los Angeles that afternoon. They rode east toward the San Gabriel Mountains. They would skirt the southern end of that range, then swing northeast. It would take about a week to reach Death Valley without pushing the horses too hard.

The swamper reported their departure to Myra. She carried the word upstairs to Tom Bellamy.

"You don't have to hide in here anymore," she told him. "Those Jensen boys are gone."

"I wasn't *hiding*," Bellamy said as he fastened his collar in front of the flyspecked mirror over the dressing table. He sounded offended that she would accuse him of such a thing. "It was your idea that I be discreet and not show myself, remember?"

"Well, either way, it's over now." She moved up behind him and rested a hand on his shoulder. "What are we going to do, Tom? I'd like to get out of this town."

"Soon, my darling girl, soon." Bellamy turned toward her, pulled her into an embrace, and kissed her. "Have faith in me."

Have faith. What an odd concept, Myra thought. She wasn't sure she remembered how to do that.

Bellamy put on his hat and strode jauntily out of the room, whistling a tune, ready to go out once more and conquer the world—even though he had failed to do so at every turn.

Four men rode into Los Angeles from the east that evening. Likely they had passed the Jensen brothers on their way toward the settlement, but they weren't acquainted with Ace and Chance, and vice versa.

Jared Foxx drew rein in front of a saloon and studied the place. His keen blue eyes under thick white brows read the words painted on the sign above the entrance. Enough light spilled out into the street from the windows to make that possible.

"This is it, all right," he said to the companions, who had brought their mounts to a stop alongside him. "This is where somebody saw Bellamy."

"What if he ain't here anymore, boss?" one of the men asked.

"Then we'll try to pick up his trail," Foxx replied. His lips drew back from his teeth in a grimace. "I won't stop looking until I find that skunk."

Jared Foxx's white hair and rawboned, angular face made him look older than he was. The hair had changed color when he was barely in his twenties, a decade and a half earlier. It was something that ran in his family. His ma was the same way, he'd been told.

The harsh life he'd led had contributed to his appearance, too. Robbing, killing, running from posses . . . those kinds of things aged a man.

He glanced over at his roughly dressed, beard-stubbled companions. They were cut from the same cloth he was. He had ridden with many others just like them over the years.

But they hadn't been with him a year earlier, when he and Tom Bellamy had ridden into Surprise Canyon with a pack of lawdogs on their heels. That day, it had been just the two of them. . . .

Surprise Canyon

Foxx clamped his teeth on one end of the bandanna and drew it as tight as he could around the blood-leaking hole in his upper left arm. One of these blasted deputies had gotten lucky and tagged him with a bullet fired from long range.

"I told you I could bind that up for you," Tom Bellamy called from the saddle of the other running horse.

Foxx spat out the bandanna end and said, "We'd have to

stop, and there's no time for that. Not until we find a good place to hole up, anyway."

"You think we'll have to fight them?" Bellamy sounded worried about that. He was clever, but he didn't have much sand.

"Can happen," Foxx snapped. "That's one of the risks men like us take."

That was true, but Foxx didn't like shooting it out with the law, either. Kill half a dozen star packers . . . hell, kill even one of the varmints . . . and it meant all the others hunted you even harder. They didn't worry overmuch about taking such a prisoner back for trial. Not if there was a suitable tree handy, or even just a good place where a "fugitive" could be shot in the back while trying to "escape."

The past couldn't be changed, though. Early this morning, Foxx and Bellamy had strolled into the bank in Bishop Creek, bent on robbing it. It wasn't their fault a couple of sheriff's deputies had wandered in while they had their guns out, and had commenced shooting at the two outlaws.

Although, if they'd had another man, they could have posted him on the boardwalk as a lookout. . . .

Lucky for them, the deputies were nervous and rushed their shots. Foxx and Bellamy threw lead back at them and knocked them down in a welter of arms, legs, and blood.

Then the bank president and the teller came up with guns from somewhere, and the outlaws had to shoot *them*, too.

By that time, the town was in an uproar. With no time to do anything except grab a few handfuls of bills from the teller's drawer, the two desperadoes rushed out, jumped on their horses, and fogged it out of Bishop Creek.

With the mountains on their left, they rode south. At first, it seemed that no one came after them. After a while, though, they checked their back trail and spotted a large group of riders topping a rise a mile back. Both men spewed bitter curses at the sight.

"All we can do is run for it," Foxx said.

Bellamy swallowed hard. His face was pale with fear. "If they catch us . . ."

"I know. Best we make sure they don't."

The posse must have had fresher horses or the devil's own luck, or both. They cut down the lead until they were close enough to take a few potshots at the fleeing outlaws. One of those slugs cut a painful furrow across Foxx's upper left arm.

They threw the pursuit off for a while by following a dry, rocky wash. Foxx started to think they had given the posse the slip, but then the group of horsemen showed up again, trailing once more but coming on steadily.

"Damn it!" Bellamy's voice was a bitter whimper. "Why can't they just give up?"

Foxx nodded toward the rugged peaks to the east and said, "Let's head for those mountains. More places to hide."

He thought those were the Panamints, but he wasn't sure. No matter what, they offered the best chance of getting away from the posse.

They had started up a narrow, twisting canyon when the blood he'd lost made Foxx feel dizzy and sway in the saddle. He got out his bandanna and tied it around the wound as best he could. He was under no illusions. The pursuers would follow them in here, and there was a good chance he and Bellamy would have to make a stand.

They would put up a good fight, but it was doubtful that they would come out of this alive.

Then Bellamy pointed up the sloping canyon wall and said, "Look at that notch. There's so much brush in it, if we could get to it, there's a chance they wouldn't spot us."

Foxx was about to dismiss the idea, but then he frowned in thought. Bellamy might be right. "That slope is pretty steep, and there's a lot of loose rock. We'll have to lead the horses. Might not be able to make it, even then."

"We should try. Otherwise, sooner or later they're going to box us in."

Foxx nodded, then grimaced as he swung down from the saddle. He took hold of his horse's reins and said, "Come on." He led the animal up the slope toward the brushy notch. The horse's hooves slipped and slid, but it stayed upright, and so did Foxx. Bellamy and his horse struggled along behind them.

Foxx looked over his shoulder. They were dislodging rocks and leaving a trail of sorts, but the slope looked like rocks rolled down it quite often. The pursuers might not notice the new sign.

Anyway, if they made it, they would have a hiding place and the high ground. No better options seemed to be available.

After a hard climb that felt like it took an hour, they reached the top. Using a gloved hand, Foxx pushed thorny branches aside to make an opening in the brush. As he fought his way deeper into the thicket, Bellamy yelped in pain behind him.

"Those stickers are better than bullets," Foxx said.

"You won't get an argument from me. I still wish they'd stop poking me!"

A minute later, Foxx came to an abrupt stop. "Well, I'll be damned," he said as he looked at what he had come to.

"What is it?"

"There's a tunnel into the mountainside back here. Looks like an old mine."

A note of eagerness came into Bellamy's voice as he said, "A place we can hide?"

"Yeah. And anybody who doesn't know it's here will have a hard time finding it."

"We found it," Bellamy pointed out as he pushed through the brush to stand beside Foxx and stare at the dark opening in the rocky wall.

"Yeah, well, we're desperate. Those possemen want to catch us, but they're not running for their lives like we are. They might not go to the same lengths we have."

Whoever had dug the tunnel had cleared a small area in front of the opening. The brush was starting to reclaim that clearing, but some open area remained. Foxx and Bellamy tied their horses to the scrubby growth at the edge of it, then approached the tunnel mouth.

Foxx fished a lucifer out of his shirt pocket and snapped it to life with his thumbnail. The flickering glow revealed that the tunnel penetrated about ten feet into the mountainside before a roof collapse closed it off. Some support beams still remained in the part that hadn't fallen in.

"I've never been in these parts before," Bellamy said. "Do you know anything about the mines around here? Could there be gold or silver in there?"

"I've heard tell of silver strikes here in the Panamints," Foxx said. "Back eight or ten years ago, some fellas on the run from the law—sort of like us—found silver and decided to bring in even bigger crooks—politicians. They sold their claim to a couple of senators. There was a boom for a while. There's even a settlement called Panamint City somewhere up the canyon, or at least there used to be. That boom died down after a few years. I don't know what happened, but I figure the veins played out. That's the usual story. Folks keep prospecting and finding color, though, from what I hear. The booms come and go." Foxx shook his head. "I don't have any idea what it's like right now."

Bellamy stared into the tunnel, with a greedy light shining in his eyes. "Then there could be a fortune in there, waiting for us to find it."

A skeptical frown creased Foxx's rugged face. "I reckon there could be," he said, "but the odds against it are pretty high. Not only that, but we've got a posse on our trail, remember? If they find us—"

"They're not going to," Bellamy interrupted him. He laughed. "Jared, don't you recognize destiny when it's staring you right in the face? Everything that went wrong today, it was meant to be. It was meant to lead us right here, to this place . . . to the fortune that's waiting for us in there!" With a dramatic gesture, he threw his arm out toward the dark hole in the mountainside.

Chapter 6

The two men led the horses as close to the tunnel mouth as they could to get them more out of sight. Then there was nothing they could do except wait and listen for the sounds of the posse closing in.

Not much time passed before that happened. Foxx silently lifted a finger to signal that he heard hoofbeats. Bellamy nodded to indicate that he heard them, too. Both men drew their guns, even though they knew that a shoot-out would almost certainly end with them dead.

The swift rataplan of hoofbeats grew louder and louder. A few shouts sounded as the posse members called to each other. The brush screened the riders, so that Foxx and Bellamy couldn't see them, but the cloud of dust the horses raised was visible. The outlaws could tell when the posse was right below them, only a few hundred yards away.

Then the dust and the noise swept on past them as the pursuit continued on up the canyon.

The two men looked at each other, but neither spoke until the sounds had dwindled to nothing. Then Foxx said, "I reckon they're gone . . . but that don't mean they won't come back."

"They'll almost have to, once they realize we're not in front of them anymore," Bellamy said. "They'll figure out that we veered off somewhere. That means they'll search even harder. Let's go back down and ride out of the canyon while we have the chance."

Foxx shook his head. "If that sheriff's got any sense, he'll have left some men at the foot of the canyon, just in case we tried to slip back past them."

"We can shoot our way out—"

"Whatever happened to your talk about destiny?" Foxx wanted to know.

That made Bellamy look at the tunnel mouth for a long moment. Then, with a slow nod, he said, "You're right. I got excited about maybe getting away and forgot all about what we have here, Jared."

"What we *hope* we have here. No guarantee there's anything in there except rock."

Bellamy's grin returned. "Only one way to find out. We just have to wait until they give up looking for us."

"There are a lot of little side canyons branching off this one," Foxx pointed out. "It'd take a week to search all of 'em. I never saw a posse yet that had the belly for that much work, especially when we didn't get a pile of money from the bank. If they thought they were going to recover a lot of loot, it might be different."

"How much *did* we get?"

To pass the time while they waited, they counted the money from the teller's drawer. It came to $847. Not much, considering they had shot and probably killed four men to get it, including two lawdogs. Life went that way sometimes. You never could tell what twists it would take.

Later, as night was falling, they heard riders go past again in the canyon, heading in the other direction this time.

"They're leaving," Bellamy whispered. "They've given up."

"We don't know that yet. Keep the horses quiet."

Darkness dropped down like a curtain. They had food and water, and a little grass grew amidst the brush, so the horses were able to graze. The two outlaws took turns sleeping and standing guard until the sun climbed into sight over the mountains again.

"It was chilly last night," Bellamy complained as he hugged himself. "I like to froze my hind end off. I'm going to build a fire for coffee."

Foxx shook his head. "We can't risk the smoke or the smell of coffee. Some of them might have stayed behind to look for us again today."

"Damn it, Jared. I'm cold to the bone. How about I build a little fire inside the tunnel to warm up? The smoke will just filter out that way without being enough for anybody to notice."

Foxx considered the suggestion and nodded. "That might work. We'll need to stay careful. Most lawmen are idiots, but a few are pretty savvy. And usually, you never know which kind it is that's after you."

Two long days and nights dragged by. The men had to ration their food and water to make it last, especially because the horses had to drink, too. They spent the time hauling broken rocks out of the tunnel. Bellamy groused about the work, but the lure of silver was strong enough to keep him laboring, anyway.

On the morning of the third day, Foxx said, "That posse's given up. Nobody's looking for us anymore."

"How do you know that?"

"That's what my gut tells me, and I trust my gut. It's time for you to go, Tom."

Bellamy frowned. "What do you mean?" A nervous look appeared on his face. His hand drifted toward his gun.

Foxx laughed. "Take it easy," he said. "I'm not gonna double-cross you and kill you. You're going to take both horses and head on up the canyon. Keep going and you're bound to come to Panamint City. When you get there, use some of that bank money to buy us enough supplies for a month, and some picks and shovels and mining equipment. You can pack it all back here on my horse."

Bellamy gave him a canny look and asked, "You'd trust me to do that? I could take the money and your horse and keep going."

"And leave behind a chance at a fortune in silver?" Foxx shook his head. "I don't think you'll do that." His voice hardened. "Besides, if you ever betrayed me like that, Tom, I'd walk out of here and track you down, no matter how long it took. I'd kill you. You know that."

Bellamy sighed. "Yeah, I reckon I do. I'll do as you say, Jared."

"And while you're gone, I'll keep working on cleaning out that cave-in. By the time you're back, maybe we'll be ready to start some fresh digging. Who knows? Maybe I'll have uncovered a vein already."

"You really think so?"

"Only one way to find out," Foxx said.

Foxx's speculation was too optimistic. It took three days for Bellamy to ride to Panamint City and return with a load of supplies and equipment.

It took three weeks for them to strike silver.

During that time, they extended the tunnel to twice its original length, being careful to shore it up better than whoever had started the mine in the first place. The obvious conclusion was that the cave-in had prompted the first prospector to abandon the diggings and move on somewhere else.

The fellow hadn't been persistent enough. Foxx and Bellamy uncovered a nice little vein of silver about two inches wide, threaded through the rock wall. They couldn't be certain the ore *was* silver until they chipped out a good number of samples and Bellamy headed back up the canyon to Panamint City with them, so they could be tested at the local assay office.

Panamint City was something of a boomtown at the moment, Bellamy had reported to Foxx after his first visit. It had several streets, fifty or sixty businesses, and maybe two hundred crude cabins, huts, and tents where people lived.

The assayer tested the samples and confirmed that the ore was silver. Not high grade, but good enough to be worth digging out, especially if there was a lot of it.

The assayer also worked for Inyo County, registering claims. When Bellamy returned to the mine the second time, he brought back not only the good news about the ore but also a piece of paper with an official stamp on it that gave whoever possessed it the right of ownership to this enterprise.

Those memories flashed through Jared Foxx's mind as he sat in his saddle in front of the saloon. With a harsh grunt, he pushed them aside and dismounted. The three men with him swung down, as well.

Foxx stepped up on the boardwalk. He had his hands on the batwings, about to shove them back, when he stopped short. He let go of the swinging doors and moved back and a little to the side. He could still see into the saloon, but he wasn't as visible to anyone in there.

"What is it, boss?" one of the men asked. "I almost ran into you when you stopped like that."

"He's in there," Foxx breathed. He couldn't believe that his search was over when it had barely begun. "Sitting at a table, playing cards."

"All right," another man said. "Let's go in there and drag him out. Then you can kick his sorry butt from one end of the street to the other."

Foxx shook his head. "No, I don't want to draw that much

attention. I've still got too many charges hanging over my head."

"What about Bellamy? He's sittin' in there big as life, ain't he? And he was with you on some of those jobs, includin' that shoot-out in Bishop Creek."

"The shifty son of a gun never let people get a good look at him," Foxx explained. "I'm not sure he ever had a reward dodger out on him. He can afford to take chances I can't." He turned his head to look at one of the men. "Kimbrough, he doesn't know you, does he?"

"We never crossed trails," Kimbrough said. "He hadn't ought to know me from Adam."

"You go on in there, then. Get in the game with him if you can. Find out where he lives."

"How will I know him?"

Foxx described Bellamy and the clothes he was wearing. "He's the only one at the poker table who looks like that. You shouldn't have any trouble." Foxx turned to the other two. "Bracken, you and Stevens don't know him, either?"

"He shouldn't recognize us, boss," the man called Bracken replied.

"All right. You can get some drinks and hang around the bar, just in case Kimbrough needs a hand. Which you shouldn't, understand?"

Kimbrough nodded. "I've got it, Jared. No commotion if we can help it. You want me to steer him out here?"

"Only if you can do it without making him suspicious." Foxx thought of something else and added, "Don't go in together. Space it out."

He walked to the end of the block while the three men went into the saloon. Foxx got out the makings and stood by the three steps leading down to the street while he rolled a cigarette. When he had the quirly lit, he took a deep drag on it and tried to calm his nerves.

He had always been this way when he got angry. Rage overtook him and made him do rash things. He couldn't afford to lose his temper with Tom Bellamy.

The treacherous skunk had something Foxx wanted. Something Foxx *needed*.

He smoked that cigarette down to almost nothing and flicked the butt into the street, then rolled another. Los Angeles was a pretty busy settlement, even at night like this. Quite a few of the stores were still open, and all the saloons and dance halls and gambling dens were doing brisk business. Standing there in the shadows, Foxx listened to the people as they walked past him. He heard mostly English, of course, but also the liquid rhythms of Spanish and the staccato beats of Chinese.

He had just finished the second cigarette when Bracken appeared at his side and chuckled.

"Kimbrough's good, boss," the man reported. "He and Bellamy are pards already, and he's talked Bellamy into showing him where the best whorehouse in town is. He came up to the bar for a minute to get a drink and whispered that to me without Bellamy seein'."

"That's perfect," Foxx said. "Tom won't suspect a thing."

He and Bracken stayed where they were, and waited. A few minutes later, the batwings swung outward. Bellamy and Kimbrough emerged and turned to walk in the other direction. A moment later, Stevens came out and followed them. Foxx and Bracken brought up the rear.

At the other end of the block, as they passed an alley's dark mouth, Kimbrough reached up without warning, looped his arm around Bellamy's neck, and jerked him into the shadows. Bellamy managed to let out a strangled cry, but it was so muffled, it couldn't have been heard for very far. The other three men charged forward and darted into the alley.

Foxx heard the sounds of a struggle. Bellamy was a cowardly weasel, but like any cornered animal, he would fight if he had to. Bracken and Stevens charged into the melee, and the whole bunch went down.

Foxx stood back and waited until they heaved up again. A man was on either side of Bellamy, each holding an arm. The third man, Kimbrough, stepped in and slammed a punch to Bellamy's stomach. Bellamy gagged and tried to double over, but the other two held him up.

"That's enough," Foxx said. "I'll take over now."

He stepped in front of Bellamy. His eyes had adjusted to the gloom enough for him to make out the surprised expression that twisted the captive's face.

Foxx drew his gun, pressed the muzzle against Bellamy's forehead, and said, "You never expected to see me again, did you, Tom?"

Chapter 7

"J-Jared?" Bellamy gasped. "Is that you?"

"It sure is."

Bellamy's eyes rolled in their sockets as he tried to look at the gun jammed against his forehead. "Wh-why are you . . . doing this?"

"Because you've got something that belongs to me." Foxx ground the gun muzzle harder against Bellamy's head. "The deed to that mine."

"But the mine's worthless!"

"No it's not, you damned fool!" Foxx took a deep breath. His jaw clenched so tight, it felt like his teeth might crack. "It's got a nice thick vein of silver in it. You just gave up too quick on finding it!"

Their disappointment had been bitter when, after a few weeks of working in the mine, the vein they had been following disappeared. More weeks of trying to uncover an offshoot of it had proven futile. Bellamy, never one to break his back with hard labor day after day, had proposed abandoning the claim and moving on. Surely the hue and cry over the bloody bank holdup in Bishop Creek had died down by now.

"Blast it, you're the one who got me started on this," Foxx had said. "I liked taking that silver out of there. I liked the money it was making us. And I don't want to give it up!"

"But the vein played out," Bellamy had objected.

"We don't know that. There could be another vein—"

"Fine," Bellamy broke in. "You go ahead and look for it, then, Jared, with my blessing."

"You don't want your half?"

"Half of nothing is nothing. It's all yours."

Foxx heard that conversation again inside his head as he stood in the shadowy alley, with a gun to Tom Bellamy's head. Bellamy whined in pain. Foxx eased off on the gun's pressure as he realized how hard he'd been digging the muzzle into Bellamy's skull.

Bellamy gasped and sobbed. He choked out, "I . . . I'm sorry, Jared. You mean . . . you found another vein?"

"Damn right I did, and it's a good one. Took me a month of mighty hard work after you lit out, but I found it. I took samples to the assay office in Panamint City, and the fella there told me it was good ore. Really good ore. But when he asked me where it was from and I told him, he said that was *your* mine! You never put my name on the claim, you son of a—" Foxx rammed the gun muzzle against Bellamy's forehead again as his words choked off in a string of strangled curses.

Bellamy whimpered. After a moment, Foxx pulled the gun away, but only so he could smash it against the side of Bellamy's head. Bellamy sagged, half conscious, in the grip of Bracken and Stevens.

Foxx stepped back. His breath hissed rapidly through teeth clenched in rage. He struggled to get control of himself. Bellamy moaned.

When Foxx trusted himself to speak, he said, "Wake him up."

Bracken and Stevens shook Bellamy out of his stupor. Bellamy's head flopped around loose on his neck for a few seconds before he groaned and said, "Stop . . . stop . . ."

"Listen to me," Foxx said. "The assayer told me I had to have that piece of paper if I was going to claim the ore from the mine. When you rode out, you told me you left it with our gear at the camp. But you didn't, did you? You took it with you!"

"Yeah, I . . . I did," Bellamy admitted. "Thought I might . . . be able to . . . get some use out of it."

Foxx grated another curse and stepped closer, raising the gun to strike again.

"Wait!" Bellamy cried. Fear seemed to have forced some of the cobwebs out of his brain. "Jared, think about it. I believed the mine was worthless. I thought you'd never get anything else out of it. You . . . you can't blame me—"

"I *do* blame you," Foxx said. "You're a low-down thief. Stealing from banks is one thing, but stealing from your *partner* . . ."

Once again, Foxx took a deep breath and forced his raging emotions under control. "All right," he said, calmer now, or at least sounding like he was. "Give me the paper . . . the deed . . . whatever the hell you call it, and we'll call it square. I told you one time I'd kill you if you ever betrayed me, but I'm willing to leave you with your life if you'll just hand over that paper."

"That's why . . . you came after me?"

"Six months I've been looking for you, following every little trail I could find. It's taken me this long, but now I've got you, and you're going to give me what I want."

Bellamy's reaction came as a shock to all three of his captors.

He began to laugh.

The laughter started quiet, then rose in intensity and volume. Foxx stood it for a second, then snapped and slammed the gun across Bellamy's face. Teeth crunched under the impact. Bellamy's head hung forward. Blood dripped from his nose and mouth.

But after a moment, he chuckled again.

"What . . . is . . . so . . . damned . . . *funny?*" Foxx asked in a voice that was almost a shout.

"I don't . . . have what you want." Blood and swollen lips made Bellamy's reply thick and hard to understand. "I . . . I lost it . . ."

"What? You lost the paper?"

Bellamy forced his head up. Blood made the lower half of his face a dark smear. "In a . . . poker game. I bet it . . . in a poker game. And the kid . . . the damn kid bluffed me!"

Foxx stepped closer and raised the gun. "What kid?"

"J-Jensen. Ch-Chance Jensen. He . . . he won it . . . bluffed me . . . almost cleaned me out . . ."

"Chance Jensen," Foxx repeated. "I never heard of him."

Kimbrough said, "I heard of *Smoke* Jensen, boss." With a nervous edge in his voice, he added, "You don't reckon this Chance Jensen could be related to him, do you?"

Foxx waved away that concern with his free hand and leaned in toward Bellamy. "Where can I find him?"

"He . . . he left town . . . him and his brother. I think . . . I think they were headed for the Panamints . . . to check out the mine . . . They rode out . . . today . . ."

Anger made Foxx feel as if he were about to explode inside or erupt like a volcano. The search for Tom Bellamy had taken him six months, and in order to find his former partner, he'd had to leave the mine. He didn't trust anybody to work it in his absence, so he had covered up the tunnel mouth with brush as best he could, hoping that no one else would come across it while he tracked down Bellamy and recovered that official document.

Along the way he had picked up Kimbrough, Bracken, and Stevens, men he had known from his days on the owlhoot trail. He had trusted them to ride with him and help him find Bellamy, and he had even told them why he was searching for the man. But he hadn't revealed where the mine itself was located. That was his secret. His alone.

But he and Bellamy had found it by blind luck. Somebody else could, too.

Now, after all this time . . . after finding Bellamy and coming so close to what he wanted . . . to discover that it had slipped out of his hands by a matter of hours . . . !

"You're sure they were going to the mine?"

"They left town, heading east . . . according to a friend of mine. Where else . . . could they be going?"

Foxx stepped back, raised his left hand, and scrubbed it over his face as he frowned in thought. Weariness and frustration surged through him, along with the ever-present anger. Finally, he drew in a deep breath.

"Is everything you've told me true, Tom? Think careful before you answer, because there's a lot riding on it."

"It's all true. I swear, Jared. So . . . there's no reason for you to hurt me anymore."

Foxx shook his head. "You're wrong about that. There's no reason for me to keep you alive."

Bellamy gasped and tried to struggle, but he was too weak and hurt to have a chance of breaking loose from Bracken and Stevens.

Foxx eared back the hammer on his revolver, then hesitated. Several tense seconds ticked past. Then he lowered the gun and eased the hammer down again.

Bellamy sighed in relief.

Then Foxx said, "A gunshot's too loud and might draw too much attention. Finish him off, boys. Fists and boots."

"No!" Bellamy cried. "No, please—"

Kimbrough's hand clapped over his mouth and silenced him. Foxx slid his gun into its holster and turned away. He heard fists thudding against flesh behind him, but he didn't think much about it. As far as he was concerned, this search was over and done with. Time to start a new search.

Time to find Chance Jensen and his brother and get that paper from him. And if the Jensens didn't like it . . . they could die, too.

* * *

Myra lost track of Bellamy during the evening. She had tried to keep an eye on him as she circulated among the saloon's customers. He was full of his usual enthusiasm and confidence again. A small pile of winnings grew in front of him as he played poker.

Then, suddenly, he was gone. He had slipped out while she wasn't looking. She didn't believe he was trying to get away from her. He had no reason to do that. But even so, she wished she knew where he was.

Hours passed, and he didn't come back.

Myra's worry grew. She told herself that he could have wandered off to some other saloon. Maybe his luck had changed and he'd decided he might do better with the cards elsewhere.

He might have even decided to visit one of the whorehouses. She would be annoyed if that turned out to be the case, but relieved at the same time.

When he did turn up again, he would be getting a piece of her mind, that was for sure.

Hours passed, and still no Tom Bellamy. The saloon closed at one o'clock in the morning. Myra went up to her room, torn between anger and worry. She had considered taking one of the customers with her, somebody who would be willing to pay for the rest of the night with her, but since she'd met Bellamy, she had been trying not to do that.

She was alone as she crawled into bed to try to sleep.

Slumber didn't come easy. She tossed and turned, seething for a while and then fretting. She was mad at herself, as well as at Bellamy. She never should have allowed herself to care enough about some man that she lost sleep over him.

After a while, somebody or something scratched at the door.

Myra didn't notice the sound at first, but after a couple of minutes, she sat bolt upright and threw the sheet aside. Somebody was out there, trying to get in.

Well, this wasn't the first time such a thing had happened, she told herself. She swung her legs out of the bed and stood up. Her thin shift fell around her hips and thighs. She fumbled around on the small table beside the bed, found a match, struck it, and lit the lamp.

Then she picked up the dagger lying beside the lamp and turned toward the door.

The scratching continued. She leaned closer to the panel and asked, "Who's out there? It's late, so you'd better—"

"*My . . . ra.*"

The voice that croaked her name didn't sound human. She gasped and took a quick step back as fear welled up inside her. Some sort of . . . monster . . . was out there in the hall, looking for her.

With a grimace, she shoved that crazy thought aside. The only monsters that existed in life were the human ones. She wondered for a second if the swamper whose help she had enlisted earlier was out there, drunk on his butt and hoping she'd be grateful enough to let him in.

"*Myra,*" the hoarse voice repeated, a little stronger this time.

She recognized something about it. Could that be Tom Bellamy on the other side of the door?

If it was, something was wrong with him.

Tightening her grip on the dagger in her right hand, she reached down with her left, twisted the key in the lock, grabbed the knob, and jerked the door open. It flew in faster than she expected, and banged against her shoulder. She caught her breath and stepped back as the man who'd been sitting on the hallway floor and leaning against the door's lower half sprawled across the threshold.

The sheet of blood covering his face glistened wetly in the

lamplight. Despite that, Myra recognized him. Her fingers opened in shock. The dagger fell and, through blind luck, missed her bare foot. The point hit one of the floorboards instead and stuck there. The dagger stood straight up about eighteen inches away from the head of the horror that was Tom Bellamy.

Chapter 8

Myra's head popped up at the sound of a groan from the bed. She had fallen asleep in a chair next to the dressing table. She shot to her feet and hurried across the room.

The wick in the lamp beside the bed was turned down low, so only a faint yellow glow revealed the battered, bruised, and cut face of the man with his head lying on the pillow. Tom Bellamy groaned again. His eyes were closed, but as Myra watched anxiously, the lids began to flutter. After a few more seconds, Bellamy forced his eyes open. The flesh around them was so swollen, they were just slits.

"M-M-Myra," he whispered. His lips were grotesquely puffy, too.

"That's right, it's me," she said as she leaned over him. "You're all right, Tom. You're with me now. You just rest."

"Wha . . . wha . . . hap . . ." He couldn't get the rest of the question out.

She knew what he wanted to know, though, so she said, "Someone beat you within an inch of your life. You made it back here to my room. Lord knows how. But you're going to be all right, so you should rest now."

"Mi . . . mi . . ."

"That's right, it's Myra."

"*Mine*!" he gasped, at last victorious in his struggle to get the word out. "Sil . . . silver . . . mine."

Myra frowned and said, "What?"

He didn't answer. His eyelids drooped and then closed all the way. He was unconscious again, or maybe this was genuine sleep, the rest he needed to start healing.

That was going to take a while, Myra thought. And even though she had assured him he was going to be all right, she didn't know that for a fact. He was in bad shape.

Earlier, as soon as she had recovered a little from the horror she had felt at the gruesome sight, she had dragged him into the room, leaving a crimson smear on the floor. Then she had gone downstairs and rousted the swamper from his cot in the storeroom. A couple of blocks away was the office and residence of a doctor who could be counted on for discretion as long as his patients paid his fee and threw in a bottle of whiskey to help steady his sometimes shaky hands. Myra had sent the swamper to fetch him, then had gone back upstairs to tend to Bellamy as best she could until help arrived.

She had soaked a cloth in the basin and wiped away some of the blood from his face. The damage he had suffered made her wince just to look at it.

It took all three of them—her, the doc, and the swamper—to lift him into the bed. The doctor warned her that the sheets were going to be ruined.

"Go ahead," she told him. "I don't care."

"This endeavor may well be doomed from the start," he told her with a grave expression on his walrus-mustached face. "This man looks as if he's been trampled by a team of twenty mules, at the very minimum. I can clean and bandage the wounds we can see, but there is no way of determining what sort of internal injuries he may have."

"Just do the best you can, Doctor."

The medico shrugged and went to work. He was known to help the working girls of the settlement with their ailments, and he had experience patching up bullet wounds. In addition to the whiskey, Myra thought he probably indulged in his supply of laudanum from time to time, too.

None of that mattered as long as he kept Tom Bellamy alive.

Well, Bellamy was alive, she thought as she moved back to the chair and sat down, but no telling how long he would stay that way. Every hour was that much, though.

Judging by the bruises on his sides, he had been kicked in the ribs numerous times. Some of those ribs were bound to be cracked. The doctor had bound up his torso tightly. His right shoulder was dislocated, but with Myra's help, the doctor had jammed it back into place and bound the shoulder, as well, so it wouldn't move around. A huge bruise covered his entire stomach and abdomen. His legs hadn't suffered as much punishment, but they appeared to have been kicked and stomped, too.

His face had looked like raw meat. Cleaning all the scrapes and cuts had helped some, but the swelling made him appear barely human. Several men had done this, Myra decided. She wasn't sure one human being could dole out that much punishment to another.

But as she knew from experience, it was best not to underestimate the capacity for cruelty in the human heart.

As she sat now and watched Bellamy breathing, his chest rising and falling slowly under the clean sheet, she leaned her head against the wall and sighed in absolute exhaustion. Her gaze flicked toward the bundle of bloody sheets rolled and wadded into a corner of the room. For a while, it had looked and smelled like a slaughterhouse in here. The swamper had worked industriously to clean everything up, though, and the sheets were all that remained. He had promised to burn them first thing in the morning.

"Tom, Tom," she whispered as she looked at him again. "What in the world did you get into?"

"Silver mine," he had said. Was it possible the Jensen brothers had doubled back to Los Angeles, caught him, and done this to him? Myra couldn't believe that. Ace and Chance were big, young, and strong, but they had a natural decency about them. Even Myra, as cynical as she was, had been able to see that. They would fight, maybe even kill, in self-defense or to protect others, but they wouldn't have beaten Bellamy like that. Not on their worst day.

Someone else must have done it. But over a silver mine? A worthless silver mine at that?

Myra had no answers. If she were the praying sort, she thought, she would say a prayer for Tom Bellamy.

On the other hand . . . what could it hurt?

She scooted the chair a little closer to the bed and spooned more stew into Bellamy's mouth. He made a face, not from the taste of the stuff but from the pain of having to open his mouth. He had lost three teeth to the beating, and now, nearly a week later, it still hurt.

Myra knew that, but she insisted that he eat, anyway. He needed the food to regain his strength. He looked better—the bruises fading, the swelling going down some—but he was still as weak as could be.

"You're a hard taskmaster," he said. His voice was almost back to normal. "I've had enough."

"No you haven't. Take a few more bites. You're never going to get stronger unless you eat . . . and you want to get stronger, don't you?"

"I have to," Bellamy said, "if I'm going to kill Jared Foxx."

Myra frowned and said, "Hush. We'll talk about that later."

He reached up and took hold of her wrist as she poked the spoon at him.

"No, we'll talk about it now," he said. "I've told you what happened. Surely you can understand why he has to die."

She understood, all right. When he had recovered enough to tell her the story, she had wanted to kill Foxx herself. If the man had been standing there in front of her, she would have plunged her dagger into his heart and been happy about it.

To be honest, her desire for vengeance on Foxx was stronger than her greed for the silver to be found in that mine. Although the silver was a mighty strong motivation, too. If Foxx had told the truth, the mine was worth a fortune. He hadn't had any reason to lie to Bellamy, who had been a helpless captive at the time.

"We have to start for the mountains," Bellamy went on. "Foxx has nearly a week's head start on us, and the Jensen brothers have been gone for longer than that." He let go of her wrist, leaned back against the pillows propping him up, and groaned. "If Foxx has already caught up to them and gotten his hands on that deed . . ."

"It couldn't have been that easy," Myra said. She set aside the bowl of stew. The mood Bellamy was in, she couldn't force him to eat any more right now. "Ace and Chance looked like they could take care of themselves."

"You underestimate how ruthless Jared Foxx is," Bellamy said. "He's perfectly capable of ambushing and murdering them both."

"To do that, he'd have to know who they are," she pointed out. "He can't just ride up Surprise Canyon, killing everybody he finds and then searching their bodies for that paper. It may take him some time to locate them."

Bellamy shook his head. "All he has to do is go to the mine. That's where the directions will lead the Jensens. Either they'll be there when Foxx shows up or they'll arrive shortly."

He might be right about that, Myra thought, but it didn't matter. The doctor was amazed that Bellamy had recovered so much, so quickly, but still, he was in no shape to travel yet . . . no matter what happened with Foxx and the Jensen brothers.

"Don't worry about that," she said. "What's important is that you're going to be all right . . . and that you're going to take Foxx by surprise when he realizes that you're not dead."

"He'll be surprised, all right. And then *he'll* be dead."

By all rights, Bellamy never should have survived that beating, according to the doctor. Foxx's men must have believed he was dead when they left him in that alley, or else they would have finished him off.

During one of his conversations with Myra, the doctor had said, "I can't guarantee that he *wasn't* dead, briefly."

"What do you mean?" Myra had asked, confused.

"There have been cases where breathing stopped and the heart ceased to beat, but then, after a short time, those activities resumed. We're talking about a matter of seconds, mind you. A minute or so, at most. And often, when such a bizarre circumstance takes place, irreparable damage occurs, anyway, so that the patient does not survive in the long term and is mentally unsound during the interval before death takes place again."

"There's nothing wrong with Tom except that he had the hell beaten out of him."

"As far as we can tell," the doctor said. "I have a theory of my own about such cases. Those who die and come back to life have seen things which mortal men were never meant to see and walk this earth again afterward."

Those ominous comments had stuck with Myra and haunted her for a while, but as the days passed, she had put them aside. Other than the physical injuries he'd suffered, Tom Bellamy seemed perfectly fine to her.

Dying would explain why Foxx's men had left him there in the alley, though.

"Two more days," Bellamy declared now. "I'll lie here and rest for two more days, and then I'm heading for the Panamints." He sighed. "So, I guess you'd better feed me the rest of that blasted stew."

Chapter 9

"This is hopeless," Chance said as he glared at the piece of paper in his hand. "None of these notations and descriptions make any sense without some sort of map to compare them to!"

"Yeah, it's a shame they don't mark latitude and longitude lines on the ground, isn't it?" Ace asked dryly.

"It certainly would help if somebody did!"

"Let me look at the deed again," Ace suggested. He took the document, ran his fingertip over the words, and lifted his head to look back and forth at the canyon walls surrounding them.

"It lists some landmarks, but I don't know what any of them are," Chance said. "We might make some guesses, but that's all they'd be."

"Yeah," Ace agreed. "I'm not making any sense out of it, either. But I have an idea what we can do." He pointed at the paper again. "This came from the assay and land office in Panamint City. We'll go on up the canyon, find the settlement, and ask the man in charge of the office. He's bound to have a map and should be able to show us exactly where the mine is."

A smile lit up Chance's face. "That's a good idea. How much farther is Panamint City?"

Ace chuckled and shook his head. "I don't have any idea about *that*, either. But if we keep going and stick to the main canyon, I don't reckon we can miss it."

They had dismounted so the horses could rest and graze while they puzzled over the deed and tried to figure out where they were. Chance put the deed back in one of his saddlebags; then they swung up and started riding along the canyon again.

The journey from Los Angeles had been uneventful. After traveling across mostly flat and monotonous country for almost a week, they found the scenery here in the rugged, snow-capped mountains beautiful. They had left the hot air behind as they'd climbed through the canyon. The air was crisp and cool now under a high achingly blue sky. A creek bubbled along the canyon floor, weaving from one side to the other, making cheerful music as it flowed over a rocky bed. A fairly good trail followed the stream's course. The wheels of count-less wagons and stagecoaches had packed the dirt hard, so the hooves of the Jensen brothers' horses didn't raise much dust as they plodded along. The canyon climbed steadily. The slope was pretty steep starting out, but it grew gentler as they went higher.

Late in the afternoon, Chance caught a glimpse of a tall, ob-viously man-made brick tower rising above the rocks a mile or so farther up the canyon. He pointed it out and said, "Look at that."

"Appears to be a smokestack," Ace said. "Probably part of the stamp mill at Panamint City. We should be there before too much longer."

They pressed on, but they had been riding for only another few minutes when they reined in again, sharply this time, as a flurry of gunshots erupted somewhere not far ahead of them.

The loud cracks echoed back and forth between the steep, brush-dotted canyon walls and set up quite a clamor. Ace and Chance looked at each other in alarm.

"Sounds like a war's broken out," Chance said.

A dull boom sounded, punctuating the other reports.

"That was a Sharps," Ace said. "If I had to guess, I'd say several men with handguns and rifles have gone after somebody with an old buffalo gun."

Chance made a face. "And you don't like that, do you? The idea that somebody's an underdog always makes you want to go rushing in to help."

"I don't like to see anybody being ganged up on."

"Neither do I," Chance admitted with a sigh. "But if we're going to see what it's all about, we'd better leave these pack-horses here, out of the line of fire."

Ace agreed. Without wasting any time, they tied the pack animals' reins to the twisted trunk of a small dead tree and then rode on up the canyon, toward the gunfire. The Sharps blasted a couple more times at spaced intervals, confirming there was only one man on that side of the fight who had to re-load after every shot.

They followed the canyon around several bends. The gun-fire got louder, and Ace caught a whiff of powder smoke. The acrid tang was very familiar to him.

The canyon had widened out as the slope had eased. It was about a hundred yards from side to side at this point. As Ace and Chance rode around another bend, they spotted a blue-gray haze of gun smoke hanging over a cluster of boulders against the left-hand wall. Another boom told them the man with the buffalo rifle was holed up in those rocks.

Directly across from him, several men hidden in a fringe of brush and more widely scattered boulders returned the fire. Ace saw tongues of flame spurt out from at least four gun muz-zles over there. Some large, dark shapes farther back in the brush probably were the attackers' horses.

Ace had no doubt those men had gone on the offensive first. Quite a few shots had rung out from the smaller-caliber weapons before the man with the Sharps had started fighting back. He'd had to make a dash for that cluster of boulders, so he'd have some cover while he mounted a defense.

Those thoughts flashed through Ace's head as he motioned to Chance. They veered toward a little notch in the canyon wall, formed by a rocky outthrust on the right.

The Jensen brothers pulled Winchesters from scabbards and dropped from their saddles. Their horses were used to gunshots and powder smoke and wouldn't bolt.

"You use the rocks for cover," Ace said. He nodded toward a dead, fallen tree a few yards away. "I'll make a run for that log. Should be safe enough. I don't think they've spotted us yet."

"Don't dawdle," Chance told him. "One of them could glance in this direction anytime."

Ace took a deep breath and lunged into the open. After a couple of long strides, he dived toward the deadfall. His hat flew off his head. He landed behind the log and came down hard enough to knock the breath out of himself for a second. But he recovered quickly and waved to Chance to show that he was all right.

Then Ace slid his rifle over the top of the log and snugged the butt against his shoulder. Aiming high, he cranked off three rounds as fast as he could work the Winchester's lever and pull the trigger.

Chance did likewise. The half-dozen bullets the Jensen brothers sprayed above the attackers' heads whipped through brush and ricocheted off rocks.

That attracted the attention of the hidden gunmen. At least a couple of them started shooting toward Ace and Chance. Ace pulled his rifle back and pressed himself as low to the ground as he could behind the fallen tree.

"Keep your head down!" Chance called to him.

"I intend to!" Ace heard bullets smacking into the fallen tree. Splinters flew high in the air and showered down around him.

The buffalo gun thundered again, and it was followed by a shrill cry from the other side of the canyon. The man in the cluster of boulders had either scored with that shot or come close enough to throw a real scare into one of the attackers.

That caused a momentary pause in their assault. Ace and Chance took advantage of that to throw more lead at the brush and rocks. Ace continued aiming high, since he didn't want to kill anyone when he didn't know for sure what was going on or which side was in the right. Chance probably wasn't being quite that careful.

It wasn't long before the attackers had had enough. Ace glimpsed men darting through the brush as they flung wild shots back across the canyon and down toward the spot where the brothers had taken cover. They leaped on their horses and burst out of the thick growth, still shooting. Ace counted five men. One slumped forward in his saddle, as if he was wounded and struggling to hang on.

One more roar came from the Sharps to hurry the riders on their way as they vanished around another bend. Then an echoing silence settled down over the canyon, broken only by the dwindling hoofbeats of the fleeing bushwhackers.

Ace and Chance stayed where they were and waited to see what was going to happen. They didn't know if they could trust the owner of that buffalo rifle, so they weren't going to expose themselves to its fire.

Finally, after several long minutes had passed, a high-pitched voice called, "Whoever you fellas are over there, I'm sure obliged to you!"

For a second, Ace wasn't sure if the voice belonged to a man or woman, but then he decided it was male. That was confirmed when it continued, "I'm comin' out now!" and a stocky figure emerged from the boulders, carrying the Sharps in one hand and leading a mule with the other. The mule had a pack-saddle strapped onto its back.

The man was short and round, with a prominent belly. He

wore high-topped boots and thick canvas trousers held up by suspenders over the faded gray upper half of a pair of long underwear. A shapeless brown felt hat with a ragged brim was crammed down on his head. White whiskers bristled out from his cheeks and chin. He waddled toward the center of the canyon.

Ace and Chance glanced at each other. "Looks harmless enough," Chance said.

"Nobody's harmless with a buffalo gun in his hand," Ace pointed out. "But he knows we were trying to help him, so it's not likely he'll blaze away at us."

Ace got to his feet and looked around for his hat. He found it and put it on while Chance led the horses out of the notch. They didn't go back for the pack animals yet. Instead, they walked toward the old man.

He stopped and waited for them. Ace had a feeling the old-timer was studying them pretty closely. As they came up to him, he nodded and said, "Howdy, boys. Thanks again for backin' my play."

"We don't like to see somebody who's outnumbered getting the worst of it," Ace said. "My name's Ace Jensen. This is my brother Chance."

"Hello," Chance said with a nod.

"Mighty pleased to be makin' your acquaintance. They call me Nick. Nick Beltz."

He stuck out a hand with fingers as short and thick as sausages. Ace and Chance shook with him; then Ace asked, "Who were those hombres?"

A flood of words in a language Ace didn't understand came pouring out of Nick Beltz's mouth. Even in the old man's curiously high-pitched, almost childlike voice, the harsh vitriol in what he was saying came through clearly.

After a moment, he broke off the tirade, chuckled, and said, "Sorry, boys. I work with some Scandihoovian fellas, and I'm so used to hearin' their lingo that sometimes it just comes outta me like that. To answer your question, son . . . I never got a good look at them skunks what jumped me, but I don't have to see 'em to smell 'em! I know good an' well they were some o' Big Dave Scranton's gun-throwers!" Beltz said the name as if he expected the Jensen brothers to recognize it.

Chance said, "I'm afraid we don't know who that is, Mr. Beltz."

"Or why his men would try to kill you," Ace added.

"Because Scranton is as low-down as the devil hisself, and he's got his heart, if you can call it that, set on stealin' my mine!"

Chapter 10

The old-timer was bound for Panamint City, and when he found out that Ace and Chance were, too, he insisted that they stick together the rest of the way.

"You young fellas made yourselves a bad enemy today," Beltz said. "When Big Dave hears how you pitched in to help me, he'll be out to get *you*, too. If those varmints double back, we can tackle 'em together."

Ace figured that he and Chance would be more protection for Beltz than vice versa, but he didn't care. He wanted to seize this opportunity to talk with someone who was familiar with the area.

"Are you a prospector?" he asked as they walked along the canyon. Since Beltz was leading his pack mule, Ace and Chance walked, too, leading their saddle horses and their own pack animals, which they had fetched before leaving the site of the battle.

"Was. Now I ain't prospectin' anymore. Got me a payin' mine that's gonna make me rich if I can keep thieves like Dave Scranton from stealin' it."

"So, Scranton's a claim jumper?" Chance asked. "Isn't that what they call it?"

"Well . . . he don't just move in and steal a man's claim right out in the open. But when Scranton sets his sights on a mine, he finds a way to get his claws on it. Bad things keep happenin' until the poor varmint what's workin' the claim decides to give up or sell out. And it's Scranton he sells out to! Or else, if a fella's too stubborn to give in that way . . . sooner or later, he just up and disappears, and Scranton takes over the abandoned claim."

"Can't the law put a stop to that?" Ace wanted to know.

"Law?" Beltz repeated. He snorted. "What law? The county seat's durned near ninety miles from here. The sheriff over there's supposed to send a deputy to keep the peace if he gets any complaints, but plenty of folks have complained and nobody's ever seen hide nor hair of any deputy! So folks are their own law in Surprise Canyon and Panamint City, and Scranton's got more gun-throwers and hard cases workin' for him than anybody else, so he gets what he wants."

"If the area's so lawless," Ace said, "I'm surprised you'd go off and leave your mine."

Beltz cackled. "Didn't say I left it unattended, did I? Them Scandihoovian fellas I mentioned are there, diggin' out the silver and guardin' the place. Nobody wants to mess with the Steingrim brothers. Scranton's liable to run outta patience and make a move against us one o' these days, but he's gonna try to run me off or kill me first. I don't run . . . and I'm hard to kill!" He patted the stock of the Sharps. "Plenty o' Injuns found that out back in my buffalo-huntin' days."

Ace enjoyed listening to the colorful old-timer, even though the wheezy, high-pitched voice got a little irritating after a while. He was about to suggest that Chance get the deed out, so maybe Beltz could tell them where their mine was, when they topped a small rise, and suddenly Panamint City was spread out before them.

The trail they had been following turned into the settlement's main street. It stretched for several blocks ahead of them, broken by cross streets. To the left, the canyon wall was steep and rocky and rose practically at the back doors of the cabins built along it. The right-hand wall was gentler and covered with brush but still pretty rugged.

The stamp mill, with its towering smokestack and cluster of large buildings with shorter chimneys, was at the far end of the settlement. It dominated the scene, but Ace and Chance saw a number of other impressive brick buildings along the street. In stark contrast, a tent or a crude tar-paper shack might sit alongside one of those brick edifices.

That was a boomtown for you: a mixture of the new and the newer, the solid and the fleeting, the squalid and the pretentious. Despite their relative youth, Ace and Chance had visited a number of raw, boisterous settlements like this. They filled Chance with eagerness and excitement. They made Ace wary.

And for the moment, with the town right in front of them, he forgot about asking Nick Beltz to have a look at the deed to Chance's mine.

"Quite a place," Chance commented as they entered the settlement.

"Yeah," Beltz said. "From what I hear, it used to be even bigger back durin' the first boom a few years ago. But then a cloudburst came along, flooded the whole canyon, and washed away most of the buildin's. What you see has been put back up since then, a little bit at a time."

"I didn't think it rained much in these parts," Ace said. "Isn't Death Valley close by?"

Beltz pointed to the east and said, "Yonder ways a few miles. It sure is dry, too. Driest desert you ever did see. But when it does rain, which ain't often, it usually comes a gusher. It's different up here in the mountains, too. We get more rain up here, and durin' the winter, it snows quite a bit. You can durned near have a blizzard up here, while less'n twenty miles away in the valley, it's dry as a bone and hot enough to melt the tallow off'n you." The old-timer laughed. "Oddest dang weather you'll ever see!"

Chance said, "I haven't seen any snow on the ground, and it's December."

"That's because we ain't had nothin' but a little dustin' most nights, and it melts away by noon the next day. But it's comin', and you can mark my words on that. I can feel it in my bones."

"A blizzard, you mean?" Ace asked with a skeptical frown.

"Could be. Could be."

That seemed unlikely to Ace, but he supposed Beltz knew more about the conditions around here than he did. He put that discussion aside in his mind and started looking for the assay and land office.

As with most boomtowns, there were more saloons than any other kind of business. Some were more substantial frame buildings with painted signs above their doors. Others were just tents with the words *saloon* or *whiskey* daubed on the canvas itself.

In addition to those drinking establishments, Ace saw a butcher shop, several general stores, a hotel called the Panamint House, a newspaper office, a blacksmith shop, a wagon yard and a freighting company, a tiny hut that served as the stage line's office, and a doctor's office. Panamint City had no churches, as far as he could see, and no school, either. The latter wasn't a surprise, since there didn't appear to be any children in the settlement. In fact, he hadn't seen anyone other than grown men.

That changed when a girl stepped out of a general store a few doors ahead of them and moved along the street at a brisk pace, with a paper-wrapped bundle in her arms.

A couple of men followed her out of the store. One of them called after her, "Say, you ought to let me carry that package for you, Miss Priscilla. I'd be plumb happy to."

Without slowing down or looking around, she said, "No, thank you, Mr. Mullen. I can handle it just fine."

The other man said in a jeering tone, "I'll bet that ain't all you can handle just fine."

"You hush that up, Webster," said the man called Mullen. "That ain't no way to talk to a lady." With a couple of long-legged strides, he caught up to the girl and moved in front of her. His solid bulk forced her to stop. "All I want to do is give you a hand, Miss Priscilla."

"But I don't need it." Her face and voice were tense. "Please . . ."

The second man, Webster, moved up closer behind her. They had her caught between them now, with no place to go unless she tried to dart to the side. And it was obvious that if she did that, the men would move to block her again.

Ace, Chance, and Beltz had come to a stop, as well, as they watched this little drama play out in front of them.

Mullen reached out and took hold of the package. "Let me have that—" he began.

"No!" The girl jerked the bundle away. She stepped back, but that made her bump into Webster as he loomed behind her. She let out a soft little cry of alarm.

"Here, I'll take it," Webster said. He reached around her with both arms to grasp the package. The move allowed him to press his forearms against her breasts.

Ace and Chance looked at each other.

Beltz saw the glance they exchanged, and said, "Hold on, fellas. You don't know—"

The Jensen brothers didn't care what they knew or didn't know. What they had just seen had both of them feeling proddy. They dropped the reins of the saddle horses and pack animals and stepped forward.

"That's damned well enough," Chance said in a loud, clear voice.

Mullen stiffened and looked back over his shoulder as Ace and Chance approached. "One of you young pip-squeaks say somethin'?" he demanded.

"My brother said that was enough," Ace replied, "and I say the same thing. Leave that young lady alone. Clearly, she doesn't want your help or enjoy your attention."

"Well, lah-dee-dah," Webster said as he tightened his arms around the girl. "Don't he talk fancy, Mullen?"

"Yeah, but he ain't sayin' nothin' that amounts to anything," Mullen said. With a dismissive sneer, he turned away from Ace and Chance. "We're not gonna hurt you, Miss Priscilla. Why don't you just come along with us? We'll go to the Silver Slipper and have a friendly drink or two. Then Webster and me'll escort you back to your place. A pretty gal like you can't be too careful in a rough place like this. You need a couple of gentlemen to make sure you get home safe."

The girl's face was flushed with anger and embarrassment as she said, "Some fine gentlemen you are!" She twisted in Webster's crude embrace. "Now, let go of me—"

Both men laughed.

Mullen stepped closer and raised his left hand to cup her chin. "I didn't figure it was possible for you to get any prettier, but damned if that's not what happens when you get mad! I swear, you're just askin' for—"

At that moment, Chance's left hand clamped on Mullen's right shoulder and hauled him around. An instant later, Chance's right fist exploded on Mullen's jaw and smashed him to the ground.

Chapter 11

Chance's punch accomplished something else besides knocking Mullen off his feet. Webster howled a furious curse and let go of the girl. He stepped around her and lunged toward Chance.

Ace was waiting for him. He threw a straight right that crashed into Webster's nose and rocked his head back on his shoulders.

Webster's momentum carried him forward despite the blow. He blundered into Ace, who tried to shove him away. Their legs got tangled, and both men fell to the hard-packed dirt street.

Not far away, Mullen recovered quickly and scrambled back to his feet. Both he and Webster were packing iron, but in the heat of anger, he didn't go for his gun. Instead, he charged at Chance and lashed out with his fists.

Chance blocked the first blow, but the second got through and clipped him on the side of his head. His hat flew off as he staggered back a step. Mullen closed in confidently.

That confidence was misplaced. Chance ducked under the roundhouse blow Mullen swung at his head. He hooked a left into the man's belly, sinking his fist almost to the wrist. That made Mullen start to double over.

Chance lifted his right hand in an uppercut that landed on Mullen's chin. Mullen straightened and went over backward. Chance followed and positioned himself to strike again if Mullen tried to get up.

But once again, Mullen recovered faster than Chance anticipated. The man snapped his leg up in a kick and sank his boot heel in Chance's midsection. Chance reeled back, suddenly sick from the vicious impact, and dropped to one knee.

Nearby, Ace and Webster rolled over several times as they slugged at each other. That raised a small cloud of dust around them. It stung Ace's eyes and choked him, and that caused him to drop his guard enough that Webster landed a hard shot to his jaw. Ace's head jerked to the side, and he was half-stunned for a second.

Webster leaped on top of him, dug a knee into his belly, and clamped both hands around Ace's throat.

Webster's lean face twisted in a vicious snarl as he began choking Ace. His fingers were like bands of iron as they dug into Ace's throat. Fireworks were exploding already behind Ace's eyes, and he knew he was about to pass out.

Desperately, he cupped both hands and drove them against Webster's ears as hard as he could. The man's thick, oily blond curls blunted the impact, but Ace still hit him hard enough to make him cry out in surprise and pain.

Webster's grip slackened a little, too. Ace grabbed the man's wrists and tore his hands away from his throat. He would have liked to lie there and gasp for air for a moment, but he couldn't afford to do that. Instead, he bucked up off the ground and hauled hard on Webster's arms, throwing him to the side.

Free of his opponent's weight, Ace rolled in the other direction to put some space between them. He came up on hands and knees and paused there with his chest heaving as he tried to catch his breath.

Chance and Mullen both reached their feet at the same

time. They were covered with dust from the street. Both had lost their hats. Chance still felt a little sick from the kick in the belly, but he tried to ignore it as Mullen came at him again.

Mullen was slightly taller and heavier, with a little longer reach. He tried to use that to his advantage as he stood off and threw punches at Chance's head and body. Chance blocked the blows he could and absorbed the others, although each time one of Mullen's fists landed, the impact seemed to rock him a little more. He darted in and threw punches of his own, but he couldn't seem to land any of them solidly.

In a stand-up, toe-to-toe battle, he was going to lose, Chance realized.

That meant he had to utilize some strategy. He gave ground and let his arms sag more and more. That boosted Mullen's confidence. He bulled in, more reckless now that he believed he was on the verge of victory. He swung another roundhouse punch, which might have taken Chance's head off if it had landed.

Instead, Chance went low, drove his head into Mullen's belly, wrapped his arms around the man's thighs, and, with a shout of effort, straightened and heaved Mullen up and over his back. Mullen turned over in midair and crashed down on his back with stunning force.

Drained of strength, Chance stumbled forward a couple of steps. He caught himself and managed to turn around. He cocked his fists to launch more punches if he needed to, but he knew they wouldn't have much force behind them.

Mullen wasn't getting up, though. He tried but then fell back and lay there groaning, defeated.

Ace and Webster were slugging away at each other again, but Ace was getting the best of it. He had gotten his second wind, and his fists lashed out with more speed and power than Webster's. He drove Webster back until the man tripped over Mullen's half-senseless form and sprawled on the ground. Ace could tell that Webster thought about trying to get up again, but then he propped himself on an elbow, extended his other hand palm out, and gasped, "Enough . . . enough."

"Durned right it is," said Nick Beltz. He had the Sharps cradled in his arms, with the barrel pointing at the two hard cases. His thumb drew back the heavy rifle's hammer. "You boys head the other direction when you get up. Either of you take a step this way . . . or reach for a gun . . . and I'll blow a hole through you."

"You'll . . . be sorry about this . . . old man," Webster told him. "This is . . . none of your business." His hate-filled glare turned toward the Jensen brothers, who now stood side by side. "Or yours . . . either. You'll all pay . . . for stickin' . . . your noses in . . . where they don't belong."

Chance picked up his hat and started brushing the dirt off it. "I wish I had a dollar, or even a nickel, for every time we've heard that."

"Yeah." Ace slapped his own hat against his thigh. "Tough talk comes cheap."

The fight had garnered the attention of a considerable crowd. Muttering curses and glaring around at the onlookers, Webster struggled to his feet, then bent to help Mullen. When both men were upright, they hobbled off, clutching their hats. The crowd parted to let them through, then began to disperse.

Several men smiled and gave approving nods to Ace and Chance before they went about their business, however. Clearly, Mullen and Webster were known here in Panamint City—and disliked by some of the citizens.

With the trouble over, at least for the time being, Ace and Chance turned back toward Nick Beltz. The old-timer stood next to the young woman, who had lingered.

Ace and Chance pinched their hat brims as they nodded to her. Ace asked, "Are you all right, miss?"

"I should be the one asking you that," she replied. "Those

two troublemakers handled you much more roughly than they did me."

"Yes, but we can take it," Chance told her. He smiled. "We're used to dealing with lowlifes like that."

"Oh?" The young woman's interest perked up more. "You wouldn't happen to be lawmen, would you?"

"Us?" Chance shook his head. "No, we're just a couple of fellows who don't like to see ladies being mistreated."

Beltz put in, "They're in the habit of stickin' up for somebody who's outnumbered, too. They jumped in and run off a bunch of Scranton's men who'd bushwhacked me."

The girl smiled. "You've been busy on your first day in these parts, haven't you?"

"As a matter of fact, we have," Ace said.

She tightened her left arm around the bundle and extended her right hand. "I'm Priscilla Lansing."

Ace clasped her hand, which was cool and smooth, and said, "Ace Jensen."

"And I'm Chance Jensen," Chance said as he took his turn shaking hands with Priscilla Lansing.

"Brothers?" she said.

"Twins, believe it or not," Ace said. "Not identical."

"She can see that with her own eyes," Chance said. His smile widened. "I'm much better looking."

"I think you both look just fine," Priscilla said. She arched a finely curved dark eyebrow. "Although a bit dusty at the moment."

She looked mighty fine, Ace thought, and not the least bit dusty. She was in her early twenties, he guessed, about the same age as him and Chance. Raven hair fell to her shoulders around a very attractive face with slightly olive skin and dark brown eyes. She wore a plain dark green dress but somehow made it look like an elegant gown.

Ace and Chance would have enjoyed talking longer to her,

but at that moment, another man hurried along the street toward them and called, "Priscilla! I heard there was trouble.
Are you all right?"

He came up to them, with an anxious look on his face. He
was in his late twenties, perhaps, and slender in a brown
tweed suit. A tan hat rode on his sandy hair. He wore specta-
cles and had a thin, intelligent face.

He also carried a black bag in his left hand, identifying him
as a doctor. He confirmed that by continuing, "I brought my
medical bag in case anyone needs attention."

"I believe everyone is all right, Dr. Drake," she told him.
She turned to Ace and Chance and added, "Isn't that correct?"

"We're fine," Chance said. "A little tussle like that is
nothing."

Ace could tell from the way Chance stood that his belly still
hurt where he'd been kicked. They would both be sore in the
morning. But Chance was right—other than the bumps and
bruises, they weren't hurt.

Priscilla said, "This is my friend Dr. Allan Drake. Doctor, Ace
and Chance Jensen. A couple of Mr. Scranton's men were being
rude and bothering me, and they stepped in to assist me."

"Well, I'm grateful to you for that, gentlemen," Drake said
as he shook hands with the Jensen brothers. "Panamint City
needs more citizens who are willing to stand up and be counted
on the side of law and order, against the elements who foster
an atmosphere of brutality and violence—"

"Speakin' of which," Nick Beltz cut in, "here comes Big
Dave."

Chapter 12

The other four turned to look. The man striding along the street toward them cut an impressive figure.

He was tall and broad shouldered, big enough that he had a lumbering, bearlike gait. His face was all planes and sharp angles and looked as if it had been hewn out of a square block of granite. He wore a black suit and had a flat-crowned black hat on his dark, gray-shot hair. A diamond stickpin glittered on his cravat, and a heavy silver watch chain looped across his vest. Despite the expensive clothes, he had the air of a man who would be more at home in work garb, swinging a sledgehammer or a pickax.

Ace was a little surprised that Scranton was alone. From everything he'd heard about the man, he figured Scranton would have some gun-wolves with him.

On the other hand, Scranton seemed like the sort of man who believed he could take care of himself. He would save his hired guns for more important work than serving as his bodyguard.

Like ambushing old-timers such as Nick Beltz . . .

Scranton came to a stop, politely raised a finger to his hat brim as he nodded to Priscilla, and rumbled in a gravelly voice, "Good afternoon, Miss Lansing. I hear you had an unpleasant encounter with a couple of my men a short time ago. I want to convey my apologies on their behalf."

"It would be more meaningful if they apologized themselves," Priscilla said.

"Yes, but they're crude brutes," Scranton said with a smile. "They have their uses, but civilized behavior isn't their strong suit. I've made it clear to them that they're not to annoy you in the future."

"Thank you," Priscilla said.

Beltz said, "How about me? Are your men gonna keep annoyin' me, Dave?"

Scranton's smile disappeared. He turned a chilly look toward the old-timer. "I don't know what you're talking about, Nick."

"Some o' your boys jumped me this afternoon. Came close to sendin' me across the divide. Would have if not for these young fellas."

Scranton glanced at Ace and Chance and said, "You're the two who tangled with Mullen and Webster."

"That's right," Ace said. "They were trying to manhandle Miss Lansing."

"So they had it coming," Chance added.

"I've already addressed that issue. What's this about you helping Nick here?"

"We came along while some of your men were trying to kill him," Ace said.

Scranton frowned. "That's a mighty serious accusation, young man. How do you *know* those men work for me?"

"Who else would bushwhack me like that?" Beltz demanded.

"I'm sure I don't have any idea," Scranton replied with a shake of his head, "but I can tell you none of my men did. They're all accounted for, all day."

He and Beltz traded cold stares for several seconds; then the old-timer let out a contemptuous snort. "I knowed it was no good tryin' to prove it. They'd all just lie for one another."

Scranton turned back to Ace and Chance and looked them up and down. "New in Panamint City, aren't you?" he asked.

"That's right," Ace said. "We just got here."

"And you've already proven that you're handy with both guns and fists. You wouldn't happen to be looking for work, would you? I can always use competent men."

Chance began, "We wouldn't work for the likes of—"

Ace put a hand on his brother's arm to stop him. "We're not looking for work," he told Scranton.

"Well, if you change your mind, you can usually find me in my office above the Silver Slipper." Scranton paused, then added, "That's the saloon I own." He nodded to Priscilla again, said, "Miss Lansing, Dr. Drake," and turned to walk away.

Beltz fondled the smooth stock of the old Sharps and said under his breath, "It'd be mighty easy to blow a hole right through that sidewindin' skunk—"

"That would be murder, Mr. Beltz," Drake said. "You don't want to do that."

The old-timer sighed. "I might want to, but I won't."

"Scranton looks a little like a bear in a suit," Ace commented, "but he's well spoken."

Dr. Drake said, "He comes from a fairly well-to-do family back East, I believe. He's had some education. But he's still a hard, ruthless man. I don't believe he intends to stop until he owns everything in Panamint City and up and down Surprise Canyon."

"Well, he ain't gonna own everything," Beltz declared. "Or if he does, he'll have to kill me and them Steingrim brothers first."

Priscilla put her free hand on Beltz's arm and asked, "How are Baldur, Folke, and Haldor?"

"They're fine, I reckon. Crotchety and cantankerous as ever."

"They should come into town more often. They can't spend all their time underground."

"Oh, they like it back in the tunnels," Beltz said. "They claim that's where they feel most at home."

"Well, you tell them to come by the mission sometime and see me."

Beltz nodded. "I'll do that."

"Mission?" Chance repeated.

"That's right," Priscilla said. "That's where I was headed when those troublemakers stopped me."

"You're not . . . a nun?" Chance asked.

She laughed. "Goodness, no. But a person can do good works without being a member of a holy order, can't she?"

"Absolutely," Ace said. "And I'm not going to try to take that package away from you like those two varmints did, but we shouldn't be standing around letting you hold it. I'll be glad to carry it for you—"

"I've got it," Drake said, moving quickly to take the paper-wrapped bundle from Priscilla before either she or the Jensen brothers could stop him. "I'll walk with you back to the mission, Miss Lansing, if that's all right. There are a couple of patients whose cases I'd like to discuss with you."

"That'll be fine, I suppose, Doctor. Thank you."

The two of them moved off along the street. Ace, Chance, and Beltz watched them go.

Ace said, "Why does he want to talk about patients with her? Is she a nurse?"

"She helps him out some from time to time," Beltz explained. "And anybody with eyes can see the doc's sweet on her."

"What's this mission she was talking about?" Chance wanted to know.

"Back durin' one o' the earlier booms, some o' the boys got together and founded one of them Odd Fellow lodges. Built themselves a hall and everything. But it didn't last, and the hall was just a-sittin' there empty until Miss Priscilla come along and bought it. She turned it into a mission to help out folks who are havin' a hard time of it, whether they're sick or hungry or both. Anybody with an ailment who can't afford to pay the doc, they can go to the mission, and Miss Priscilla'll see that it gets took care of. She's been talkin' about tryin' to start a school there, too."

"A school?" Ace repeated. "What for? I haven't seen any children around."

"Oh, there's a whole passel o' young'uns in Panamint City and up and down the canyon! You just ain't seen 'em, because they're all inside workin', either in one o' the businesses here in town or out in the mines. The scrawny ones are good for gettin' into narrow spaces in the tunnels." Beltz pursed his lips. "I don't much care for that myself. Hate to see the little 'uns workin' so hard. Seems like they ought to have a chance just to be kids. But there ain't much I can do about it."

"I'll bet Miss Lansing doesn't like it, either," Ace said.

"No, she sure don't. She does what she can to help 'em out. That's why she hopes to get a school goin'."

"If there's anything we can do to help her, we'd be glad to."

Beltz wheezed and chuckled. "A mite took with her yourself, are you, lad?"

"That's not what I said." Ace felt his face warming. "I just admire someone who tries to do good like that."

"Especially when she's a pretty girl, eh, brother?" Chance said. "I don't reckon you'll be much competition for that handsome doctor, though."

"I'm not competing with anybody," Ace said through clenched teeth. "I just like to help folks."

Beltz gave him a hard slap on the back and said, "Come on to the store with me, then! You can help me load up the supplies I come to town to get. And then if you want, you can help me pack 'em back out to the mine."

"Are *you* offering us jobs now?" Chance asked.

"Nope, but I never turn down volunteers!"

Chapter 13

Ace and Chance walked on to the store with Beltz, as the old-timer had suggested. Ace spotted the assay and land office across the street and felt the urge to head in that direction, but at the same time, he was curious about a few things and decided to scratch that itch instead.

"You and Scranton seem to know each other fairly well," he commented. He already knew Beltz well enough to figure that would be enough to get the man talking.

"Oh, sure," Beltz said. "Not that long ago, Dave was just another prospector like the rest of us, diggin' in the dirt and gougin' rocks outta the ground. It ain't like we were friends or anything, mind you, but we knowed each other and got along well enough, I reckon. The doc mentioned that Scranton comes from a rich family back East, and that may well be true. But judgin' by things I've heard him say, he was the black sheep o' that family and was as hard up when he got here as any other desert rat!

"Then, a few months back," Beltz went on, "he struck a mighty big vein of high-grade silver, and it wasn't no time a'tall until he was struttin' around here in them fancy duds, buyin' up businesses and claims and hirin' fellas to work in his mines while he sits in his office, spinnin' a web like a danged ol' spider. He made no secret o' the fact that he figures on bein' the biggest man in Surprise Canyon. Maybe, before it's all said and done, one o' the biggest in the whole darn state of Californy!" The old-timer tugged on his whiskers and frowned in thought. "Might have somethin' to do with the way his family turned their backs on him and he got run off where he comes from. Reckon he's out to show all the folks back home that he's better'n them, even if he has to run roughshod over ever'body in these parts to do it!"

They had reached the store and tied up their horses and the mule at the hitchrack while Beltz was talking. Now they went inside, and Beltz headed for the counter at the back of the store to give the clerk the order for his supplies. Ace and Chance hung back.

"I've been thinking about something," Chance said quietly. "Scranton didn't look too happy with old Nick when he walked off."

"I thought the same thing," Ace agreed. "He must really want Mr. Beltz's mine, if he would send men to ambush him like that."

"A man who'll have somebody bushwhacked once will do it again."

"That's right. So it might be a good idea for us to make sure he gets back to his claim safely."

"Is that all right?" Chance asked. "I mean, I know we came all this way to check out my mine . . . I mean, *our* mine—"

Ace held up a hand to stop him. "You're the one who bluffed Bellamy out of that pot. It's your mine, Chance."

"The hell with that! You know it's always been share and share alike with us, Ace."

"We can talk about that later," Ace said. "For now, I agree that there's no real hurry about finding the mine. I saw the assay and land office across the street. Why don't you take the deed over there and see if the man who runs it can give you directions? I'll wait here with Mr. Beltz and help him with his supplies. Then we can all go back down the canyon to his mine and make sure he gets there all right before we go looking for the other one. That sound all right to you?"

"Almost, but not quite," Chance said. He reached inside his coat and slipped out the folded piece of paper. As he held it out to Ace, he went on, "I got this out of my saddlebag and brought it with me because I didn't want to leave it out there on the street. You've always had a lot better sense of direction than I do, brother. *You* go talk to the fella at the land office while I help old Nick load his supplies."

"Are you sure?" Ace asked with a slight frown as he took the document.

"You're the brains of this outfit, Ace. Always have been." Chance grinned. "I'm the handsome one, remember?"

Ace hesitated. Chance was plenty smart, and they both knew it. But he was also right that Ace had the better sense of direction and an instinctive awareness of where he was.

"All right," he said. "I'll go see what I can find out."

He slipped the deed into the inner pocket of his denim jacket and left the store. Panamint City's main street was still busy. Wagons and buckboards rattled along its rough surface. Men on foot clogged the boardwalks, and riders on horses and mules added to the traffic in the street. Ace weaved his way across, toward his destination.

The sign above the frame building's door read ASSAY SERVICES – LAND RECORDS AND CLAIMS – INYO COUNTY, CALIFORNIA. A window to the right of the door revealed a chest-high counter inside. Ace went in and saw a man sitting at a desk on the other side of that counter. An open door behind him led into a room with a table and some apparatus on it. Ace figured that was where the assaying work took place.

A little bell above the door rang when Ace opened it. The man looked up from the paperwork he was doing and then got to his feet. He came around the desk, approached the counter, and said in a friendly voice, "Good afternoon. What can I do for you?"

He was stocky, a little below medium height, with curly dark hair. He wore a white shirt and gray vest. His suit jacket was hung over the back of his chair. Ace figured the man was in his midthirties.

"I need some information," he said as he took out the deed. He had already spotted a large framed map on the right-hand wall. Nodding toward it, he went on, "And I'd like to study that for a spell, if that's all right."

"Certainly," the man replied. "That's an official county map, for use by the public. Can I help you find something on it?"

Ace unfolded the document and spread it on the counter, turning it so that it faced the man. He put a finger on the part that detailed the mine's location and said, "I'm looking for this place—"

That was as far as he got before the window glass crashed behind him and he felt the wind-rip of a bullet as it sizzled through the air only inches from his left ear.

The man on the other side of the counter let out a startled, frightened yell and made a dive for the floor, suggesting that the shot hadn't hit him. Ace flung himself down, as well. As he did, however, he grabbed the deed and stuffed it back under his jacket.

Two more shots rang out in quick succession. The slugs thudded into the wall separating the front and back rooms. Ace rolled and caught a glimpse through the broken window of a man standing on the boardwalk outside, with a smoking gun in his hand.

Ace had drawn his Colt as he'd thrown himself to the floor. He angled the barrel up and squeezed the trigger. The gun roared and bucked in his hand as he sent a slug toward the bushwhacker lurking on the other side of the window. The man yelped and jerked backward. Ace didn't know if his shot had scored. That seemed unlikely, because the next moment, heavy footsteps pounded the planks as the gunman fled.

Ace leaped to his feet. He darted to the door, threw it open, and risked a look outside. As he did, the man running along the street to his left twisted and flung a shot back at him. Ace ducked instinctively as the bullet chewed splinters from the jamb, not far from his head.

Then he gave chase. He wasn't going to allow anybody to take potshots at him and get away with it.

The gunfire had alerted people on the street that something was going on. Some of the bystanders scurried to get out of any potential lines of fire, while others jumped forward, wide-eyed with interest, and yelled questions.

The fleeing man leaped around some of them and shoved others aside. Indignant shouts followed him. Ace twisted and darted through the crowd but tried to avoid knocking anyone down.

The bushwhacker glanced back again. This time Ace got a good look at his face. He recognized Webster, the man he had battled with earlier.

Webster might have been following Ace, waiting for a chance to try to kill him, or he might have been walking along the street and spotted the young man in the assay and land office, then acted on impulse to take a shot at him.

Either way, Ace wanted to catch up to him and make sure it didn't happen again.

He holstered his gun so he could run harder. If he got close enough, he could bring Webster down with a flying tackle. Then he would force the man to talk, because a *third* possibility had just occurred to Ace.

Big Dave Scranton could have sent Webster after him. Since the Jensen brothers had sided with Nick Beltz and then turned down Scranton's offer of a job, Scranton might have decided it was in his best interest to get rid of them.

That thought made a surge of fear for Chance's safety well up inside Ace, but he had to deal with this threat before he could check on his brother. More of the crowd had cleared away ahead of Webster. He stumbled a little as he ran through the open space.

Just then, the first youngster Ace had seen in Panamint City appeared. A little girl stepped out from the boardwalk in front of a building, evidently unaware of the desperate gunman pounding toward her. When she saw Webster looming in front of her, she cried out in fear.

The next second, his left hand clamped on her shoulder. He twisted and started to drag her in front of him as he brought up the gun in his other hand.

Ace knew instantly what Webster was doing. The man intended to use the little girl as a shield while he gunned down Ace. While he still had a relatively clear shot at Webster, Ace came to a sudden stop and his hand flashed to the Colt on his hip.

Ace didn't possess the same gun speed as his father and uncles, but he was pretty fast. His Colt came up and slammed out a shot before Webster could pull the trigger again. Webster's head jerked back as the .45 slug struck him in the center of the forehead. That was a risky shot on Ace's part, but if it was successful, it would put Webster down and render him no longer a threat faster than anything else.

That was exactly what happened. The gun flew out of Webster's right hand, his left hand let go of the girl's shoulder, and his knees buckled, all at the same time. He fell to his knees and then pitched forward as the terrified girl scrambled back onto the boardwalk. A woman waiting there grabbed her and held her tightly.

Ace trotted forward, holding his gun ready, even though he

knew Webster was dead. A small dark pool appeared under the man's head, with the dirt sucking up the blood almost as fast as it welled out through the hole in his forehead.

Ace looked over to the boardwalk, saw that the woman hugging the little girl was Priscilla Lansing. A sign on the large building behind them read PANAMINT CITY MISSION. He hadn't had time to notice that until now. Priscilla's face was pale with shock under its healthy olive tint.

"Is she all right?" Ace asked as he nodded toward the little girl.

"I . . . I think so." Priscilla put her hand on the girl's shoulders and moved back a little. "Lucy, are you hurt?"

The girl was shaken and crying, but she shook her head to indicate that she hadn't come to any real harm.

Priscilla looked up at Ace and said, "She's all right—"

More shots blasted somewhere up the street. Ace hadn't forgotten that Chance might be the target of an ambush attempt, too. He whirled around and ran through the crowd that had started to gather behind him. His heart slugged with fear for his brother as he ran toward the general store.

Chapter 14

"Where'd your brother go?" Nick Beltz asked Chance when the old-timer had finished giving his order to the clerk.

"Oh, he just had to go run an errand," Chance replied with a casual wave of his hand. After thinking about it, he believed it was best not to reveal to the old-timer why he and Ace were here in Panamint City. After all, they didn't really know Beltz that well. Not well enough to reveal to him that they were the owners of a potentially lucrative silver mine.

"Well, if he's not back in time, the two of us can handle loading those supplies. If you want to come out to the mine with me, I'll introduce you to those Scandihoovians, and you can have supper with us and spend the night." A grin added extra wrinkles to the old-timer's face. "To tell you the truth, it'd be nice to have somebody else around to talk to. Them Steingrims savvy English all right, but mostly they palaver in their own lingo." He paused, then added, "Best I ever seen with picks and shovels, though. They can go through rock like it ain't hardly there."

The two men ambled toward the front of the store as Beltz continued talking. He pulled a pipe and a tobacco pouch from his pocket and began filling the gnarled old briar. He had just swiped a match across the seat of his canvas trousers and held the flame to the bowl when gunshots sounded somewhere else in town.

Chance stiffened and muttered, "What in blazes?"

Beltz puffed on the pipe to get it going. As a cloud of smoke wreathed his head, he clamped his teeth on the stem and said around it, "This here's a boomtown, remember? Not a day goes by when there *ain't* some shootin'. Sometimes there'll be three or four different ruckuses in a day. Most folks just duck their heads and go on about their business when one o' them corpse-and-cartridge sessions breaks out."

Chance made a face and said, "Yeah, but Ace is out there somewhere. I'd better go check on him."

"Sure, it won't hurt—" Beltz began.

They had just turned toward the front door when it swung open and the burly gunman called Mullen stepped into the store. He had a revolver in each hand and pointed them at Chance and Beltz, who stopped in their tracks.

Chance's first impulse was to reach for the ivory-handled Smith & Wesson .38 he carried in a cross-draw rig under his coat. It was impossible to outdraw an already leveled gun, though, and since Mullen hadn't started pulling the triggers immediately, it might be better to wait and see what happened.

"Don't move, you two," Mullen snarled. "Just stand right there and listen to those shots."

"What the hell are you doin'?" Beltz demanded. "Put those hoglegs down, you dang fool, before I blow a hole the size of your head through you with this Sharps o' mine!"

"I can put half a dozen bullets in you before you can lift that blunderbuss, you old pelican," Mullen said.

The store had a few other customers, in addition to the clerk, who called, "What's going on up there? Is this a holdup?"

"No holdup," Mullen replied, "and nobody's gonna get

hurt except these two if you all just stay back and keep your heads down. But if anybody tries to stop me from doin' what I came to do, then you can die, too, damn it!"

"Take it easy," Chance said. He kept his hands where Mullen could see them and didn't make any sudden moves. "Nobody has to die here."

Mullen's face twisted in an ugly grin. "That's where you're wrong, kid. You didn't think Webster and me were gonna let you and that other pip-squeak get away with what you done, did you?"

"You mean thrashing both of you soundly?"

Mullen's grin turned into a scowl. "You took us by surprise!" he said. "You never would've whipped us otherwise."

Irregularly spaced shots continued to crash somewhere not far off in Panamint City. Each one felt like a punch in the gut to Chance. He said, "Is that shooting—"

"That's Webster finishing off your pard," Mullen said. "And when he's done, I'm gonna send you and the old coot to hell. I just wanted you to hear your friend dying first."

"You're one o' the varmints who bushwhacked me today!" Beltz accused. "Big Dave sent you to do it, and he prob'ly sent you here to throw down on us now!"

"You run your mouth too much," Mullen snarled. He lifted the left-hand gun a little. "I think I'll go ahead and close it right—"

Chance knew he couldn't bide his time any longer. He lowered his shoulder, dived to his right, and crashed into Nick Beltz, knocking the old-timer sprawling in one of the store's aisles.

Mullen opened fire with both guns. Flame and lead spewed from the muzzles. Bullets ripped through the space Chance and Beltz had occupied only a heartbeat earlier. Chance hoped everybody behind them in the store had gotten out of the way.

Bellowing incoherently in rage, Mullen charged forward

and swung around toward the aisle where Chance and Beltz had taken cover. Chance had fallen on top of the old-timer. He pushed himself up on his left hand and drew the Smith & Wesson with the other hand.

Mullen triggered first, with his left-hand gun, but when the hammer fell, it produced just a futile click. In the wild volley he had fired, he had emptied that weapon.

Chance's .38 cracked. The bullet, on an upward trajectory, caught Mullen under the chin. It bored on through his throat and the base of his brain. Mullen toppled backward and fired the final round in his right-hand gun. It went harmlessly into the store's ceiling because Mullen's fall had pulled his arm up. Both guns clattered to the floor as they slipped from his nerveless fingers.

Chance sat up and kept his gun trained on Mullen, even though he was sure the hard case was dead. He climbed to his feet, stepped over to the fallen man, and kicked well out of reach both guns that Mullen had dropped. He looked down into the man's staring, sightless eyes for a second, then turned his attention back to Beltz.

"Are you all right, Nick?" he asked.

"I'm fine, I'm fine," Beltz wheezed in his querulous, high-pitched whine, "except I'm gonna have a big bruise where you plowed into me!"

"Better a bruise than a bullet hole."

Beltz waved a hand. "Oh, that rapscallion never would've hit me. I'm quicker and nimbler than I look!"

Chance ignored that and turned to look toward the rear of the store. "Everybody all right back there?" he called.

"We all ducked when the shooting started," the clerk replied. "Mullen did some damage with all that lead he was throwing around, though."

Beltz had gotten to his feet. He leaned the Sharps against some shelves and slapped dust off his trousers.

"You can send the bill for the damages to Big Dave," he told the man. "You can bet he was behind this!"

"And *I'll* bet there's no way to prove that," Chance commented. "Men like Scranton are good at shielding themselves from all the trouble they cause."

"Yeah, you may be right," Beltz grumbled. "But we all know who's to blame for this, and I ain't gonna be shy about expressin' that opinion to anybody who'll listen, either!"

"Which will give Scranton even more of a reason to hold a grudge against you," Chance pointed out.

Beltz snorted. "Things have gone way too far already for me to worry about that!"

He probably had a point. Before Chance could say anything else, running footsteps sounded just outside the door. Chance started to lift the .38 again, then lowered it as Ace appeared in the doorway, Colt in hand.

Ace's keen eyes took in the scene instantly. "Looks like I got here a little too late for the action," he said.

"Was that some action of your own I heard a minute ago?" Chance asked.

"Yeah, that fella Webster took a couple of shots at me," Ace replied with a nod.

"He get away?"

"He did not." Ace looked down at Mullen, who lay in a pool of blood that had leaked from his bullet-torn throat. "I see this hombre didn't, either." Ace's gaze lifted to his brother. "You're not hurt?"

"No, and neither is Nick. Mullen threw a lot of lead around but didn't manage to hit anything except merchandise."

"Which somebody's going to have to pay for," the clerk put in.

"Go talk to Scranton, like I told you," Beltz growled. "But wait until after you've got that order o' mine ready to go."

"It's ready, it's ready," the clerk said with an exasperated note in his voice. "In fact, it'd be fine with me if you'd take it and go."

"Well, then, what're we standin' around for?" Beltz waved a thick-fingered hand at the Jensen brothers. "Come on, boys. Let's get 'er loaded up so's we can rattle our hocks outta this unfriendly town!"

Chapter 15

Because of his worry about Chance, Ace had rushed back to the general store without checking on the man who ran the assay and land office. After pleading one more errand to run, he left Chance to help Beltz—once the local undertaker had arrived to get Mullen's body out of the way—and returned to the office on the other side of the street.

The pudgy, curly-haired man looked up and got a look of alarm on his face when Ace walked in.

"No one is going to try to shoot you this time, right?" he asked.

"Not that I know of," Ace said, "but to be honest, I wasn't expecting to get shot at the last time, either."

The man pointed at the broken window. "I'm going to have to board that up, you know. And boards aren't that easy to come by in Panamint City! I'll probably have to just tack some tar paper or canvas over it, and then I won't get any light or air in here."

"Sorry," Ace said. "I should've been more considerate and asked that hombre to wait and bushwhack me when I came back out."

"Yeah, you should've," the man said, but this time a hint of a smile lurked around his mouth. "Don't worry about it. I'll bill Inyo County for part of the cost of a new window, since I run the land office for them. The assaying part is a private business. *My* business." He stuck his hand over the counter. "I'm Theodore Whittier."

"Nice to meet you, Mr. Whittier," Ace said as he shook hands. "My name's Jensen. Ace Jensen. And if I can make a suggestion . . . ?"

"Please do."

"You might ask Mr. Dave Scranton to kick in for some of the cost, too. That fella who opened fire through your window works for him. *Worked* for him."

Whittier grunted. "Yeah, I heard you caught up to him down in front of the mission. That was good work, saving that little girl. Risky, but good."

Ace shrugged. "Wasn't really time to do anything else. Standing around and trying to talk sense into a fella like Webster never does any good."

"Amen to that." Whittier put his hands flat on the counter. "Now, you came in here for something earlier . . . ?"

Ace reached into his jacket and found the paper he had stuffed in there. It was pretty crumpled up now, but he placed it on the counter and smoothed it out.

"I was trying to find out where this mining claim is located," he explained. "There's no map on it, and those coordinates and landmarks don't mean anything to me."

"Well, let's see," Whittier said as he leaned over the paper. "This is dated before I took over this office, so I don't have any personal knowledge of it . . . but we should be able to find it on the map, like you suggested . . ."

He picked up the paper and carried it over to the map. Ace followed and watched over his shoulder as Whittier rested a fingertip on the map and looked back and forth between it and the deed.

"Here . . . and here . . . and here." Whittier's finger moved each time he spoke. "Coffin Rock . . . Buzzard's Notch . . . the Spider Hole . . ." He leaned closer to the map on the wall and squinted, then tapped his fingertip against it. "Right here, on the north side of the canyon. That's approximately three and a half miles from here. Look for this little double peak here, and then this sawtooth ridge . . ." He turned away from the map and held up the deed. "This is your mine?"

"My brother's. He wants to put it in both of our names, but I don't really care about that."

"You might, if it turns out to have any color in it." Whittier shrugged. "But that's none of my business. Have him come in when he gets a chance, and I can record it officially for him."

"I'll do that," Ace said. "It might be a day or two."

That bit of business could wait until they were sure Nick Beltz made it back safely to his mine. As late in the day as it was, more than likely they would take him up on his offer to spend the night, too. But they could find Chance's mine tomorrow and get it recorded.

Whittier handed the deed back to Ace. "Be sure to hang on to that," he advised. "When your brother registers it, I can make a copy and keep it here, but for the time being, that's the only way to prove he owns that particular claim."

Ace slid the document back in his pocket. "We'll take good care of it."

"Try not to get any blood on it if anybody starts shooting at you again."

"I'll remember that," Ace said with a smile.

He said so long and left the office. As he stepped out into the street, he looked toward the general store, where Chance and Beltz were lashing several bundles of supplies to the old-timer's pack mule.

Then he heard someone say, "Mr. Jensen," he turned the other way, and saw Priscilla Lansing coming toward him.

Ace took his hat off and went to meet her. As he came up to

her and they both stopped, he said, "That little girl . . . she's all right?"

"She was terrified, of course, but is unharmed, thank goodness."

"I'm mighty sorry she was put in danger, even briefly, because of me."

Priscilla cocked her head to the side. "Why do you say that? It wasn't your fault. In fact, your quick action saved Lucy from being in even greater danger, I'd say."

"I'm the one Webster was trying to kill."

"Which makes *him* to blame and you a victim, as well."

"There's no arguing with that logic."

"Don't misunderstand," Priscilla went on. "I hate the idea that gunplay is so common in this town that a young girl . . . or anyone else . . . can't step outside without risking getting in the way of a bullet. I suppose men such as you and your brother . . . men who are accustomed to such violence . . . contribute to it simply by existing."

"At the same time, without men like us to step in and try to protect folks, things might be a lot worse."

Priscilla sighed. "Unfortunately, that's true, as well." She smiled. "At any rate, I'm glad you're all right, and I appreciate what you did. Even though I wish it hadn't been necessary."

"Can't argue with you there."

"What are you going to do now? Are you and your brother planning to stay in Panamint City?"

"Today we're going back out to Mr. Beltz's mine with him, to make sure he gets there without any more trouble from Scranton's men. After that . . ." Ace shrugged. "We haven't made any firm plans for after that."

"Well, if you're around . . . I hope to see you again. Without any gunplay going on next time."

"Amen to that," Ace said. He nodded politely, put his hat on, and turned to head back to the store.

Chance and Beltz had finished tying down the supplies. Chance grinned and said, "If I had known you were going to go chasing off to flirt with young ladies, I would have told you to stay here and help us."

"She hailed me," Ace pointed out. "It wasn't my idea."

"But you didn't argue overmuch, did you, son?" Beltz asked. He cackled with glee. "Went scurryin' right down the road to talk to her. Not that I blame you, no sirree! Any gal who looked like Miss Priscilla called out to me, I'd go a-runnin' to answer her! Afraid those days is long since over for the likes o' me, though."

The old-timer took up the mule's lead rope and started walking. Leading their mounts and packhorses, the Jensen brothers fell in alongside him.

The sun was fairly low in the western sky ahead of them as they headed back down the canyon. Beltz assured them that they would reach the mine before nightfall, though.

"It'll take about an hour and a half to get there," he said. "It's right at three and a half miles from Panamint City to the mine. Wouldn't take that long except that the ground's so rugged and you can't rush this dang mule. Ain't that right, Mehitabel?"

The mule didn't say anything.

Ace did, though. With a slight frown on his face, he asked, "Three and a half miles, you say?"

"Yep. Ain't ever measured it to the foot, of course. Be hard to do that. But that distance is pretty dang close, mark my words."

Ace nodded slowly.

After a while, he pointed to a distinctive rock formation jutting up from the canyon wall on their right and asked, "Does that have a name?"

"Folks around here call it Coffin Rock."

Chance said, "It's shaped a little like a coffin, isn't it?"

"Yep."

A little farther on, Ace called the old-timer's attention to a gap in the rimrock on the southern side of the canyon. "That's interesting."

"Buzzard's Notch," Beltz said. He laughed. "I've come by here and seen nigh on to a dozen of them ugly critters sittin' up there, just a-waitin' for somethin' to die. Ain't sure why they like that spot so much, but they do."

"Is there a place called the Spider Hole around here, too?"

"Sure is. How'd you know about the Spider Hole?"

"I heard somebody mention it in town," Ace said. "The name just struck me as distinctive."

"Yeah, it ain't far from my mine. I'll point it out when we go past."

They walked on. As they did, a disturbing conviction grew stronger inside Ace.

The Spider Hole was just that, a hole in the canyon wall filled with spiderwebs. Chance looked at it and shuddered.

"I never did have much use for creepy-crawlies," he said.

"Me, neither," Beltz agreed. "They can plumb stay away from me."

After they had gone a few hundred more yards, Beltz pointed to a switchback trail that had been hacked into the northern canyon wall. It led up to a brushy notch where a thread of smoke was rising from a fire.

"That's it," he announced with a note of pride in his voice. "That's my mine. Let's go on up and say howdy to the Stein-grim brothers."

Ace looked down at the ground. Those latitude and longitude lines he had mentioned to Chance earlier may not have been marked on the earth, but despite that, he was certain of one thing.

That mine up there . . . the mine claimed and worked by Nick Beltz . . . was the same one described on the deed that was still in his pocket.

Chapter 16

Ace almost blurted out the realization, but he clamped his mouth shut at the last second. Thoughts raced through his brain. Beltz had never said how long he had been working this mine. He could have come along and taken it over after Tom Bellamy abandoned it. Obviously, Beltz and his helpers were taking silver ore out of the mine, which would mean that Bellamy had given up on it too soon.

The more Ace considered the situation, the more evident it was to him that that was what had happened. Beltz hadn't filed a claim, had just moved in and started mining the silver.

Ace didn't know if that was legal or not. They would have to hash that out later. For now, he wanted to talk to Chance and tell his brother what he'd figured out, before either of them said anything to Beltz about the matter.

"Ace?" Chance said. "Something wrong?"

"What?" Ace realized that Beltz had started up the trail and Chance had followed him. He was still lost in thought at the bottom, though. "Sorry. I guess my mind wandered."

A few yards up the trail, Beltz laughed. "He's just thinkin' about Miss Priscilla, that's all. Nothin' like a pretty gal to get a fella all distractified."

Ace tightened his grip on the reins of his saddle horse and

the second packhorse and muttered, "All right, all right. I'm coming." He started up the trail after Chance.

The slope wasn't difficult, but the climb took several minutes because of the switchbacks. When the three men reached the top, Ace saw that the notch was about fifty yards across at the front, its widest point. The sides angled back to a cliff, where the mine was located. Except for the gap where the trail ended, brush had been left along the front, to provide some protection from the elements, but had been cleared out farther back. Ace saw two tents, one larger than the other, and a brush corral, where several more mules grazed on the scanty grass. A campfire burned between the tents and the corral. A man knelt beside it, frying bacon in a pan. A coffeepot sat at the edge of the flames, too, and a pot of beans bubbled near it. Biscuits baked in a Dutch oven. The mingled appetizing aromas reminded Ace of how long it had been since he and Chance had eaten.

The sound of a pickax ringing against rock drifted from inside the tunnel. Ace figured the man at the fire was one of the Steingrim brothers and the other two were working in the mine. As he, Chance, and Beltz approached, the man at the fire set the pan aside, straightened, and came toward them.

Ace had heard folks describe some men as being "as wide as they were tall," but this fellow was the first one he'd laid eyes on who almost fit that description. He doubted if the man topped five feet, but his shoulders were very broad, and his arms and legs were enormous with muscle. They strained the red-checked flannel shirt and the canvas overalls he wore. His feet in work boots were huge. Between a wild thatch of reddish-brown hair and a bushy beard of the same shade, not much of his face and head was visible.

"Who are dese fellows?" he asked Beltz. His voice was so low pitched and rumbling that Ace had a little trouble making out the words.

"New friends I ran into on the way into town," Beltz said. "They pitched in and gave me a hand when some o' Big Dave's men jumped me. Boys, meet Folke Steingrim. Folke, this is Ace and Chance Jensen."

"Howdy," Chance said with a smile and nod. "It's good to meet you . . . Folke." He hesitated a little over the name but tried to pronounce it the way Beltz had. He stuck out his hand.

Folke's massive paw, which looked like it might not fit in a five-gallon bucket, swallowed Chance's hand. Chance looked apprehensive, as if he feared that Folke might crush every bone in his hand, but then he relaxed. Folke must have taken it easy on his grip, Ace thought.

That was the case, he found out a moment later, when he shook hands with the man, as well. He could sense the incredible power, but Folke kept it restrained.

"Thank you for helping Nick," Folke said. "You stay, eat with us, yah?"

"That's the idea," Beltz said. "I invited 'em to spend the night." He eyed the Jensen brothers. "As handy as they are with guns and fists, I wouldn't mind if they decided to stick around even longer. There's no tellin' what sort o' deviltry Scranton will get up to next."

Folke waved a big hand toward the corral. "You can put horses away. Supper be ready soon. Plenty for two more!"

"We're obliged to you," Ace said.

He and Chance led their mounts and the packhorses toward the brush enclosure. Behind them, Folke started unloading the supplies from Beltz's mule Mehitabel.

Quietly, Chance said, "Sooner or later we're going to have to tell Nick that we have a mine of our own to tend to, so we can't work for him. He's just such a colorful sort that I've enjoyed spending time with him."

"Yeah, me, too," Ace agreed. "But about that mine of ours . . . yours . . . whatever you want to call it . . ."

"Yeah?" Chance prodded when his brother's voice trailed off. "What about it?"

Ace drew a deep breath, nodded toward the tunnel mouth, and said, "I'm looking at it."

Chance frowned at him in confusion for a few seconds, then turned his head and stared at the tunnel before swinging his startled gaze back to Ace.

"You mean . . . *this* mine?"

"I'm afraid so. I talked to the fella in the land office and studied the map there, and there's no doubt in my mind. This is the claim that goes with this deed." Ace tapped his jacket, where the important paper rested in an inner pocket.

"But how's that possible?" Chance wanted to know. "Beltz acts like this is *his* mine."

"I know. All I can figure is that he came along and started working the claim after Tom Bellamy abandoned it. Maybe he figured since nobody was here, the place was up for grabs." Ace shrugged. "Legally, maybe it was. I don't know. I don't know much about the laws that govern mining claims."

Chance rubbed his chin and frowned in thought. "Smoke could tell us. He's got a mine on the Sugarloaf."

"Yeah, but Smoke's not here. He's all the way over in Colorado, or off somewhere else, doing who knows what. You know how Smoke is."

Ace unhooked the crude gate made out of dried brush and swung it open. As he and Chance led their horses into the corral, Chance said, "We have to tell Mr. Beltz about this."

"Why?" Ace said. "I mean . . . eventually, sure. But why right now?"

"Because that's not his silver he's taking out of there!"

"He and the Steingrims are doing the work for it," Ace

pointed out. "It wouldn't be fair, after all the effort they've put in, for us to just waltz in and insist that all the profits belong to us."

Chance frowned as he started unsaddling his horse. "But legally—"

"There's what's legal, and there's what's right. And we both know those aren't always the same thing."

"Yeah, yeah," Chance muttered. He sighed. "I see what you're saying, but if that mine actually belongs to us, it's not fair for us to get nothing out of it, either."

"That's true. I'm just suggesting that we mull this over a little before we do anything."

After a moment, Chance nodded. "I suppose I can go along with that. Anyway, no matter who really owns this mine, we don't want that skunk Scranton taking it over!"

"We sure don't," Ace agreed. "Mr. Beltz talks a good fight, but I think he might be in over his head here. Scranton struck me as a bad man to have for an enemy."

"Yeah, I'm not convinced he didn't send Mullen and Webster gunning for us, although I guess they had a grudge of their own to settle."

Ace nodded and said, "The same thought crossed my mind."

"So," Chance said as he turned to face his brother, "are we going to throw in with Nick and his friends, help them fight off Scranton and his gunmen, and see how things go with the mine?"

"That's what I'd do . . . but in the end, it's not up to me. You're the one who bluffed Bellamy and won that deed."

Chance laughed. "Yeah, but like I've said all along, we don't have to be anywhere . . . or do anything . . . at any particular time. Let's just play out *this* hand, why don't we, and see where the cards we've been dealt take us?"

"That sounds good to me," Ace said with an emphatic nod.

They unloaded the supplies from their pack animals and carried them to the camp. If they were going to be staying around for a while, they would contribute their provisions to whatever Beltz and the Steingrim brothers had on hand. That was the way things worked out here on the frontier.

The noises from the tunnel had stopped. The sun was down now, although an arch of rose gold remained in the western sky. Ace and Chance saw that the other two Steingrim brothers had emerged from the mine to join Beltz and Folke.

The old-timer performed the introductions. "Boys, meet Baldur and Haldor Steingrim. Fellas, this here is Ace and Chance Jensen, some new pards of ours."

They shook hands all around. Baldur and Haldor were built like their brother Folke, short but almost unbelievably broad. Baldur's hair and beard were a faded blond, while the thatch on Haldor's head, cheeks, and jaws was a much brighter red than Folke's. The family resemblance was in the way they dressed and their massive stature; not enough of their facial features were visible to tell much from them.

They seemed friendly enough, although polite and restrained, probably due to their Scandinavian heritage. They all had thick accents but were understandable when they spoke English, as they seemed to do fairly well.

Chance grinned and said, "So, are you fellas triplets? Ace and I are twins, you know, although you might not think it to look at us."

"Triplets, no," Haldor said. "I am the oldest, then Folke, and Baldur is the baby of the family."

Beltz laughed and slapped his thigh. "Some baby, eh?" he said. "Can you imagine the poor woman who gave birth to these three behemoths? I admire her and pity her at the same time!"

Baldur said, "Our mama is Viking woman! Give birth to warriors, then go back to work!"

"Aye, I don't doubt it! Come on, lads. Let's all sit down and eat. Folke, pour the coffee! And then, afterwards, we'll talk about settin' some guard shifts." Beltz looked around at the others. "I don't know about you boys, but I wouldn't put it past that no-good scoundrel Big Dave to try somethin' else tonight!"

Chapter 17

With six of them in camp, it made sense to split up into three guard shifts with two men in each. Beltz asked for a volunteer to take the first watch with him. Ace spoke up, saying that he'd do it. He wanted to get to know the old-timer, in the hope that this might give him a better idea about what to do about Beltz taking over Chance's mine.

Baldur, Haldor, and Folke drew lots to determine the other shifts, and Chance, unable to resist anything that bore even a faint resemblance to a competition, threw in with them. Haldor and Folke claimed the second shift, while Chance and Baldur would take the final one.

While they'd eaten, night had fallen with the stunning suddenness that it always did in this high mountain desert. The Steingrim brothers went into the large tent they shared to get some sleep, while Chance spread his bedroll on the ground.

"It gets mighty chilly up here at night year-round," Beltz warned him. "This time o' year, it's even colder."

"I'll be all right," Chance said. "Ace and I have spent plenty of nights out on cold trails."

"Suit yourself," the old-timer said. "You're young. Likely you won't freeze to death."

As the others settled down for the night, Ace and Beltz

walked out to the edge of the notch. Ace had gotten his heavier sheepskin jacket from his gear and had it on instead of the denim jacket. He turned the collar up.

Beltz wore a long buffalo coat with a distinctive musky odor about it but left the shaggy garment hanging open for now. He had exchanged his battered old felt hat for a fur cap with a long top that dangled down the side of his head almost to his right shoulder. A decorative ball of white fur was attached to the end of it. He carried his Sharps and was also armed with an old Walker Colt stuffed behind his broad leather belt.

Ace had his Winchester tucked under his arm. He stood at the top of the trail and looked up and down the canyon. The moon hadn't risen yet, but so many stars floated in the ebony sky overhead, and those stars seemed so close, that plenty of silvery illumination filtered down into Surprise Canyon. The air was crisp and cold enough to make the men's breath fog in front of their faces.

It was a peaceful scene. Ace didn't see anything moving in the canyon. But he knew better to believe everything was as tranquil as it appeared to be. Danger could lurk in the middle of apparent serenity. He and Chance had seen plenty of examples of that and sometimes found themselves ducking bullets because of it.

"Now that we've had a look around, we'd best move back in the brush a mite," Beltz said. "As bright as it is, we might be makin' targets of ourselves out here."

"I was just thinking the same thing," Ace agreed. They stepped away from the edge so that the brush gave them some cover.

Beltz surprised Ace then by saying, "I want to talk to you about Miss Priscilla, son."

"What about her? Honestly, I wasn't flirting with her—"

Beltz stopped him with a wave of his thick-fingered hand. "Yeah, you were, a mite, and that's what I want to talk to you about. A little innocent flirtin' amongst young folks ain't gonna hurt nothin', but I just want you to know . . . I set a heap of store by that gal, and I wouldn't take it kindly if anybody was to take advantage of her."

"Mr. Beltz, are you being serious now?"

"I surely am. I like to josh around with folks, but I'm plumb serious about this. Miss Priscilla's doin' her dead level best to help folks in Panamint City and hereabouts. Not many are steppin' up to give her a hand, neither. Doc Drake does, some, but that's 'cause he's sweet on her. Most folks, all they care about is gettin' as much as they can for their own selves."

"That's true," Ace said. "Chance and I have seen that a lot of times. But we've come across plenty of people who try to help others, too."

"Yeah, well, helpful natures sorta go by the board when silver's involved. That shiny ore makes too many folks forget about everything else. Anyway, what I'm tellin' you is, you'd better be careful o' Miss Priscilla's feelin's, or else you and me are gonna have trouble."

Ace smiled in the darkness. "I give you my word, Mr. Beltz, and I'm being serious about this, too, I don't have any improper intentions where Miss Priscilla is concerned. In fact, if there's anything I can do to help her with her mission in town, I'd be happy to."

"Well, as a matter o' fact, I've been thinkin' the same thing, and I reckon I've come up with somethin' I can do. She's got some kids livin' with her there at the mission, young'uns whose folks have died or moved on and abandoned 'em here or what have you. There are others who still have a ma or a pa but no money, and they're barely scrapin' by. It's a mighty hard way to live, especially for kids. So I thought . . . what with Christmas comin' up and all . . ."

"That you'd make sure all those children got some presents," Ace said, taking a guess when the old-timer paused and didn't go on, apparently overcome by embarrassment. "I think that's a wonderful idea, Mr. Beltz."

Beltz waved a hand again and said, "Oh, shoot, I don't know. Seems kinda show-offish to me. I've been tryin' to figure out if there's some way I could handle it without too many folks havin' to know I had anything to do with it. Like . . . I don't know . . . maybe sneak in there beforehand, in the middle o' the night, say, and just leave the presents so the young'uns'd have 'em in the mornin'. I'm sure the Steingrim brothers'd help me. Them Scandihoovians like to drink and fight, but they're good hearted."

"That sounds like something Chance and I would like to help with, too."

"You speak for your brother?"

"We're twins, remember? We agree on most things, most of the time."

Beltz chuckled. "I'll bet that when you *don't* agree, though, it's a plumb knock-down, drag-out battle, ain't it?"

"That's been known to happen," Ace said with a laugh. "Anyway, when you make up your mind what you're going to do, be sure to let us know. We'll pitch in if we can."

Beltz cocked his head to the side and peered at Ace in the starlight. "You figure on bein' around that long?"

"I think we just might be," Ace said.

"I'm mighty glad to hear it. I realize I ain't known you and your brother for very long, but I can tell already what sort o' fellas you are. If you want to join up with this outfit . . . work on the mine and help keep it outta the greedy paws o' Big Dave Scranton . . . I could cut you in for . . . say . . . two percent o' the profits."

"Each?"

"Well . . . you drive a hard bargain, but . . . oh, shoot, why not?"

"I'll think about it," Ace promised, "and I'll talk it over

with Chance. For now, let's just say that we're giving you a hand because we enjoy the company."

"Meanin' me, o' course. I *am* pretty entertainin' to be around. Them Steingrims can be a surly lot, though, I'm warnin' you."

Ace laughed.

On the other side of the canyon and back to the west a hundred yards or so, Jared Foxx heard the laughter drifting faintly through the cold night air. His jaw clenched in anger until it felt like his teeth might crack.

He forced himself to relax as Kimbrough said quietly, "Sounds like they got at least two men standin' guard, boss. There must be more hombres up there than just those brothers Bellamy told us about."

"I don't understand," Bracken said from behind them. "Those Jensen boys weren't that far ahead of us. How did they get here, take over the mine, and find some other fellas to throw in with them?"

"We don't know that's what happened," Foxx rasped. "We don't know a damned thing . . . except that somebody's squatting at my mine, and I want it back!"

"We'll get it, boss," Kimbrough assured him. "We just have to figure out the best way to do it, that's all."

Foxx nodded, not thinking about whether the other men could see him in the darkness. He was too busy trying to control the anger he felt toward the interlopers on the other side of Surprise Canyon.

Things in the canyon had changed in the months that he'd been gone. They had passed other mines and seen men working on those claims. When he and Tom Bellamy had first stumbled on the old tunnel, not many people had been in these rugged mountains on the edge of Death Valley. That was why it had been a good place for a couple of outlaws on the run to hide. Panamint City had been the next thing to a ghost town in those days.

The silver strike he and Bellamy had made, along with other such discoveries, had drawn more fortune seekers into the area. Panamint City had started to grow again, to regain some of its former luster, although it hadn't really boomed until after he started trying to track down Bellamy, Foxx had heard. This was a big country, and it still wasn't crowded, by any means, but it might get to that point one of these days.

Foxx had been counting on the hope that nobody else would have come along and happened upon the old mine, though. It wasn't that easy to find, after all. He and Bellamy never would have come across it if they hadn't been hunting for a good place to hide from that posse.

Even so, he'd been angry but not shocked when they'd approached the mine earlier that evening and seen the light from a campfire up there in the notch. They had withdrawn a short distance back down the canyon to keep an eye on the mine.

The Jensen brothers may have beaten him to the mine, Foxx thought. But it didn't really matter, he told himself, since he planned to kill both of them, anyway. Anybody who tried to steal something that rightfully belonged to Jared Foxx had it coming.

Tom Bellamy had found that out—the hard way.

But Kimbrough was right: the best thing they could do right now was bide their time, find out what kind of odds they'd be dealing with. . . .

Those thoughts were going through Foxx's mind when a huge wave of gun-thunder suddenly rolled through the canyon and a host of orange muzzle flashes tore the night apart.

Chapter 18

Ace and Nick Beltz had split up a minute earlier, Ace staying where he was to the left of the opening in the brush, Beltz moving over to the right side of the notch. The roar of gunfire was like the sudden crash of thunder, but no storm was moving into Surprise Canyon tonight—other than the storm of lead that tore through the brush around Ace.

He threw himself to the ground and landed on his belly. The thick brush meant that the attackers couldn't see him, but the gnarled branches wouldn't do anything to stop rifle bullets. He could tell from the sharp cracks that the men firing at them were using Winchesters.

"Mr. Beltz!" he called over the uproar. "Are you all right?"

"Fine as frog hair!" the old-timer yelled back. "Keep your head down, boy!"

The boom of Beltz's Sharps punctuated the order as he began returning the fire.

Ace wriggled forward until he could thrust his Winchester's barrel through a gap in the growth. A branch snagged his hat and pulled it off his head, but he didn't worry about that. Although the brush screened his view to a certain extent, he saw a number of muzzle flashes coming from approximately the same elevation on the other side of the canyon, a hundred yards away.

It looked like perhaps a dozen bushwhackers were over there. They raked the notch with withering fire. Ace hoped Chance and the Steingrim brothers had sense enough to stay low.

Those were Big Dave Scranton's men over there. Ace had no doubt about that. After the earlier failed ambush attempt, the confrontation in town, and the deaths of Mullen and Webster, Scranton had declared open war on Nick Beltz and his allies.

Scranton's men had a fight on their hands, though. Beltz's old buffalo gun blasted again, and Ace began peppering the opposite slope with rounds from his Winchester, too. He cranked off three swift shots, then pulled the rifle back and rolled quickly to the right.

He figured the bushwhackers would target his muzzle flashes, and he proved to be correct about that. A hail of bullets shredded the bushes around the spot where he'd been lying a moment earlier.

Ace propped himself up on his elbows and took aim at one of the orange tongues of flame licking out into the darkness. He raised his rifle just slightly and squeezed the trigger, then rolled again.

He had no way of knowing whether he had hit his target—but he noticed that no more muzzle flashes came from that exact spot.

The Sharps boomed again. As the echoes rolled away, Ace heard somebody over there screaming. Whoever it was, Ace didn't think he was faking. The bushwhacker was hit, and those cries were genuine sounds of agony.

Ace knew that a Sharps could blow a man's arm clean off his body if the slug hit him right, so he wasn't surprised Beltz had inflicted some damage. He scrambled back the other way, staying as low as he could while he did so, and once he was farther left than he had been before, he stretched out and fired three more rounds toward the far side of the canyon.

A faint sound behind him made him start to twist around.

Chance said, "It's just me!"

"What are you doing up here?" Ace asked. "You should have stayed farther back, where it's safer."

Chance laughed. "What in blazes makes you think it's any safer back there? Those bushwhackers are throwing enough lead over here to blanket the whole place!"

Ace knew his brother was right. At the same time, because of the brush and the darkness, the attackers across the canyon were shooting blindly. That heavy fire was enough to make the men at the mine keep their heads down, and a stray bullet might find a human target by pure luck, but unless they had enough ammunition to keep shooting all night, Ace couldn't see what they hoped to accomplish. . . .

And then he did see. The realization jolted him. He exclaimed, "Come on, Chance!" and started crawling toward the gap in the brush at the head of the trail just as quickly as he could.

He heard Chance following him and twisted his head around to make sure his brother was staying low. Chance was, which was a good thing, because numerous bullets whipped through the brush not far above them.

As he reached the gap, Ace heard heavy footsteps and rapid breathing not far down the trail. *That* was the reason for the bombardment from across the canyon. It was a distraction so that some of Scranton's hired gun-wolves could make it up the switchback trail and charge into the camp itself to wipe out Beltz and his friends.

In order to do that, the men on the other side of the canyon would have to stop shooting. Some sort of signal must have been passed, because the guns over there suddenly fell silent.

As soon as they did, Ace snapped, "Cover me!" to Chance, rolled out onto the trail, and lay so that he faced down it.

Half a dozen dark shapes were less than twenty feet from the top of the trail. Ace still had eight rounds in his Winches-

The shooting resumed from the far side of the canyon, but was no longer a concentrated assault. The firing was more spread out and sporadic. The men over there would have been able to tell that their allies' thrust up the switchback trail had been not just repulsed but also broken up completely.

The only options remaining to them were a siege or withdrawal.

From the other side of the notch, Nick Beltz called, "Are you boys still all right over there?"

"For now," Ace replied as he thumbed fresh cartridges through the Winchester's loading gate. "How about you, Mr. Beltz?"

"Oh, I'm havin' a joyous time!" the old-timer said. "I've been needin' some target practice, and those polecats over yonder are givin' me plenty of it! I'm pretty sure I've ventilated at least a couple of 'em."

Ace and Chance went back to returning the attackers' fire, staying low and shifting after each shot to keep Scranton's men from drawing a bead on them. On the other side of the gap, Beltz did the same. The shots dwindled more and more and finally stopped.

"Think they're giving up?" Chance asked in a whisper.

"I don't know," Ace replied, "but I reckon if we're patient, we'll find out."

Sure enough, a few minutes later, a swift rataplan of hoofbeats sounded down in the canyon and headed off toward Panamint City.

Beltz hooted with laughter and called, "They've lit a shuck! We beat 'em, boys!"

"Better keep your head down for a little while, anyway, just in case it's a trick," Ace advised.

Beltz snorted. "You reckon I don't know that? Hell, I was fightin' Injuns before you boys was born! And there ain't nobody trickier than them critters!"

ter. He emptied the rifle as fast as he could work t
squeeze the trigger. It was a devastating ons   it
knocked several attackers off their feet and sent so   s
tumbling back down the trail or off to the side, s   b
rolled down the canyon wall itself.   h

At the same time, Chance came up on one knee
and swung his rifle from left to right, firing just as t
and spraying lead among the men on the other si   c
canyon to keep them occupied.

The hammer of Ace's Winchester clicked dow
empty chamber. Two men still remained on the t
flame bloomed redly in the shadows as they fired des
at the Jensen brothers.

Ace dropped the empty rifle and yanked out his C
bullet plowed into the trail not far in front of him and
dust into his eyes. He winced and blinked rapidly to
clear his vision. Another bullet whined past him, mu
close for comfort. He pushed himself up a little with h
hand, thrust the Colt out in front of him, and fired, aim
much by instinct as by sight.

The attacker in front yelled and reeled back, drille
Ace's bullet. He blundered into the man behind him,
cursed and shoved him to the side, sending him topp
down the slope. Then the second attacker yanked up his
and fired.

But that brief respite had given Ace's sight time to cl
and his Colt blasted a split second before the other man's. T
slug's impact twisted the attacker to the side and sent his sh
screaming harmlessly down the canyon. He fell to his kne
and then rolled off the trail, too.

Chance reached down, grabbed the collar of Ace's sheep
skin coat, and hauled his brother back behind the brush. Ac
barely had time to snag the barrel of his empty Winchester
and drag it with him.

Fifteen minutes passed before Beltz said, "You fellas stay up here and keep your eyes open. I'm goin' back to check on them Steingrims."

The moon was rising now. It gave off enough light for Chance to see Beltz dart back toward the camp in a crouching run. The old-timer was surprisingly fast and nimble for his age, just as he had proclaimed in town after the shoot-out in the general store.

Quiet descended over the canyon again. After a while, Beltz trotted out to the edge and reported, "Folke, Baldur, and Haldor are all right. They kept their heads down and crawled off behind one o' the rock piles from the tunnel, so they had some good cover. They feel bad about not gettin' in on the fight, but none o' them boys is worth a lick with a firearm. Nobody can beat 'em when it comes to wrasslin' or bare-knuckles brawlin', though."

Ace could easily imagine that was true, given the way the Steingrim brothers were built.

He turned quickly toward the canyon again, as did Chance and Beltz, when someone shouted, "Hello, the camp! Are you up there, Beltz?"

"Do you know that voice?" Ace asked.

Beltz nodded and said, "Yeah, that's Hobie Wright. He's got a claim a mile or so down the canyon." The old-timer lifted his voice. "Yeah, Hobie, we're fine."

"Sounded like a real war broke out up here!" Wright called. "I don't reckon I've heard that much shootin' since Chickamauga!"

"Some fellas tried to part our hair with lead, but we discouraged 'em. They took off with their tails twixt their legs."

"Well, I'll pass the word that you're all right. Good night, Nick."

Beltz turned to Chance and said, "You might as well go on back to camp and see if you can get some more sleep, son. Won't be time for you to stand guard for quite a while yet."

"Yeah, but it's kind of hard to doze off again when you've been shot at that many times," Chance said.

"Not for me," Beltz chortled. "I've caught me a catnap in the middle of a battle plenty o' times. Why, one time in the Texas Panhandle, when me and some other fellas was pinned down in a buffalo waller by about five thousand screamin' Comanch', I had me the best dream about this little ol' gal who lived back in Wichita—"

"Maybe I *will* try to get some more sleep," Chance said, then hurried off toward the camp.

But Ace knew that he would hear the rest of the story.

Chapter 19

Kimbrough, Bracken, and Stevens wanted to go see what all the shooting was about, but Jared Foxx told them to stay put.

"I don't know who those bushwhackers are, but maybe they'll wipe out the varmints who moved in on my mine," he said. "I'll be happy to let them do the work for me, even though I kind of wanted to settle that score myself. The important thing is getting that mine back."

"But what if *they* take it over?" Kimbrough asked.

"Then we'll kill *them*," Foxx said.

It really couldn't get much simpler than that.

From where they were, they had almost a front-row seat to watch the battle, including the close-range shoot-out at the top of the trail leading up to the notch.

That trail hadn't been there when Foxx set out to find Tom Bellamy. Whoever had taken over the mine had put some work into improving conditions.

Foxx didn't care about that. Whoever they were, whatever they had done, they were still thieves and would be dealt with accordingly. Foxx knew that he was an outlaw, but nobody was going to steal from *him* and get away with it!

When the shooting was over, Foxx and his companions saw

several men who had been firing from this side of the canyon cross it on foot, leading horses so they could recover the bodies of their slain companions who had tumbled back down. Then the whole group rode away noisily.

"Might be a good time to jump those fellas up at the mine," Bracken suggested. "They probably won't be expecting any more trouble this soon."

Foxx considered the suggestion for a moment, then shook his head. "I want to," he said, "but I still think it's best we wait until we have a better idea what we'll be dealing with."

"And there are at least three hombres up there who are full of fight, too," Kimbrough said. "We saw that with our own eyes. No telling how many more there are."

Foxx mulled things over for a minute or two more, then told his companions, "Get the horses. We're going to ride on into Panamint City. I want to find out what happened here tonight, and I've got a hunch that's where the answers will be."

It wasn't just Big Dave Scranton's office that was above the Silver Slipper Saloon. He had his living quarters up there, as well. He paced back and forth across the sitting room in his suite. His teeth were clenched on the unlit cigar in his mouth.

"Dave, honey, I swear, you're fixin' to worry yourself to death," said the blond woman sitting on a fancy divan on one side of the room.

Scranton swung around toward her and glared. Normally, it made him feel better to look at Natalie Fairchild and know that the honey-haired Southern beauty was one of his possessions, just like the mine, the saloon, and half of the other businesses in Panamint City. Her fair-skinned loveliness and the lush curves of her body, amply displayed by the low neck of the gown she wore, would set any man's pulse to racing and make him proud to have her as his own, to do with as he wanted.

Tonight, however, it didn't help one damned bit, Scranton thought.

"I'm sure Porter will be back soon and will tell you that everything went fine," Natalie continued in her sensuous drawl, a legacy of her Mississippi heritage. "That dreadful old man will be dealt with, and that mine will be all yours."

"It had better be," Scranton growled as he took the cigar out of his mouth. "I'm tired of messing with Nick Beltz. He's stood in my way long enough." He waved the cheroot to indicate not only his luxurious surroundings but also the bigger picture. "Panamint City is my town, and pretty soon the rest of Surprise Canyon will belong to me, too."

Six months ago, he wouldn't have dreamed that such grandiose ambitions were even possible, let alone that they might be fulfilled. But things had changed, and now he was on the verge of success. "Big Dave" wouldn't be just his nickname anymore. He would be truly *big*.

It had started with the silver strike he'd made, the sort of strike he had been after all his adult life. But as the ore had begun to flow from the mine and the money had piled up, his dreams had grown. Not just grown, but exploded. He had started buying businesses, including this saloon. The previous owner hadn't really wanted to sell it, but a visit from Anse Porter and a couple of Scranton's other men had convinced him otherwise.

The success of that tactic had emboldened Scranton to use it again. He had gotten his hands on a few other lucrative mining operations that way. Like a stream flowing downhill, his wealth and power had grown, and at some point, he had realized that no limits applied to a man who was strong enough—and ruthless enough—to do whatever was necessary to get what he wanted. If a few stubborn holdouts had to be beaten up—or worse—well, that was their own damned fault, wasn't it?

The idea that some scruffy, eccentric old coot could stand in his way was ludicrous. He'd made Nick Beltz a couple of perfectly good offers for his claim. They weren't as much as what the mine was worth potentially, of course, but they were better than nothing, and Beltz should have taken one of them and moved on. When he'd refused, Scranton had started pondering other actions to take against him.

Oddly enough, that skirmish earlier today, when Mullen, Webster, and a few of his other hired gunmen had jumped the old man, had been a spur-of-the-moment thing on their part. Scranton hadn't ordered it. They had come across Beltz on his way to the settlement and decided that the boss would like it if they got rid of him.

Scranton took that as an omen. He should have disposed of Beltz before now, and he wouldn't hesitate any longer.

Unfortunately, Beltz had gotten some help out of nowhere in the form of those two young drifters. Scranton didn't know what to make of them, but clearly, they were tough and capable. They had to be, to have handled Mullen and Webster the way they did. Because of that, now it might be harder to get rid of Beltz than it would have been if he had acted sooner.

But they were just temporary obstacles, Scranton told himself as he went to the sideboard and picked up a bottle to pour some whiskey into a short, heavy-bottomed glass. In fact, there was a good chance Beltz was dead by now, along with his Scandinavian helpers and those two young saddle tramps.

He had just tossed back the drink when a knock sounded on the door.

Scranton turned in that direction with a frown and jerked his head toward the door. Natalie uncoiled herself like a cat from the divan and crossed the room to open it. She knew he didn't like opening doors.

He caught the little sigh of annoyance she gave when she stood up, too. Later, he'd have to have a talk with her about that show of disrespect.

"Hello, Anse," she said. She stepped back to let Porter walk into the sitting room. He had his hat in his left hand and nodded deferentially to Scranton—who was just about the only man to whom Porter would ever defer.

Tall, lean like a wolf in midwinter, with a hungry gray face, Anse Porter didn't know a blasted thing about mining, but he knew how to handle a gun. More importantly, he knew how to handle *men* who could handle guns. If he had been with Mullen, Webster, and the others earlier in the day, more than likely old Nick Beltz would have died then and there, no matter how many gun-tough strangers had shown up out of the blue.

Porter had something wrong in his guts that was eating away at him. He carried a little bottle of laudanum and took a nip from it now and then, when the gnawing got too bad. He looked like he wouldn't have minded doing that now, as he faced Scranton and said, "Bad news, boss."

"That's not what I want to hear," Scranton snapped.

"I know it's not, but I can't change what happened."

"Beltz and his friends are still alive?" Scranton sounded as if he couldn't believe that was even possible.

"I'm afraid so, and we lost half a dozen good men."

Scranton let out a bitter curse and threw the cigar on the rug at his feet. As he stalked toward Porter, Natalie moved in behind him and bent to pick up the cigar before it could burn a hole in the woven fabric.

"How can that be?" Scranton demanded. "You took almost twenty men out there. Why didn't you just ride in and . . . and wipe them out?"

"Because there's no way to reach that mine without going up the trail," Porter replied with a trace of anger in his voice. "A couple of men with rifles could hold off an army from up there. That's why I sent six fellas up the trail while the rest of us opened fire on Beltz's bunch from the other side of the canyon. I figured that way, they could make it all the way up to the notch before Beltz and his friends knew what was going on."

Porter shook his head ruefully and continued, "It almost worked, too. But then somebody . . . one of those drifters, I'm thinking, because the Steingrims aren't smart enough for that . . . figured out what we were doing. Our men ran right into a wall of bullets."

Scranton stared at him for a long moment without saying anything. Then, in a voice dripping with scorn, "So you just gave up after that?"

"I'd already lost a couple of men on our side of the canyon, and a couple more were wounded. Beltz is a damn sharp-shooter with that old buffalo rifle of his, and those saddle tramps aren't bad, either. When the men on the trail were wiped out, I knew that was all the others had the stomach for. We collected the bodies and got out of there."

"It was all *somebody* had the stomach for," Scranton said with a sneer. "But then, we both know about your stomach problems, don't we?"

For a second, anger burned brightly in Anse Porter's eyes. Scranton wondered if he had pushed the gunman too far. He still held the heavy glass. If Porter reached for his gun, Scranton would throw the glass in his face and then tackle him. In a hand-to-hand battle, Scranton could break Porter in half, and they both knew it.

Then the flames receded in Porter's gaze, and he shrugged.

"You pay me for my experience in dustups like this, boss," he said. "I wasn't going to waste the lives of more men in a fight we probably couldn't win."

"Fine, fine," Scranton said in a sullen voice. "There'll be another day, I suppose. But I've run out of patience with Beltz. I want that obnoxious old coot gone, and good rid-dance."

Porter nodded. "It'll be taken care of. It's just a matter of figuring out the best approach. You've got my word on that."

"Even though he has more help now?"

"You're talking about those two youngsters? Don't worry about them." Grim trenches appeared in the gunman's cheeks. "I'm gonna take special pleasure in getting rid of Ace and Chance Jensen."

Chapter 20

Jared Foxx reined his horse to a stop in front of the Silver Slipper Saloon. He frowned up at the sign that stretched along the second floor, above the boardwalk awning. The fancy curlicues and the letters painted on it in bright, garish hues were visible in the flickering light from torches that burned along the street at regular intervals.

The saloon had been called the Silver Slipper the last time Foxx was in Panamint City, but the big sign was new and so were the words underneath the saloon's name: DAVID SCRANTON, PROPRIETOR.

That couldn't be Big Dave Scranton, could it? Six months earlier, Scranton had been just another prospector trying to chip a smidgen of color out of Surprise Canyon's walls. Foxx had known who he was but hadn't been friends with him, hadn't even nodded to him when they passed each other on the streets of the settlement. He couldn't remember ever exchanging half a dozen words with the man.

But he knew how quickly and dramatically a person's circumstances could change. If Scranton had made a big strike, he might have become rich enough to buy the Silver Slipper from its previous owner. Foxx couldn't recall that man's name.

"Looks like the biggest and best saloon in town, boss,"

Kimbrough said from where he and the other men had reined in alongside Foxx. "Might be able to get an idea of what we want to know in there."

"And even if we don't, we can get a drink," Bracken said. He dragged the back of his hand across his mouth. "I've got a powerful thirst."

"Yeah, we'll go on in and see what we can find out," Foxx said. He swung down from the saddle and looped his reins around the hitch rail. They had been lucky to find such a handy place to tie up their mounts. Panamint City was a busy place tonight. It appeared that most of the stores were still open, and the saloons were doing a brisk business, of course.

Foxx stepped up onto the boardwalk in front of the saloon but paused before going in. Something on the other side of the street and a little farther down had caught his eye. He turned his head and studied the big building. It had been there before he left these parts to hunt down Tom Bellamy, but he had the impression that it had been empty then.

Now it was the Panamint City Mission, according to the sign on it. What was a mission doing in a place like this, and what sort of crazy do-gooder would think you could start such a thing in a boomtown? Nobody around here gave a damn about anything except themselves.

"Boss?" Kimbrough said.

"Yeah, I'm coming," Foxx said. He lingered a few seconds longer and watched as several snowflakes spiraled down between him and the mission, twirled by the inconstant wind that drifted through these mountains. It was cold tonight but not cold enough for the snow to stick, and, anyway, not enough was falling to amount to anything.

Because of the chill in the air, the batwings were tied back and the double wooden doors were closed. Foxx opened one of them and stepped into the saloon, followed by his men.

The air inside was warm and filled with the familiar mix of

tobacco, beer, whiskey, bay rum, cheap perfume from the saloon girls, and unwashed human flesh. A piano sat unplayed in a rear corner, but the babble of talk and laughter, the whisper of cards, the click of poker chips, and the clink of bottle against glass combined to make appealing music for men who had spent a great deal of time in places such as this.

A few spaces were open at the bar, but Foxx made one big enough for himself and his men by glaring at a couple of customers until they uneasily moved over to give them more room. Like most of the Silver Slipper's patrons, these roughly dressed men looked like miners. A few townspeople were on hand in the saloon, as well.

As Foxx and the others stepped up to the bar, a chunky bartender with a few strands of black hair plastered over the big bald spot on top of his head polished the hardwood with a rag and asked, "What can I get for you boys?"

"Beers for all of us," Foxx said, "along with a bottle of rye and four glasses. And make it the good stuff."

"That's all we sell here, friend," the bartender said smoothly. He drew the beers and set the mugs in front of the newcomers. Then, as he reached for glasses under the bar, he paused and frowned at Foxx. "Don't I know you?"

"You look a mite familiar to me, too. Didn't you used to work here a year or so ago?"

"That's right. I quit for a while to do some prospecting, but that didn't pan out." The man laughed at his own joke.

Foxx didn't laugh. He said, "Judging by the sign outside, this place has changed hands since I was here last. How'd that come about?"

"Same way as usual," the bartender replied with a shrug. "New boss bought the business from the old boss."

"And that new boss is Big Dave Scranton?"

"That's right." The bartender got the glasses, put them in front of Foxx and the others, then reached to the back bar to snag a full bottle of whiskey. "Like I said, your face is familiar, mister, but I can't put a name with it." He glanced at Kimbrough, Bracken, and Stevens. "I don't reckon I know your friends."

"My name's Foster," Foxx said, falling back on the alias he had used while he and Bellamy were working the mine. The name Jared Foxx had turned up on too many wanted posters over the years to be safe.

The bartender grinned and pointed a blunt finger at him. "Sure, I remember you now! You and another fella used to have a claim a few miles down the canyon, didn't you?"

"That's right." Foxx took a drink of his beer. Might be useful to keep this lout talking, he thought.

"What happened? Vein play out?"

"Sooner or later they always do, don't they?"

"Ain't that the truth," the bartender responded with a chuckle. "What brings you back to Panamint City? Going to try your luck again?"

"I'm thinking about it. If Big Dave Scranton can get rich and start buying saloons for himself, I don't see why I can't. He was just a hardscrabble pick-and-shovel man the last time I heard anything about him."

"Well, that was before the big strike he made six months ago."

Six months, Foxx mused. Scranton's discovery must have happened very soon after Foxx had set out to find Tom Bellamy.

"A lot's changed since then," the bartender went on. "Mr. Scranton has expanded his mining operation and bought quite a few of the businesses here in town. He owns this saloon, the hotel, a couple of restaurants, the livery stable, and he has an interest in the bank and several of the stores. The way he's going, he's gonna be the richest, most important man in this whole part of the state! Wouldn't surprise me if he winds up with his eye on being governor, or maybe a senator."

"Wouldn't that be something," Foxx said, shaking his head slowly. "From a lowly prospector to an important man like that. I'm a little surprised everybody just went along with him and let him gobble up the things they had worked for."

"Well . . ." The bartender suddenly looked and sounded more reticent. His eyes cut back and forth, and he leaned forward and lowered his voice slightly as he went on, "To tell you the truth, the boss didn't give some of them all that much choice in the matter."

"Ahhh," Foxx said in understanding. He knew exactly what the bartender meant.

When Big Dave Scranton saw something he wanted, he didn't allow anything to stop him from getting it. Foxx not only understood, but he could sympathize with that attitude. He looked at life the same way himself.

Foxx nodded to the whiskey bottle and told the bartender, "Fill us up from that."

"Sure, Mr. Foster." The man pulled the cork and splashed amber liquid into the four glasses.

Foxx picked up his and lifted it. "Here's to fellas getting what they want."

"I'll drink to that," Kimbrough said.

The other two muttered agreement, and then all four threw their drinks back.

Foxx thumped the empty glass on the bar, picked up the beer again in his left hand, and turned to lean back against the bar and rest his right elbow on it as he looked around the room. That put his right hand in position to make a quick grab for his gun if he needed to.

That seemed unlikely, though, since nobody in the room had paid much attention to the four of them after they'd come in, other than the men Foxx had stared into moving aside.

He sipped the beer and studied the faces of the other men in the saloon. Some of them looked vaguely familiar to him.

He knew he remembered them from when he'd been around Surprise Canyon before. He had no friends here, though, and didn't try to fool himself into thinking he did.

Despite Foxx's casual pose, the wheels of his brain were turning rapidly inside his head. The conversation with the bartender had suggested a strong possibility to him. If Big Dave Scranton was a powerful man now and had his heart set on taking over everything worthwhile in these parts, it stood to reason that he might be interested in Foxx's old mine. Interested enough that he would send men to bushwhack whoever was there. It seemed unlikely that anybody else in these parts would have the manpower to mount such an attack.

He turned his head and said to the bartender, who was still hovering nearby, "Where does Big Dave keep himself these days? Out at his mine?"

"Uhhh . . ." The bartender looked a little hesitant about answering. He cast a nervous glance at Kimbrough, Bracken, and Stevens, who were all regarding him with cold, reptilian interest. Finally, he must have decided that a threat right in front of him was worse than a potential one somewhere else. He said, "The boss stays here in town most of the time. He, uh, has his living quarters on the second floor, as a matter of fact."

"In this saloon?" Foxx grinned. "You don't say."

"If anybody was to ask you, mister, I'd just as soon that was the story you told. That I didn't say, I mean."

"Sure," Foxx agreed. "It's nobody else's business, is it?" He turned, took a twenty-dollar gold piece from his pocket, and slid it across the hardwood. "Is Scranton up there now?"

Deftly, the bartender made the coin disappear.

"I think so," he replied, "but I can't say for sure, Mr. Foster. There's a back door and an outside staircase on the second floor, so it's possible he could've left without me knowing."

"Well, I'll take a chance on that." Foxx drained the last of the beer in the mug and slid it across the bar, too. He said to the others, "Finish up, boys. We're going to pay my old friend Big Dave a visit."

The bartender looked alarmed. "You . . . you can't just go up there unannounced like that," he said. "The boss won't like it."

"He won't mind. In fact, I think he'll be happy about it. You see, I've got a notion that he and I can help each other out with a certain matter."

And if that proved to be the case, Foxx thought, he wouldn't mind at all helping Scranton deal with the interlopers who had come in and taken over his mine. Then, when the mine had been restored to its rightful owner . . .

Not even Big Dave was big enough to withstand a bullet.

Chapter 21

Anse Porter was about to leave the second-floor suite when someone knocked on the door. He and Scranton hadn't come to any conclusions about what to do next concerning Nick Beltz, the Steingrim brothers, and those Jensen boys, but they would figure out a new course of action over the next few days. Porter was certain of that. Big Dave Scranton wasn't going to allow anybody to defy his will for very long, no matter how lucky they might have been so far.

But for tonight, Scranton was willing to let that defiance go, despite the bitter disappointment and anger he felt because Porter and his men had failed to wipe out the old-timer and his allies. Porter knew that, more than likely, Scranton would use a session with Natalie Fairchild to soothe his raging emotions.

That might or might not be pleasant for the blonde—Porter didn't know her well enough to say—but she was paid well to supply Scranton with whatever he wanted . . . just like Anse Porter was.

For himself, Porter just wanted to go back to his rented room, suck down a couple of swallows of his medicine, and let it carry him off to a temporarily pain-free oblivion for a while.

Whoever was at the door had damned well better not threaten that respite, Porter thought.

Annoyed, he was about to reach for the doorknob and jerk the door open when he reminded himself that his employer had enemies. That was why Scranton kept a guard with a shotgun posted out there. Tonight it was Mort Milligan. Porter had nodded a hello to him when he'd come upstairs earlier to report to Scranton. Milligan had been sitting in a chair at the end of the hall, only a few steps away from the suite's door.

Porter rested his hand on the butt of his gun and called through the panel, "Who's there?"

"It's me, Anse," Milligan's familiar voice replied. "Mort."

"What do you want?"

"There's a fella out here who wants to talk to the boss. Claims he's an old acquaintance."

Acquaintance, thought Porter. That was odd. Usually when somebody showed up to try to "borrow" money from Scranton, with no intention of ever paying it back, they claimed to be an old friend.

"What the hell is it now?" Scranton demanded impatiently. He was back at the sideboard, pouring himself another drink. Natalie had returned to lounge on the divan.

"Somebody who wants to see you, Mr. Scranton," Porter said as he turned his head to look over his shoulder at the boss.

"Well, who is it?" Scranton snapped. "Get a name."

Through the door, Porter asked, "What's his name, Mort?"

"Says it's Foster. *Whoa!*"

Something crashed out in the corridor, hard on the heels of Milligan's startled exclamation. Porter jumped back, away from the door, and drew his gun. He expected somebody was about to bust through there and start shooting.

Instead, the door opened, all right, but the man who shoved it back stood there just outside the threshold, with his hands held in plain sight. He was a tough-looking hombre in black. The white hair under his black hat stood out in sharp contrast, but he didn't really look old enough to be that snowy headed. Something about his rawboned face struck Porter as familiar, but at the same time, the gunman was convinced he had never seen this man before.

"Sorry about the commotion," the man drawled. "I got a little tired of waiting while all the palavering went on. I'm afraid I knocked your man out here on his butt. He's a mite groggy at the moment."

"He's alive, though?" Porter asked.

"Sure."

"I'll make sure he's sorry for being so careless, then." Porter motioned slightly with his gun barrel. "What's your name?"

"Foster," the stranger replied.

Scranton had moved over so he could get a good look at the white-haired man. He jabbed a finger at the visitor and said, "I remember you."

"You ought to," Foxx said. "We were both working claims in the canyon at the same time." His mouth quirked. "From the looks of it, you were more successful than I was."

Without taking his eyes off the man, Porter asked, "You want me to let him in, boss?"

"Yes, that's all right. If he wanted to cause trouble, he would have done it before now."

"That's right," Foxx said as he lowered his slightly raised hands. "I'm just here to talk, Dave. I have a . . . let's call it a business proposition for you."

"I'm doing plenty of business on my own," Scranton said.

"Yeah, I can tell that," Foxx said. He walked into the room, then paused as he noticed Natalie on the divan. His hand came up, and his index finger ticked the brim of his hat. "Good evening, ma'am."

"Hello, Mr. Foster," she said coolly.

He smiled. "I don't believe you were in Panamint City when I left these parts a while back."

"No, she wasn't," Scranton said. "She's here because I brought her here. And you came to talk to me, remember?"

Natalie stood up and, with a slight trace of insolence in her voice, said, "You could at least offer the man a drink, Dave. There's no need for us to be rude."

Scranton glared and told her, "Pour him a drink, then."

She smiled sweetly. "I'd be happy to."

Out in the hall, Mort Milligan groaned as he began to recover his senses. Porter took a step in that direction, but Scranton said sharply, "Stick around, Anse. Milligan can take care of himself."

"Sure, Mr. Scranton," Porter said. He knew Scranton didn't fully trust the visitor and wanted his top gunhand close by. Couldn't blame a man for being cautious. Porter took hold of the door and closed it.

Natalie handed Foxx the drink she had poured. He smiled and said, "Thank you kindly, Miss . . . ?"

"Fairchild," she told him. "Natalie Fairchild."

"The name certainly suits you."

"What happened to you, Foster?" Scranton asked. "You just dropped out of sight. Not that I gave it much thought, mind you, but if I had, I would have wondered if something happened to you. Or if you had a reason to disappear, like maybe the law was after you."

Foxx stiffened a little, but he kept the easy smile on his face. "Now, why would a man worry about that around here?" he wanted to know. "When was the last time you saw an Inyo County lawman anywhere in Surprise Canyon?"

"I don't reckon I've *ever* seen one up here," Scranton said. "But I've heard that posses used to chase outlaws into these mountains from time to time. Hell, according to the stories, that's how silver was first found here seven or eight years ago, by some owlhoots on the run from the law."

Foxx sipped the drink in his hand and nodded in appreciation of the smooth, fiery liquor. "Things like that can happen," he said. "But why I left didn't have anything to do with that." He took another sip, then said grimly, "My partner ran out on me."

Scranton pointed a finger again and said, "That's right. You had a partner. Benjamin? Belton?"

"Bellamy," Foxx said. The hate in his voice was plain to hear.

"That's right. Tom Bellamy. You say he ran out on you?"

"Yeah. And he took the deed to the mine with him."

Scranton frowned. "That mine never amounted to much, did it? A little color, but it didn't last long?"

"That's what Bellamy thought. He figured the mine was worthless."

"But he took the deed, anyway?"

"Yeah."

"That's a pretty sorry thing to do." Scranton drew in a breath and looked shrewdly at Foster for a moment, then said, "But it *wasn't* worthless, was it?"

"Bellamy gave up too soon. I'm stubborn."

Scranton laughed. He tossed off the rest of his drink and then laughed again. "Now, that's pretty ironic," he said. "Bellamy takes off with the deed out of . . . what? Sheer meanness?"

"He thought maybe he could get some use out of it," Foxx explained. "As things turned out, he wound up using it as stakes in a poker game . . . and lost it."

Scranton's laughter was loud and hearty this time. He said, "Let me get this straight. You found more silver, but you didn't have the deed to the mine, so you couldn't legally claim it. Why didn't you just take the ore, anyway?"

"I could have, if there had been just a limited amount."

Scranton's eyes narrowed suddenly. "But it was a big vein," he said, taking a guess. "A bonanza."

"I believed it had the makings of one. That's why I wanted to do things aboveboard. So I had to go find Bellamy and get that deed back."

"Since you said that about him losing it in a poker game, I'm guessing you found him."

"I did," Foxx said. Porter heard the finality in the man's voice and thought that he wouldn't have liked to be Tom Bellamy in those circumstances.

"All right, it's an interesting story," Scranton said. "Even an entertaining one. But what does it have to do with me? Why are you here, Foster? If you have the deed now—"

"I don't," Foxx broke in.

"You didn't just track down whoever Bellamy lost it to and take it back?"

"The kid who won it and his brother had already started up here to claim the mine before I found out what was going on."

Scranton regarded him coolly and said, "You look like a man who knows how to handle a problem like that."

"I like to think I am. I imagine you like to think that you are, too. But you have a problem, too, and *you* haven't been able to do it."

Scranton's face darkened with anger. Natalie eased back over to the divan, well out of the way if trouble erupted.

"What in blazes are you talking about?" Scranton demanded.

"You sent a bunch of gunmen down the canyon tonight to take over a claim, didn't you? And either put the run on the men working it . . . or kill them?"

Scranton stiffened. The empty glass in his hand clattered as he set it roughly on the sideboard. "Are you telling me that this . . . this so-called claim of yours . . . is the same one that crazy old man is squatting on? And that the damned Jensen brothers are the ones who wound up with the deed to it?"

"I don't know anything about a crazy old man," Foxx replied, "but Ace and Chance Jensen are mixed up in this deal, that's for sure. And you're right . . . That's *my* silver mine you're trying to move in on, Scranton."

The air in the room was charged with tension now. Porter had holstered his Colt after he'd let Foxx into the room, but he hooked his fingers into claws near the gun butt now, ready to make a play if he needed to. Foxx had his drink in his left hand. His right hovered close by his gun.

The two men locked cold stares with each other for a long moment. Then, abruptly, Scranton's granitelike face relaxed as much as it could.

"It sounds to me," he said, "like we need to make some sort of mutually profitable arrangement, you and I."

Foxx lifted his glass and swallowed the rest of the whiskey in it.

"That's exactly what I was thinking," he said. "And *that's* why I'm here."

Chapter 22

"The old man is named Beltz," Scranton said a few minutes later, after he and Foxx had taken seats, Scranton next to the good-looking blonde on the divan, Foxx in an armchair on the other side of the sitting room, near a small fireplace, where embers glowed redly.

The gray-faced gunman—Porter, Foxx thought his name was—stood to one side, between him and Scranton. Porter had his arms folded across his chest, which would slow down his draw a little if he had to make one, but Foxx would be willing to bet that he could shuck that Colt from its holster pretty swiftly, anyway.

The blonde looked both interested and greedy. More than likely, even without knowing the details, she was trying already to figure out some angle she could use to turn this situation to her advantage.

Scranton took a cigar from his vest pocket and put it in his mouth. He looked over at Natalie Fairchild. The blonde took a match from a polished wooden box on a small table next to the divan. The movement made the neckline of her gown drop a little lower and gave Foxx an enticing view from where he was. He didn't consider such things of vital importance, but he could still enjoy them when he got the chance.

Natalie lit the match by scraping it on a rough strip attached to the box. She leaned the other way to hold the flame to the tip of Scranton's cigar. He puffed it to life, then leaned back and exhaled a cloud of smoke.

He didn't offer a cheroot to Foxx, which was kind of offensive, but again, Foxx didn't care all that much. It would have been nice if Scranton had ordered Natalie to bring him a cigar and light it for him, though. Foxx figured he ordered her to do plenty of other things.

Foxx shoved that thought out of his head and asked, "What old man?"

"The one who's taken over your mine," Scranton replied. "He was already around when you were here before. Pudgy little man with a white beard and a high-pitched voice."

Foxx shook his head. "I don't remember him. But I kept pretty much to myself."

For good reason. He didn't want anybody recognizing him from a wanted poster.

"Beltz has worked claims up and down the canyon," Scranton went on, "but he never had any luck with them until he stumbled on the one you say belongs to you."

"I don't just say it," Foxx snapped. "It's the truth."

Scranton had the fat cigar between two fingers of his right hand. He waved that hand to put aside what Foxx had just said.

"I didn't know anything about that. You and I weren't ever friends, Foster. I didn't know where your claim was. All I knew was that Beltz started taking out a considerable amount of silver . . . and I figured a claim that produced like that ought to belong to me. I made a couple of offers to buy it, but he turned me down."

"Because he couldn't legally sell it to you," Foxx pointed out. "He's just squatting there, and if he'd tried to sell it, people would have found out. He's nothing but a claim jumper!"

Scranton's burly shoulders rose and fell. "What he's doing may be against the law, but who's going to enforce it?"

"I am," Foxx said. "I aim to take that mine back." He paused. "But if you were to help me do that, Scranton, I'd be willing to share part of it with you."

"Half?" Scranton asked without hesitation.

Foxx shook his head. "Not hardly. It was my mine to start with."

"Then you take it back from Beltz and his friends." Scranton put the cigar in his mouth and puffed on it again before he added, "Anyway, if you want to talk about what's legal and what's not . . . from what you told me, it sounds like Chance Jensen actually owns that mine."

Foxx snorted dismissively. "Jensen's just a kid."

"A tough kid. He and his brother tangled with a couple of my men today. They beat them with fists, and then later they swapped lead . . . and my men wound up dead. Then, tonight, they were out there at the mine when more of my men tried to move in."

"Yeah, my friends and I were close by," Foxx said with a thin, humorless smile. "We watched the whole thing. They put the run on your boys, that's for sure."

Porter had been leaning against the wall. He straightened, an angry look on his gaunt face. "They were lucky—" he began.

"Not from where I was sitting," Foxx broke in harshly. "It looked to me like they shot fast and straight, and you couldn't root them out, despite outnumbering them four or five to one."

"They had the high ground," Porter said. "That mine's easy to defend—"

Foxx interrupted him again. "Damned right it is. How many men does Beltz have up there with him, anyway?"

Scranton said, "As far as I know, there are six men holding the mine right now, including Beltz himself. The Jensen brothers just went out there with him this evening. He has three *other* brothers working for him. They're from Norway or Sweden or somewhere over there. Steingrim is their name."

Porter added, "I've never seen any of them carrying a gun, though. I think it was just Beltz and the Jensens defending the place tonight."

"Like I said, outnumbered four or five to one," Foxx gibed.

"We'll catch the Jensens away from there sometime. It'll be different then. And once they're dealt with, Beltz and the Steingrims won't be able to hold us off for long at all," Scranton said.

Foxx sat back in the armchair and cocked his left ankle on his right knee. "Sounds to me like you waited a little too long to jump in with both feet, Scranton," he said. "You should have dealt with the situation before the Jensens showed up."

"They may complicate things . . . Hell, they've already complicated things . . . but this is nothing I can't handle," Scranton insisted. "And I don't need your help, Foster." He shook his head. "As far as I can see, you don't really have anything to offer me, so I don't see any reason to take you up on that deal, no matter what percentage you're willing to give up."

Foxx put his left foot back on the floor and leaned forward. His face was set in hard lines now. "That's *my* mine."

"You don't have legal right to it any more than I do," Scranton said. "I'd say it belongs to whoever has that piece of paper. And right now, that's Chance Jensen."

With an effort, Foxx controlled the anger that seethed inside him. "If you go after the deed, and my friends and I go after the deed, we're liable to just get in each other's way," he said. "And if we're not working together, Scranton, then we're working against each other. That means you'll have me and my boys to contend with as enemies, too." Foxx shook his head. "That's just going to make the job tougher for you."

"Tougher for *you*, you mean," Scranton snapped. "I have more men than you do."

"Maybe." Foxx's tone was noncommittal. He wasn't going to admit to a potential rival how many men he could call on. Better to let Scranton wonder about that. "It's already pretty clear, though, that rooting out those fellas at the mine isn't going to be easy. Why make it any harder than it has to be?"

Scranton glared at him for a long moment. Then, "Forty percent."

"Twenty," Foxx countered.

"Thirty," Scranton said. "And by the Lord Harry, I won't go any lower! If that's not agreeable to you, you can get the hell out of here and watch your back, because it won't be just the Jensens who are out to get you!"

Foxx glared just as hard, but after a couple of seconds, he shrugged and said, "I'd rather have seventy percent of what's mine by rights than nothing. You've got a deal, Scranton."

Scranton chewed the cigar and asked, "You want me to have a contract drawn up?"

"There's no court around here to enforce it," Foxx replied with a humorless chuckle. He nodded toward Natalie Fairchild and the gun-wolf called Porter. "We have witnesses to the arrangement."

"Witnesses who work for me."

"I trust them to be fair about things," Foxx said easily.

"Very well," Scranton said. "If we're working together, what's our first move?"

"The Jensen brothers know you by now, but they don't know me. As far as I'm aware, we've never laid eyes on each other. Beltz might recognize me, though, since we were around the canyon at the same time. What I need to do is catch those boys away from the mine sometime and make their acquaintance. That way I can find out exactly what the setup is out there."

Scranton grimaced. "There's no telling how long that will take."

"Are you in a hurry, or do you want results?"

"I want results, blast it. But every day that goes by is another day Beltz and his helpers dig more silver out of that mine."

"What have they been doing with the ore?" Foxx asked. "Are they shipping it out on the stagecoach?"

Scranton shook his head. "The old man brings in enough to trade at the store for supplies, but that's all. If he's telling the truth about how much the mine is producing, he must have a pretty good cache out there by now."

"Then sooner or later, that cache will be ours," Foxx declared. "A pile of silver's not going to get up and walk away on its own two feet."

"No, I suppose not." Scranton sighed. "Just don't take too long to make your move, Foster. I'm not a patient man."

"Don't worry about that. Neither am I." Foxx pushed himself to his feet and took off his hat. He inclined his head toward Natalie and went on, "Even though we didn't get a chance to visit much, Miss Fairchild, it was a pleasure meeting you."

"Likewise, Mr. Foster," she said. "Perhaps we can get to know each other better some other time."

"I'd like that," he said, aware of but ignoring the scowl Scranton sent toward him. Porter didn't look too happy, either. "I'll let myself out."

Foxx clapped his hat back on and went out of the room, then closed the door behind him. He paused for a second in the corridor and grinned. He was reasonably happy with the way the meeting had gone. Scranton was a crude, greedy son of a gun, and Foxx didn't like having to agree to give him even 30 percent.

But in the long run, it didn't matter. As soon as he had what he wanted, he would kill Scranton, and Porter, too, for that matter.

Then maybe he and Natalie Fairchild actually would get to know each other better.

"I know that fella, boss," Anse Porter said to Scranton as he stared coldly at the closed door. He knew their visitor hadn't had time to reach the stairs yet. Porter could jerk the door open and put a bullet in the troublemaker's back before he knew what was going on.

"What do you mean?" Scranton asked.

"As soon as I laid eyes on him, I knew I'd seen his face somewhere before."

"You know him?"

Porter shook his head. "No, I'm sure we never crossed trails. But I recognized him, anyway, and there's only one way that's possible." He paused. "I've seen his pictures on reward posters. You know I've done some bounty hunting in my time."

Scranton frowned. His voice was quick with interest as he asked, "You're saying the man is an outlaw?"

"I'm convinced of it. I don't think his real name is Foster, either. That just doesn't sound right to me."

"Real names don't mean a great deal out here," Scranton replied with a shake of his head.

"I know that, but if I can recall what else was on that wanted poster, we'll have a better idea who we're dealing with . . . and what we'll have to do about him in the long run."

Scranton put the cigar back in his mouth and clenched his teeth on it, so it stuck up at a jaunty angle.

"Oh, that's simple," he said around the cheroot. "I know exactly what we're going to do. In the long run, we're going to kill him and any men he has riding with him. Once that's done, all that silver will be mine." Scranton turned toward the divan and jerked his head toward the bedroom door as he looked at Natalie. She sighed, stood up, and moved in that direction as Scranton added to Porter, "You can let yourself out, too."

"Sure, boss," Porter said. He would go along with what Scranton told him to do. That was what he always did.

For now.

Chapter 23

For the next several days, Ace and Chance worked at the mine with Nick Beltz and the Steingrim brothers. Neither of them said anything to the old-timer about the piece of paper that was stowed safely away now in Chance's gear. Ace and Chance both liked Beltz, and they didn't see any reason to upset him at this point. The mine was producing silver. They could work out all the details later.

At the very worst, Beltz had promised them 2 percent each, after all. The Jensen brothers had never set out to become silver tycoons.

Even though the work was hard, Beltz's colorful personality and seemingly endless supply of stories made him entertaining to be around. Some of the yarns were violent and bloody, others were ribald, and occasionally one of his tales was funny and heartwarming.

His talking made up for the taciturn nature of the Steingrim brothers. Baldur, Folke, and Haldor were incredibly productive workers, but they labored in silence for the most part, broken only by occasional grunts of effort when one of them would bear-hug a chunk of rock that it would have taken both Ace and Chance to lift and carried it out of the tunnel.

They were a little more forthcoming in the evenings,

around the campfire. Folke proved to be a pretty good raconteur as he spoke of Thor, Loki, Odin, Heimdall, and the other gods of the old religion.

"One day we shall all go to Valhalla," he declared one night. "And there the fighting and the drinking and the wenching will never end."

Chance looked up from the cup of coffee in his hand and asked, "Where is this Valhalla place? Back in the country where you come from?"

"Valhalla is where Vikings go after they've died in battle," Ace said. "I read about it a time or two in books."

"Oh. Well, that doesn't sound bad. I suppose if you've got to go somewhere, it might as well be there."

Beltz slapped his thigh and laughed. "Don't let these boys lead you astray, Chance. They're pagans. Miss Priscilla tried once or twice to convert 'em whilst they was in town, but it never took."

"A fella's got a right to believe what he wants, I suppose, and some of it's not that different," Ace said. "The Indians sometimes talk about the happy hunting grounds in the spirit world. That sounds sort of like Valhalla."

"Yah," Haldor said, "and if the Indians be there, we will give them a good fight!"

"Plenty of battle for everyone!" Folke added.

"I'll drink to that!" Beltz said as he lifted his coffee cup, which Ace had seen him spiking from a flask earlier.

Such camaraderie was a welcome thing for the Jensen brothers. It looked like they weren't going to be with family for Christmas, which was only about a week away, but this year they could celebrate with their newfound friends. Ace wondered if there would be anything special for the holiday going on in Panamint City.

Of course, it wouldn't be a good idea for all of them to go into town and leave the mine unprotected. Scranton hadn't tried anything else since the attack the night Ace and Chance had gotten here, but probably he was just biding his time, waiting for a good opportunity to strike. They were still standing guard every night, even though nothing had happened.

The second morning after the Jensens arrived, they got up to a thin coating of white on the ground. The snow had fallen during the night. Once the sun rose, it began to melt, and most of it was gone by the middle of the day. A few pockets remained in the shady places all the time, since the temperature never climbed enough to melt it off completely. And every night more fell, so that the world was white when they got up in the morning.

It could get warm inside the tunnel, however, as the men labored to extend it and extract silver-bearing ore from it. Ace and Chance had used picks and shovels before, but not recently. For a few days, their muscles ached considerably, and they were stiff every time they climbed out of their bedrolls, but the work began to harden them up.

When they had been there a week, Beltz announced, "We need some more supplies. I ain't sure it's a good idea for me to go into town by myself, though."

"One of us can go with you," Ace said without hesitation. "And the other one should stay here, just in case Scranton tries something." He smiled at the Steingrim brothers. "No offense, fellows, but I'm not sure how well you'd stack up against Scranton's hired gun-wolves."

"If they would come up here and face us like men," Haldor rumbled as he clenched his hands into huge fists, "we would defeat them. But no! They stand off and shoot at us like the cowards they are!"

"That's why you need somebody here who can shoot back at them," Chance said. "Ace, I'll match you to see who goes into town. We can flip a coin or draw straws or—"

"Or you can just go, and I'll stay here," Ace interrupted

him. A chuckle came from the older—by a few minutes— Jensen brother. "I know that after being out here for a week, you probably can use a dose of civilization."

"Well, that does sound pretty good," Chance admitted. "Thanks, Ace. I promise not to look up that Miss Lansing and flirt with her. You've already got enough competition from that doctor fella."

A blush spread over Ace's face. "It doesn't matter to me what you say to Miss Lansing, as long as you're polite to her. I'm not in any sort of . . . of competition for her!"

"Sure," Beltz said, with a cackle of laughter. "We all seen for our own selves how you wasn't interested in her a'tall! Ain't that right, Chance?"

"My brother's problem is just that he's so dang shy," Chance said.

Ace glared at them and said, "Are you going to stand around all day hoorawing me, or are you going to town to get those supplies?"

"We're goin', we're goin'," Beltz said. "Come on, Chance. Help me get the pack saddle on that ol' mule o' mine."

A short time later, Chance and Beltz left the mine. Beltz was riding Ace's horse and leading Mehitabel the mule this time, so the trip wouldn't take as long as if they had to walk all the way to Panamint City and back, as Beltz normally did.

The Steingrim brothers went into the mine to work. They didn't need Beltz's supervision to know what to do. Ace tucked his Winchester under his arm and took up a position behind the brush, near the gap at the head of the trail. He would stand guard there, watching and listening for any potential threats.

Down in the canyon, Chance was equally alert as he rode alongside the old-timer. Beltz was yammering about something, as usual, but Chance listened with only half an ear. His keen eyes scanned both rugged sides of the canyon ahead of them, searching for any sign of an ambush. They stuck to brushy areas when they could and followed gullies, even though that made the going harder, just so they wouldn't be such good targets out in the middle of the canyon.

The temperature hadn't climbed much today, since a thick gray overcast blocked most of the sun's warmth. Chance wore a brown overcoat and had the collar turned up. Beltz was in his usual shaggy buffalo coat. He wore his floppy-brimmed hat rather than the tasseled fur cap.

"Maybe not today, but it won't be long, mark my words," he said, drawing Chance's attention back to his harangue.

"Won't be long until what?" Chance asked.

"Boy, were you not listenin' to a word I just said? There's a snowstorm a-comin'! A big one, accordin' to what my bones tell me. Could be a plumb blizzard!"

"When?"

"Sometime in the next few days. It's hard to tell exactly when somethin' like that is gonna happen, but I know it's comin'. Knowed it as soon as I crawled outta my blankets this mornin'. That's why I figured it'd be a good idea to head for town and lay in a few more supplies."

Chance felt a jolt of alarm. "You don't think we're going to get snowed in for a long time, do you?" He knew that in some places, the snow drifted so deep that people couldn't get in or out for months.

"No, it ain't like we're up in the really high country," Beltz told him. "We might get enough snow to make the trail impassable for a few days, but then there'll be a warm breeze off the desert to the east, and some of it will melt. I'd be mighty surprised if we ever got snowed in for more'n a week."

"A week's plenty long enough," Chance said. "I don't like it when I can't just pick up and go whenever I want to."

Beltz laughed. "That's the fiddle-footed nature you got, boy. I can see it in both you and your brother. You're on the drift, and you like it that way."

"I reckon we do," Chance agreed. "We've never really known any other way of life. Even when we were young, the fella raising us never settled down for long."

"Prospectin's the same way," Beltz said with a nod. "The lure of the unknown always drawin' you on."

That was the truth. Chance wondered if it would ever change for him and Ace . . . and whether or not they would want it to. That uncertainty was one reason why he had gone along with Ace's suggestion that they not tell Beltz about the deed Chance had won from Tom Bellamy.

That, and the fact that both brothers genuinely liked the old-timer and hadn't figured out a way to break the news to him without upsetting him.

A short time later, they came in sight of the stamp mill's smokestack, looming high at the head of the canyon. The thick column of smoke that came from it was darker than the gray clouds and just seemed to add to the chilly gloom. Chance was going to be glad when they reached the warmth and light of the buildings in the settlement.

The cold had driven some people inside, so Panamint City's main street wasn't as busy as it had been the last time Chance was here. Wagons were parked in front of the businesses, and a few men hurried along the boardwalks, huddled in their coats, but Chance and Beltz had no trouble finding places at the hitchrack in front of the store for the two saddle horses and Mehitabel.

Chance looked along the street to a café with yellow light gleaming through its windows and said, "You shouldn't need my help for a while, Nick. I'm going down there to get a cup of coffee and warm up a mite."

"I thought you was supposed to be protectin' me from Scranton and his gunnies," Beltz protested.

"What's he going to do right here in the middle of town in broad daylight? Well, what passes for broad daylight when it's this cloudy, anyway."

Beltz shrugged and said, "All right, but if I get ventilated, it ain't my fault."

Chance made a face. "Dadgum it. If you're just going to make me feel guilty—"

He broke off as he spotted a woman hurrying along the boardwalk toward the store. She wore a thick coat, with a fur collar turned up around her ears and cheeks. The coat had a hood, which she had pulled up over her head. Because of that, he couldn't get a good look at her face or figure, but he liked the graceful way she moved, even though she didn't waste any time getting out of the cold wind and going on into the store.

"I reckon I'd better come with you, after all," Chance said. "We can get some coffee later, before we head back out to the mine."

"Sure, I reckon." Beltz looked confused by Chance's sudden change of mind. He probably hadn't noticed the woman going into the store.

The fire burning in a potbellied stove in a rear corner had warmed things up inside the building. It felt good as Chance and Beltz went in. Chance turned his coat collar down and thumbed back his hat. He looked around for the woman who had just entered the store.

She was standing at the counter, talking to a clerk. The hood of her coat was still up, and the fur collar still nestled around her face. Chance moved up behind her and heard the rich, slightly husky tone of her voice as she said to the aproned man, "Already tried the doctor's office, and he's not there. I was hoping you might have something that would help."

She sounded worried, and not only that, Chance thought that her voice was familiar, although he couldn't place it right away.

"Sorry, ma'am," the clerk said. "We've got a few potions and nostrums, but they're not real medicine. To be honest with you, if the fella's really in pain, you might be better off going to one of the saloons and getting a bottle of whiskey."

With an exasperated sigh, the woman reached up and pushed the hood back from her head. She said, "Whiskey's not going to be strong enough. I need laudanum or opium."

"The doc's probably around town somewhere," the clerk said. "Unless he got called out to one of the mines in the canyon because somebody's hurt."

Chance stood behind the woman and a little to the side. From there he had a partial view of her left profile.

That was enough to make a shock of recognition go through him. He was right about hearing her voice before, and now that he could see her, he recalled where and when he had met her: in a saloon in Los Angeles a couple of weeks earlier.

He stepped up beside her, took his hat off, and said, "Hello, Miss Malone. Maybe I can give you a hand."

Chapter 24

Myra Malone exclaimed in surprise and turned toward him. "Who—" Her eyes widened in recognition. She had recognized him, too. "Mr. Jensen!"

"In the flesh," Chance said with a smile. "I'm not sure what you're doing up here in the mountains, but you sound like you're having a problem. I'd be glad to help, if I can."

She shook her head. "No. I appreciate the offer, but I can handle things—"

"You're looking for the doctor, aren't you?"

The worry in her eyes deepened. "That's right. But he's not at his office."

"Are you hurt?"

"No, it's for a . . . a friend of mine . . ."

"Well, I have an idea where we might be able to find him, if you'd like me to help you look. It wouldn't be a problem at all."

Myra caught her bottom lip between her white, even teeth and chewed it for a second before she said, "If you're sure you don't mind . . ."

"Not at all," Chance assured her. "Give me just a minute."

He turned to Nick Beltz, who was looking at some new pickaxes hanging on hooks on the wall. "Nick, I have to help an old friend for a few minutes, but you should be all right here in the store."

"Runnin' out on me again, are you?" Beltz asked. "I'm old, and I'm a friend, ain't I?" He glanced past Chance. His shaggy eyebrows rose, and Chance knew he was looking at Myra. "Ohhh. I reckon there's friends, and then there's *friends*."

Chance lowered his voice and explained, "She's looking for the doctor. He might be at the mission, so I thought I'd take her down there."

"You could just tell her where it is."

"I'm not sure a lady needs to be walking around Panamint City alone."

He wasn't sure Myra Malone was actually a lady, either, considering that when he met her, she was working in a saloon and calling herself Trixie, but that didn't really matter at the moment.

Beltz chuckled and waved a hand. "I'm just joshin' you, son. You go on ahead. I'll be here when you get back, and if I ain't, that'll be because I got darin' and went down to the café for that cup o' hot coffee. You're right, Scranton won't try nothin' here in town. He's still tryin' to look halfway re-spectable . . . for now."

"Thanks, Nick," Chance said. He turned back to Myra. "Let's go. Panamint City's not really a big town. We ought to be able to find Dr. Drake, even if he's not where I think he might be."

"Do you know the doctor?" Myra asked as they started to-ward the door.

"We've met," Chance replied, not offering any details be-yond that.

"Is he a good doctor?"

"Well, I don't actually know. But he seems like he probably knows what he's doing."

"I hope so," Myra said with a sigh. She pulled her hood

over her head again as they stepped out onto the store's front porch.

Chance turned his collar up and tugged his hat down against the biting wind. He put a hand on Myra's arm. There wasn't anything particularly intimate about the gesture, under the circumstances, but Chance enjoyed doing it, anyway.

He led her across the street, dodging piles of horse and mule droppings and frozen puddles that had resulted from previously melted snow. When they reached the opposite boardwalk, they went along it until they came to the former Odd Fellows hall, now converted to the Panamint City Mission.

"The doctor helps out here sometimes," Chance explained to Myra as he reached for the doorknob. He heard music and singing coming from inside.

The pleasant sounds welled up as he opened the door. Warmth flowed out along with them. Chance ushered Myra inside and pulled the door closed behind them to keep the cold from snatching away any more of the heat than necessary.

As Chance patted his gloved hands together to warm them up, he looked around the big room. Priscilla Lansing had been right: there were children in Panamint City. A group of two dozen of them stood at the front of the room, in two rows, singing as Priscilla played a piano that sat off to one side. Although Chance was far from an expert at judging such things, he estimated that their ages ranged from five or six to the mid-teens.

Their voices were untrained. Some of them were off-key, and others were having trouble keeping up with the words, but they were singing "Silent Night," and it sounded mighty nice to Chance, anyway. Although he tried to keep it buried, like all Jensens, he had a sentimental streak. He couldn't help but smile a little as he listened.

Two sections of benches were set up like pews in a church.

A man in a dark suit and hat sat on the front bench to the right, not far from the piano. Even though the man had his back to the two newcomers, Chance recognized Dr. Allan Drake.

He leaned closer to Myra, pointed to Drake, and said, "That's him. That's the doctor."

"Thank you. I'm glad your hunch was right." She started to take a step forward, then stopped. "I suppose we should let them finish their song before we interrupt them."

"Can your friend wait?"

Myra looked torn. Chance had been thinking about what she'd said, about how she had a friend who needed medicine from the doctor, and he recalled that back in Los Angeles, she had seemed to be close to the gambler named Tom Bellamy.

Was it possible that *he* was the friend who'd accompanied her to Panamint City? The former owner of the mine now being worked by Nick Beltz?

Myra was saved from having to make a decision, as the song came to an end. Priscilla Lansing turned on the stool in front of the piano and smiled at the two rows of youngsters.

"You did very well, children," she told them. "I'm sure your families and friends will be proud of you when you perform on Christmas Eve."

She must have spotted Chance and Myra from the corner of her eye as they stood in the back of the room, because she turned more on the stool and stood up.

"Hello? Can I help you?" Then she smiled and went on, "Mr. Jensen! It's good to see you again."

Chance took off his hat and held it in his left hand. He touched Myra's left arm with his right hand as both of them started along the aisle between the two sections of benches. Up at the front, Dr. Drake stood up and turned toward them, as well.

"Hello, Jensen," he said. "Where's your brother?"

"Ace didn't come into town with me today," Chance replied, which didn't really answer the doctor's question. Drake didn't need to know their business. Chance went on, "This lady is looking for you, Doctor. This is Miss Myra Malone."

"Miss Malone," Drake said with a polite nod. His hat was on the bench, next to where he'd been sitting, or else he probably would have tipped it. "Are you in need of medical attention?"

"No, it's a friend of mine," she told him. "He . . . he was injured a while back, and he's still in a great deal of pain at times. I was hoping you could give me some medicine for him . . ." Her voice trailed off as Drake began shaking his head.

"I'm sorry, but I'd have to examine the patient first," he said. "If you'd like to bring him to my office, I can meet you there in a few minutes." He glanced around at Priscilla and smiled. "I knew that Miss Lansing's choir was going to be practicing this morning, so I thought it might be nice for them to have an audience."

"And we appreciate that, Doctor," Priscilla said. "But we certainly don't want to keep you away from your duties."

"I don't know," Myra said. "I can try . . ."

"I'll go on back to the office," Drake said. "I'll be there in a few minutes, if your friend wants me to take a look at him."

Myra didn't look happy about it, but she said, "All right. I'll tell him. Thank you, Doctor."

Priscilla moved closer to Chance and asked, "How are you and your brother doing, Mr. Jensen?"

"We're fine. Ace was busy today, or else he would have come into town, too." Chance didn't explain that Ace was standing guard at the mine. He smiled and added, "He's going to be sorry he missed talking to you. And, uh, hearing that nice song, of course."

Priscilla appeared pleased to hear that. She said, "The children will be performing on Christmas Eve. Everyone in the area is invited. I hope both of you will be able to attend."

"We'll have to wait and see, I reckon. But I'll tell Ace about it. I can promise you that."

Drake looked a little annoyed. Chance figured that probably was because he didn't like Priscilla asking about Ace.

Myra turned toward the door. She paused when Priscilla said, "It was nice to meet you, Miss Malone."

"You, too, Miss Lansing."

"I hope your friend gets to feeling better."

"So do I," Myra said. "I'm not sure he'll be willing to see the doctor, though. He doesn't like to admit that there's anything wrong with him."

Chance put his hat on and said to Priscilla, "I'll tell Ace you said hello."

She smiled. "Thank you, Mr. Jensen."

Chance turned to follow Myra. Even though he had done what he had said he'd do—help her find the doctor—he intended to stick with her. He wanted to know if Tom Bellamy was here in Panamint City and, if so, what the man wanted here.

Maybe he planned to try to get his hands on that mine again. If that was the case, he'd have to get in line! Big Dave Scranton already had his eye on it, not to mention how Nick Beltz and the Steingrim brothers had moved in and started working it.

"Are you headed back to the hotel?" Chance asked as he moved alongside Myra. Without waiting for her to answer, he went on, "I can walk with you. Panamint City may look a mite peaceful today, but it's still a boomtown, and a lady probably shouldn't be walking around by herself."

With a faint smile, Myra said quietly, "Being a lady is one thing I haven't been accused of very often, Mr. Jensen."

"Call me Chance."

"All right . . . Chance."

He reached for the doorknob and was about to grasp it

when someone outside turned it. The door swung open. Cold wind blew in Chance's face. He saw the man standing in the doorway, a lean figure silhouetted against the gray daylight outside. Instantly, Chance recognized Tom Bellamy, even though the man's face was pale and haggard. His eyes seemed more deep-set and haunted than they had been when Chance faced him across a poker table in that Los Angeles saloon.

Bellamy recognized Chance, too. That was obvious from the way his eyes widened and a scowl twisted his gaunt face.

"You!" he exclaimed. Then his gaze flicked to Myra. "You're going to try to steal *her*, too? Damn it, no!"

With that harsh cry, he stepped forward swiftly and snapped a punch that landed squarely on Chance's jaw.

Chapter 25

Even though Bellamy didn't weigh a lot and the blow didn't have much power behind it, it took Chance by surprise. The impact was enough to knock his hat off and make him take a step backward, away from Myra.

She cried, "Tom, no!" as Bellamy rushed forward, swinging again at Chance, who caught his balance and set himself to meet the man's attack.

Chance blocked the first couple of punches Bellamy launched at him. He could have landed a solid blow of his own, but Bellamy looked so frail, Chance was afraid he would do some real damage if he hit him too hard. He might even kill Bellamy, and he didn't want that.

Chance feinted to his right, and Bellamy bit on it completely. That allowed Chance to dart back to his left and lunge forward. He clapped a hand on Bellamy's right shoulder and shoved. That twisted Bellamy even farther around.

"Don't hurt him!" Myra cried. Chance assumed she was talking to him, pleading with him not to hurt Bellamy.

That wasn't his intention. He grabbed the man from behind, wrapping his arms around Bellamy's torso and pinning his arms to his sides. Bellamy raged and writhed. Curses flew out of his mouth, along with spittle.

But he couldn't free himself from Chance's firm grip.

"Blast it, settle down!" Chance said. He was tall enough that when he lifted, Bellamy's feet came off the floor a couple of inches. The man tried to kick back at him.

The children who had been singing "Silent Night" a few minutes earlier rushed along the aisle between the benches, eager to get a closer look at the fight. Some of the boys yelled encouragement, even though they didn't really know what was going on. Priscilla Lansing raised her voice and told them to return to the front of the room, but they were caught up in the excitement of the struggle and ignored her.

Chance stumbled back and forth as he tried to avoid the kicks that Bellamy aimed at his shins. He cast a desperate glance at Myra, pleading with his eyes for her to do something.

Otherwise, he was going to have to hurt Bellamy just to get him to quit fighting.

"Tom, stop it," she pleaded as she came closer, with both gloved hands outstretched. "Please, Tom, don't carry on like this." She reached in and gripped his shoulders, so that he had to stop flailing his legs around. If he hadn't, he probably would have kicked her.

Bellamy's shoulders slumped, and his head sagged forward. Chance lowered him until his feet were on the floor again, and said, "If I let go of you, are you going to stop fighting?"

"Yeah," Bellamy replied in a dull voice. "There's nothing left for me to fight for, is there? You've already taken everything that matters away from me."

"That's not true, and you know it."

Chance released Bellamy and took a step back from him.

Bellamy's dejected, defeated attitude vanished as soon as he was free. He whirled toward Chance. A hate-filled snarl twisted his face. His hand darted under his coat and reappeared, clutching a small pistol. "I won't let you get away with it!" he yelled, then added a filthy epithet.

"Tom, no!" Myra cried.

Bellamy was fast, but Chance had seen the man's draw happening as soon as Bellamy started it. He could have unleathered his own gun swiftly enough to beat the gambler's shot. But Chance knew he wouldn't have time for anything fancy. He'd have to kill Bellamy, more than likely.

So instead of reaching for his Smith & Wesson, he threw the punch he had been reluctant to launch earlier. His right fist smashed into Bellamy's jaw and knocked the man off his feet. Bellamy went over backward, his legs flying up in the air. Myra had to leap aside to keep him from crashing into her. Instead, he landed with a heavy thud on his back. The gun sailed out of his fingers and spun around as it slid across the floor toward the group of avidly watching children.

One of the bigger boys took a step forward. His eyes lit up with eagerness as he started to bend over and reach for the pistol.

Priscilla was too quick for him. She got there first and scooped the gun from the floor.

"Shame on you, Seth," she said. "What were you thinking? You don't need this gun!"

"Aw, Miss Priscilla," the boy muttered. "I wouldn'ta done nothin' with it. I just wanted to hold it."

Bellamy groaned as Myra dropped to her knees beside him and slipped an arm around his shoulders. She raised his head and said, "Tom, are you all right?"

Dr. Allan Drake moved in, all business now. "Let me take a look at him, miss," he said.

He went down on one knee on Bellamy's other side, grasped his chin, and moved his head back and forth, probably checking to see if his jaw was broken.

Bellamy moaned again and said, "Wha . . . wha . . ."

"Open your eyes," Drake told him. When Bellamy did so, Drake studied each eye in turn. Then he said, "Can you move your arms and legs?"

Bellamy moved his legs, raised his arms, and dropped them. He still seemed only half-conscious, but he had understood what Drake said.

"No sign of serious injury," Drake declared with a satisfied nod. To Myra, he added, "You can help him sit up."

Chance was glad to see that he hadn't done any major damage to Bellamy, even though throwing down on Chance like that meant that whatever happened, Bellamy would have had it coming. Chance looked over at Priscilla, who still held the pistol, and he said, "I'm sure sorry for this disturbance, Miss Priscilla. Your choir practice was mighty nice."

"This altercation was hardly your fault, Mr. Jensen," she said. "You had no way of knowing that man was going to come in here and attack you."

"Maybe I should have guessed something like that might happen," Chance mused as he watched Myra help Bellamy into a sitting position. The doctor had stood up and moved back to give them room.

Chance still didn't know what Tom Bellamy was doing here in Panamint City, but the fact that Myra had come here with him was a pretty clear indication something was going on between them. He should have guessed that Bellamy was liable to be jealous if he saw Chance and Myra together.

He had figured Bellamy was at the hotel, though, since Myra had indicated that he needed medical attention. He shouldn't have been wandering around town. But maybe he had been asleep, had woken to find that Myra was gone, and had gone out to look for her, despite his condition.

The whys and wherefores of it didn't really matter, Chance told himself. What was important was the furious glare Bellamy directed toward him.

"I should have known it'd be you," Bellamy rasped. "I should've known."

"Tom, don't upset yourself—" Myra began. She still knelt beside him, with a hand on his shoulder.

Violently, he shrugged that hand away. He turned his glare toward Myra and said, "Didn't take you long to find somebody else once you figured out the shape I'm in, did it?"

Myra's mouth tightened. "That's not what happened."

"No? Then how come when I went to look for you, I saw you traipsing in here, hanging all over Jensen—"

"She wasn't hanging all over me," Chance snapped. "I was just trying to help her find the doctor, so he could take a look at *you*, you blasted idiot. You're the one she was worried about, was trying to get help for."

Bellamy shook his head and muttered, "I don't believe it."

Dr. Drake said, "It's true. I told the young lady to bring you to my office so that I could examine you and prescribe some medication for the pain you're in, if I deem it necessary." He looked at Myra. "The offer still stands."

"Forget it!" Bellamy said. "I don't need any help."

As if to prove that, he reached over and grasped the nearest bench, which was the rear one on that side of the hall. Grunting with effort, he began trying to climb to his feet.

Myra stood up and took a step toward him. She reached out tentatively, only to halt the gesture when Bellamy gave her a cold, angry stare. She stood there watching as he struggled upright with the help of the bench to steady himself. They all watched, knowing that Bellamy would reject any offers of help.

When he was standing, he scowled at Priscilla and said, "Give me my gun."

"Hold on," Chance said. He stepped forward, held out his hand, and Priscilla placed the pistol in it.

It was a top-break weapon with no trigger guard and a five-round cylinder. Chance opened it, turned it up, and shook the five bullets out of their chambers. Then he snapped the empty gun closed and turned to Myra.

"You might want to hang on to this for a while," he said as he handed her the pistol. He trickled the cartridges into her other outstretched hand and added, "Along with these."

"Thank you, Chance," she said. "I . . . I'll try."

A sneer twisted Bellamy's face. "You two are mighty cozy. Just like I thought. I trusted you, Myra."

"As far as I can see," Chance said, "all she's done is try to look out for you. I don't reckon you deserve it, either."

Myra had slipped the gun into a pocket. She laid that hand on Chance's arm for a second and said, "It's all right. He's just upset and in pain. He's not thinking straight right now."

"Don't make excuses for me, damn you," Bellamy barked at her. "I'm thinking just fine, and I know good and well what I'm doing." He pointed a finger at Chance. "And I'm telling you right now, Jensen, this isn't over."

"It had better be," Chance responded. "It's liable not to end as well for you next time."

Bellamy snarled a curse at him, turned, and started toward the door, which had been open all this time, letting cold air into the hall.

Myra gave Chance a helpless little shrug, told Priscilla, "I'm sorry," and went after him.

"I'm sorry, too," Chance told Priscilla again, then added with a slight smile, "I reckon that wasn't how choir practice was supposed to turn out."

Instead of answering him, Priscilla said, "Please go back to the front of the room, children. We still have several songs to learn before the performance."

Dr. Drake said, "I had better return to my office, in case that, ah, gentleman changes his mind or someone else is in need of my services. I'll drop back by later, Miss Lansing."

"Of course, Doctor," she told him. "We're always glad to see you."

She made it *we*, Chance noted, instead of saying that *she* was always glad to see the doctor. Might not mean anything, but again, he would mention it to Ace.

And he needed to tell Ace that Tom Bellamy was in Panamint City, too, and was clearly bearing a grudge against him. Probably against Ace, too, as his brother. The man was in bad shape, and Chance wasn't sure just how much of a threat he really was, but they couldn't ignore the possibility of trouble.

After all, it didn't take much to pull a trigger, especially when the gun was aimed at somebody's back. . . .

Chapter 26

By the time Chance got back to the general store, the supplies Nick Beltz had bought were already loaded on the mule.

"Well, you weren't any help at all," the old-timer accused, but the grin on his face took any sting out of the words. "Too busy gettin' into ruckuses inside a mission, of all places."

Chance frowned at him. "How'd you know about that?"

"The door was standin' wide open while you and that fella were waltzin' around. Folks passin' by saw what was goin' on. The word's already spread around town. Was it just a fistfight, or did gunplay break out, too? I didn't hear no shots."

"Nobody did any shooting," Chance replied with a shake of his head, not adding that gunplay had only narrowly been avoided. "And it really wasn't much of a fight. The other fella was sick. He probably should have been in bed, resting, instead of being out, starting trouble. I was just trying to keep him from hurting anybody."

"What was his grudge against you? Lemme guess . . . He was jealous on account of that gal you left here with?"

Chance shrugged and let it go at that. Under the circumstances, he couldn't very well explain how he had won the deed to that mine from Bellamy . . . the very mine that the old-timer believed belonged to him now.

Beltz finished settling up with the clerk. As he told Chance, he didn't believe in running a tab at the store, preferring to pay for his supplies as he bought them. With that done, they stepped outside.

Beltz nodded toward the café and said, "How about we go get that cup of coffee now? We can warm up our insides a mite before we start back to the mine."

The overcast showed no sign of breaking, so the temperature hadn't risen much. Chance nodded and said, "That sounds like a good idea. It's late enough in the morning that we might go ahead and have something to eat, too."

"I like the way you think, son!" the old-timer said with a laugh. He slapped Chance on the back as they started toward the café.

"I want a drink," Tom Bellamy complained as Myra Malone tried to steer him back to the hotel.

"It's too early for a drink, and besides, it's not good for you," she told him. She had her left arm hooked through his right one as they moved along the boardwalk.

"What does it matter?" Bellamy muttered. "What does anything matter?"

He stumbled suddenly, and from the way his face contorted, Myra knew that a fresh wave of pain had just gone through him. The beating he had suffered at the hands of Jared Foxx's men back in Los Angeles had damaged something inside him. Damaged it badly. The pain wasn't always so bad that it almost incapacitated him, but such spells were becoming more and more frequent as the days passed.

Bellamy forced himself to straighten up and walk. He said, "Did you make plans with Jensen back in Los Angeles to meet him here?"

"You know better than that, Tom. You're the one who wanted to come up here to Panamint City. It was your idea, remember? I just came along to take care of you."

"Didn't ask you to. If I'd known what you were really up to, I would've left you back there."

Myra told herself it did no good to argue with him. Once he got an idea in his head, it was unshakable—even if it directly contradicted something he had believed five minutes earlier.

"Let's just get out of this cold wind," she said. "I'm chilled to the bone."

"Fine. I—" He stopped short, and his knees buckled. He would have fallen if Myra hadn't reacted quickly enough. She grabbed his arm with her other hand, too, and braced her legs. Holding him up wasn't easy, but she managed somehow.

She looked around on the boardwalk and the street, thinking that she might see someone who could help her, but nobody was nearby. And in this inhospitable weather, most folks had their heads down and were hurrying along on their own business, wanting to get it done and to get back inside as quickly as possible.

"Help me . . . over to . . . that post," Bellamy gasped.

It was only a few steps to one of the posts that held up the awning over the boardwalk. Myra managed to get Bellamy there. He wrapped one arm around it to help hold himself up, which relieved some of the strain on her. A couple of minutes passed, and then Bellamy drew a deep breath and sighed.

"It's getting better now," he said. His voice was barely above a whisper. "I think . . . maybe it would be a good idea . . . to see that doctor, after all."

"I'm glad to hear you say that, Tom. I really am," she told him. "We can stay here and let you rest for as long as you need to. When you feel like you're ready to give it a try, we'll go."

He nodded weakly.

He continued leaning on the post for a couple more minutes, then told her he thought he was strong enough to make the effort. She held on to his arm with both hands as they moved away from the support. Bellamy stumbled a little as he stepped down from the boardwalk to the street, which they had to cross to reach Dr. Allan Drake's office.

They made it there a short time later. Myra was relieved to see a light in the front window of the small frame building. A sign with Drake's name on it hung from a post in front of the office.

When they reached the porch, she didn't knock, just grasped the doorknob, turned it, and pushed. Welcome heat washed out over them. Drake sat at a desk in the front room, with a thick book open in front of him. He stood up quickly as Myra and Bellamy stumbled in.

"Good heavens," he said. "I'm glad you decided to bring in your friend, Miss Malone. He doesn't look well at all."

"He had another spell just a few minutes ago, when we were trying to get back to the hotel," Myra explained. "I convinced him to let you take a look at him."

Drake moved in on Bellamy's other side. "Let me help you with him. We'll get him into the examination room. I was just reading up on internal injuries. It seems that's what Mr. Bellamy may be suffering from. You said he was beaten?"

"Yes. Badly," Myra said as they supported Bellamy between them and led him into a small room to one side, with a sheet-covered table in it. They got him onto the table, and Drake positioned a pillow under Bellamy's head.

Myra stepped back and went on, "I'm pretty sure he was kicked and stomped, too. He was in terrible shape when those horrible men got through with him."

"He must have some very bad enemies," Drake said.

If he wanted more of an explanation, he wasn't going to get it from Myra. She said, "The doctor in Los Angeles told him he ought to stay in bed for several more weeks, but Tom was insistent that we come on up here."

"There must be something here that's very important to him," Drake said, prying again.

Myra continued to ignore the hint.

After a moment, the doctor went on, "A man in his condition really shouldn't have been traveling." He made shooing motions with his hands. "Please go and wait in the other room, Miss Malone. I'll examine the patient and then let you know what I think is the best course of action."

"All right. Thank you, Doctor."

With a weary sigh, Myra left the room. She had noticed a small divan in the front room and sat down on it. She certainly didn't intend to doze off, but the thickly cushioned divan was comfortable, the room was warm, and she hadn't slept well in a long time, because of her worry over Bellamy.

Without her even being aware of it, slumber claimed her.

Jared Foxx stood on the boardwalk across the street and listened to the blood pounding in his head as his heart slugged heavily in his chest. He didn't doubt the evidence of his own eyes. He knew that what he had just seen was real. And yet he still struggled to believe it.

That had been Tom Bellamy stumbling along the street, though, with the help of some woman. Bellamy, who was supposed to be dead back in Los Angeles.

Thieving, treacherous Tom Bellamy.

Foxx had watched as they went into a building he now saw was a doctor's office. The strong impulse was to charge across the street, bust into the office, and put a bullet in Bellamy to make absolutely certain he was dead this time.

Foxx fought down that urge. He wasn't a man who acted rashly or recklessly. Never had been. He had tried to plan his crimes, which was why they had always gone well, until the botched bank robbery that had ended with him and Bellamy outracing a posse into Surprise Canyon.

Kimbrough had told him they'd left Bellamy dead in that alley. Obviously, Kimbrough had been wrong. Well, mistakes happened sometimes, Foxx told himself.

He was curious who the woman was. There might be a way to find out, Foxx told himself. He crossed the street and peered through the window into the doctor's office. The curtain was pushed back, so he had no trouble seeing the woman come out of another room, sit down on a divan, and push back the hood of the coat she wore.

She was pretty, that was for sure, with thick brown hair and nice features. She looked vaguely familiar. Foxx thought he might have seen her through the window of the saloon in Los Angeles. One of the girls who worked there, he decided.

But she wouldn't have seen him, since he hadn't gone inside and had sent Kimbrough to lure Bellamy out of the saloon. Foxx craned his neck to look around the doctor's office as best he could. He didn't see Bellamy. More than likely, his old partner was in that other room with the medico. Out in the street, Bellamy had looked like he was in pretty bad shape.

Good, Foxx thought. Whatever had happened to Bellamy, he'd had it coming.

The woman's head was leaning back against the divan. She had gone to sleep. Foxx told himself to be patient, even though it wasn't easy, and he waited to see what was going to happen.

Myra jerked upright as the examination-room door opened. She looked around wildly for a second, disoriented because she had been jolted out of sleep.

"I'm sorry," the doctor said quietly as he stepped into the office. "I didn't mean to startle you, Miss Malone."

"That . . . that's all right, Doctor," she said. "How's Tom? What did you find?"

"As I suspected, I believe he has internal injuries and perhaps some bleeding somewhere inside, but it's impossible to determine the extent of either." Drake sighed. "That's the problem with the human body. We can't just open it and take a look inside. Surgery is so fraught with risks that it has to be reserved strictly for life-threatening emergencies."

With a grim look on her face, Myra said, "The way Tom's been acting, I'm not sure but what his life *is* threatened by whatever's wrong with him, Doctor."

"You may well be correct," Drake said, nodding. "But to be perfectly forthright . . . I lack the necessary skill to perform such a procedure. As things stand, it's still possible that he might recover on his own. But if I were to attempt to operate . . ." He shrugged. "I'm afraid his chances would be almost nil."

Myra looked intently at him for a long moment, then nodded slowly. "I appreciate you being honest with me, Doctor," she said. "Under the circumstances, what do you suggest?"

"Continue caring for Mr. Bellamy as you've been doing. The most important thing is that he get as much rest as possible. Going out and, ah, getting into fights is just about the worst thing he could be doing."

"I'll make sure he understands that," Myra said. "What about something for the pain . . . ?"

"I'll give you a bottle of laudanum. Make sure he uses it sparingly, though. In fact, it would probably be a good idea if you keep it with you and dispense it yourself, rather than trusting Mr. Bellamy to do so. No more than one spoonful every four hours."

"All right," Myra said with a nod. "Can I see him now?"

"Of course. Go ahead in. I'll fetch the laudanum."

Drake went over to a cabinet behind the desk while Myra

turned toward the door to the examination room. As she opened it, a gust of cold air hit her like a slap in the face. She gasped in surprise and threw the door back more.

An empty examining table and an open window greeted her, along with the frigid air.

"Doctor!" she cried. "He's gone!"

Chapter 27

Tom Bellamy pulled his coat tighter around himself, although the thin garment didn't do much to keep the cold wind from slicing through him.

It was mostly just habit that made him do so. He didn't really feel the chill that much. It was nothing compared to the fiery blaze of pain inside him. That warmed him all the way through, if you could call it that.

Mealymouthed doctor telling him to stay in bed and rest, he thought bitterly. He couldn't do what needed to be done if he followed those orders. He couldn't stay in bed and find the man he needed to kill.

Chance Jensen.

The very name was stupid and hateful. Who named somebody *Chance*? Jensen deserved to die just for that, even if there weren't any other reasons.

But there were plenty of reasons, starting with the way Jensen had stolen Bellamy's mine from him. The kid must have cheated somehow. Bluff or no bluff, there was no way Jensen had beaten him fair and square.

Then, on top of that, the mine had turned out not to be worthless, after all! Back in the nooks and crannies of Bellamy's mind lurked the knowledge that Chance hadn't had anything to do with that twist of fate, but he ignored it.

The mine was one thing, but Myra was something else entirely. Jensen was guilty as hell of trying to steal her away. That was his worst crime of all, Bellamy told himself. Bellamy wasn't going to let him get away with it. He would kill Jensen first, as soon as he found him.

Bellamy reached inside his coat pocket and closed his fingers around the handle of the scalpel he had taken from a cabinet in the examination room before he climbed out the window.

Jensen wouldn't be so damned pretty by the time Tom Bellamy got through with him!

Myra ran to the open window and leaned out, then jerked her head from side to side as she looked frantically in both directions. She didn't see any sign of Bellamy.

"Good grief!" Dr. Drake said as he came up behind her. "What's he done? He shouldn't be out of bed!"

Myra turned away from the window and rushed past him.

"I have to find him!" she said over her shoulder. "The shape he's in, he's liable to pass out and freeze to death!"

"Miss Malone, wait!"

Something about the urgency in Drake's voice made Myra pause and look back at him. "What is it?"

He was standing in front of a cabinet positioned against one wall. The door was open. Drake pawed through several items inside and said, "I keep some of my instruments in here. It looks like one of my scalpels is gone. Yes, it is. I'm sure of it!"

Bellamy was the only one who could have taken it. Myra said, "So he has a scalpel. It's just a little blade, isn't it?"

"And sharp enough to slice a man's throat wide open, if you took him by surprise and moved quickly enough."

The shape Bellamy was in, Myra didn't know if he was capable of that. But she didn't know that he wasn't, either. And there was someone who had been in Panamint City a short time earlier whom Bellamy hated enough to kill.

Chance must have left town with that old miner by now, she thought. He must have. But she had to be sure. If Bellamy murdered Chance, that would be the end of everything, of any hope they might have for a normal life.

Without saying anything else, she ran out of the doctor's office, leaving the front door open behind her. She didn't look back to see if Drake was following her.

Her rapid footsteps carried her toward the mission. That was where she had seen Chance last. When she reached it and jerked the door open, she heard piano music coming from inside once again. With the agitated state she was in, she didn't recognize the song and didn't care what it was.

The melodic notes stopped as soon as Myra rushed inside. She looked along the aisle between the rows of benches and saw the group of children standing at the front of the room. They had fallen silent and were gaping at her. Off to the side, Priscilla Lansing took her hands away from the piano keys and turned on the bench to stare at her in surprise, as well.

"Miss Malone," Priscilla said. "What are you doing back? Is something wrong?"

"Chance Jensen," Myra gasped, a little out of breath from fear and her mad dash along the street. "He . . . he's not here?"

"No. He left a little while ago, not long after you did."

"Did he say where he was going?"

"I think he was headed back to the store to find Mr. Beltz, the man he works for."

That made sense, Myra thought. She should have started at the store, she realized, but some instinct had made her return to the last place she had seen Chance.

Without explaining what was going on, and ignoring the

questions that Priscilla Lansing called after her, Myra turned and ran out of the mission, back out into the cold.

Warmed up not only by the two cups of coffee he'd had but also by the large bowl of beef stew and the four fluffy biscuits he'd consumed, Chance leaned back in his chair and sighed.

"Amen to that, boy," Nick Beltz said. He patted his round stomach. "When you get to be my age, a meal like that makes you want nothin' more than to unbutton your trousers and sit back to take yourself a nice nap." He sighed. "I reckon we'd best be gettin' back to the mine, though. As it is, it'll be late enough 'fore we get there that your brother and them Stein-grims are gonna be wonderin' what happened to us."

"You're right," Chance said as he reached for his hat, which sat on the table to his right. He stood up and settled it on his head, then pulled on the heavy overcoat, which he had taken off while he and Beltz were in the warm café. Beltz donned his shaggy buffalo coat. Chance thought that he must have gotten used to the garment's smell. He barely noticed it anymore.

The waitress called, "Merry Christmas!" to them as they headed for the door. Chance returned the sentiment, and Beltz chortled.

"Yeah, the holiday's comin' up pretty quick now," the old-timer said. "Did your brother say anything to you about what I'm plannin' to do?"

"He said you wanted to provide presents for the children at Miss Lansing's mission," Chance replied as they stepped out into the chilly, overcast afternoon. "But you want to do it with-out her or the youngsters knowing where they come from."

"That's right. Them Steingrims are pretty good at whittlin'. I thought maybe I could get 'em to whittle some toys for the young'uns, and next time we come to town, I'll pick up a few things at the store, too. O' course, if I put Folke and Baldur and Haldor to work doin' that, they won't have as much time to dig in the mine, but I figure we can all afford to take off a little time for a worthwhile cause."

"If there's anything Ace and I can do to help, we'd be glad—" Chance began.

He had his head down so his hat brim would protect his face from the wind. Because of that, he didn't see the person hurrying toward him until they ran smack together. Chance took a quick step backward, tensing to protect himself from attack.

Then he relaxed slightly when he recognized Myra Malone standing in front of him, pale and trembling.

"Oh!" she exclaimed. "I'm sorry. I didn't see . . . You're all right!"

"Yeah, last time I checked," Chance said with a smile. He grew more serious as he went on, "But are you? All right, that is? You look pretty shaken up, Miss Malone."

"Yes, I . . . I'm fine. I'm just . . . looking for Tom."

"Bellamy?" Chance said, his voice hardening.

"Have you seen him?"

Chance shook his head. "Not since you left the mission with him earlier. Did you ever get him to go see the doctor?"

"Yes, he finally agreed to do that after he almost collapsed in the street. But then he disappeared from the doctor's office. I . . . I was worried that he might come after you again. He doesn't have that pistol anymore. I've still got it. But he . . . he stole one of the doctor's scalpels."

"I haven't seen him, but I can help you look for him," Chance offered impulsively. Nothing moved him to volunteer faster than a pretty girl who was distraught. However, he glanced at Beltz and added, "If that's all right—"

The old-timer didn't let him finish before waving a hand and saying, "Sure, sure, go ahead. I'll even pitch in. If all three of us spread out, we can cover more ground. This fella's sick, ain't that right?"

"Very sick," Myra said.

"Then we better find him. It's pert near freezin'."

Myra put one hand on Chance's forearm, touched Beltz's shoulder with the other hand. "Thank you," she said. "Thank you both."

Chance nodded and gave her an encouraging smile. He wasn't quite sure why he was worried about Tom Bellamy, but if finding him would make Myra feel better, he supposed the effort was worth it.

In the shadowy depths of an alley across the street, Tom Bellamy caressed the scalpel's handle and watched Myra flirting with Chance Jensen. As if that wasn't bad enough, she started playing up to the old man, too. She'd rather be with a fat old codger than him, Bellamy thought. Well, he'd just have to kill the old man along with Jensen.

If Myra kept up this wanton, shameless behavior, he might have to teach her a lesson. A few swipes with the scalpel, and she wouldn't be pretty enough to go after other men.

Bellamy suppressed the urge to charge across the street and attack all three of them. His mind was still clear enough for him to realize that if he tried to do that, Jensen would gun him down before he made it halfway. No, he needed to wait until he could catch Jensen alone.

And it looked like he might get his opportunity soon, because the three of them over there split up and went in different directions. Bellamy faded back along the alley and turned to follow the backs of the buildings, heading the same way Jensen had gone. After he had passed behind a couple of buildings, Bellamy scurried up another alley, unaware of how badly he was stumbling. In his mind, he was moving swiftly and surely, an implacable avenger of all the wrongs that had been done to him.

There he is! Bellamy crouched behind a stack of crates and watched as Jensen turned and started to cross the street, coming generally toward him. His hand tightened on the scalpel.

Then someone grabbed him from behind, taking him completely by surprise. An arm went around his neck and jerked him back. Bellamy couldn't cry out, because of the incredible pressure on his throat.

But his madness gave him the strength to twist in the brutal grip, bring his arm up, and stab up and back over his shoulder with the razor-sharp scalpel.

Chapter 28

Chance didn't know where to start looking for Tom Bellamy. As sick as the man was, he might well be out of his head, just wandering around Panamint City, not really knowing where he was or what he was doing. Myra had been to the mission already, though, without finding Bellamy, so Chance didn't see any reason to go there.

After striding along the street for a short distance without seeing any sign of the man, Chance decided to cross over to the other side. There were more alleys over there—and rats liked alleys. That wasn't a very generous thought, Chance chided himself, but Bellamy had been acting like a rat, scurrying around and causing trouble.

Chance had just reached the opposite boardwalk when someone called his name and made him pause. He turned to look and saw Dr. Allan Drake coming toward him briskly.

"Are you looking for that man Bellamy?" Drake asked after he came up to Chance and stopped.

"That's right. Miss Malone found me and told me he'd escaped from your place."

"Well, I don't know if *escaped* is actually the proper word. I mean, he wasn't a prisoner or anything. But he *did* climb out a window without us knowing what he was doing, so I suppose you could say that he—"

"What is it you want, Doctor?" Chance broke in.

"I thought I might accompany you on your search. If you *do* find Bellamy, he's liable to need more medical attention."

"It might be better if you looked for him on your own," Chance suggested. "Miss Malone and Nick Beltz and I have split up so we can cover more ground. You're welcome to do that, too. Just give a holler if you find him."

Drake didn't look too happy about that idea, but he nodded and pointed along the street. "All right. I'll go this way."

"And I'm going to check out these alleys," Chance said. He nodded to the doctor and started down the nearest narrow passage between buildings.

Not much light penetrated these close confines even on the brightest day. As thick as the overcast was today, it was like twilight in the alley. Chance peered intently into the shadows but didn't see anything unusual. Some empty crates were stacked against the wall of the building on one side, and trash littered the ground here and there.

Chance's hand drifted over to hover near the butt of the Smith & Wesson he carried in the cross-draw rig under his coat. He hadn't forgotten that Bellamy had a grudge against him and had, in fact, tried to kill him earlier in the day. Myra had said that Bellamy didn't have the pistol anymore, but he might be armed with one of Dr. Drake's scalpels.

Chance didn't want to do anything to cause Myra grief, but if Bellamy jumped out of the shadows and tried to stab or slash him, Chance intended to stop him—permanently, if necessary.

That didn't happen. Chance reached the back end of the alley without coming across Bellamy or anyone else. He paused there, looked back and forth.

To his left, what looked like a pile of garbage huddled against the building's rear wall. Details were hard to make out in the gloom, but Chance's gaze almost moved past the pile before he realized there was something vaguely humanlike about the shape.

With instinctive alarm bells suddenly going off in his head, he drew the Smith & Wesson and moved quickly along the wall. Somebody had thrown a few pieces of tar paper and some other trash on top of whatever was lying there motionlessly, but the closer Chance came, the more it looked like a man.

His heart thudded in his chest as he kicked away some of the garbage to reveal the body of a man in a dark suit. His hat lay next to his head. Even in the bad light, Chance recognized Tom Bellamy.

Bellamy wasn't moving or making a sound, didn't appear to be breathing. Chance slipped a hand inside the man's coat and rested it on his chest. It didn't rise or fall.

Bellamy was dead, all right, but he hadn't been so for long. His body still retained a little warmth, and on a day this cold, it would cool off quickly. Chance figured Bellamy hadn't been dead for more than a few minutes.

He'd come so close to finding the man in time. Chance wasn't going to waste a lot of sympathy on Bellamy, but he was sorry for the grief this was going to cause Myra.

As he straightened, a familiar voice called his name. "Chance! Chance, is that you, boy?"

"Yeah, it's me, Mr. Beltz," Chance replied as the round figure of the old-timer hurried toward him from the rear mouth of another alley.

"I got to thinkin' somebody ought to look back here, but it appears you beat me to it." Beltz stopped short a few yards away and stared. "Holy Toledo! Is that . . . ?"

"Yeah, it's Bellamy," Chance replied with a grim sigh. "I guess his injuries caught up to him. Either that or the cold did him in."

"Or *somebody* did. Lookee there!" Beltz pointed.

Chance leaned over to study Bellamy's corpse more closely. Right away, he spotted the same thing the old-timer had.

Bellamy's throat was dark and mottled. His eyes bulged, until it seemed they were about to come out of their sockets. His tongue protruded slightly between his parted lips.

"What the devil?" Chance muttered. He took a match from his pocket and snapped it to life with his thumbnail. When he held the flickering flame closer to Bellamy's face, it was clear what had happened. Chance could even see how the bruises on Bellamy's neck formed the shape of hands.

Somebody had choked Tom Bellamy to death.

"Lord have mercy," Beltz said. "Somebody must've really hated this fella to do that to him. Looks like they squeezed the life outta him, slow and painful-like."

Chance moved the match so its light did a better job of illuminating the bruised neck. He said, "You can tell it was a man who did the job. Those marks are too big for a woman's hands to have made them."

"No offense, boy, but that seems like one o' them whatcha-callems, foregone conclusions. A gal wouldn't be strong enough to choke a man to death."

"You might be surprised. And Bellamy was sick enough that he may have been too weak to put up much of a fight. But overall, yeah, I agree. There's no question a man killed him."

"The question is . . . who?"

Chance had no answer for that.

The match had burned down almost to his fingers. When a harsh voice suddenly asked, "Who's back there? What's going on here?" he dropped the match and straightened. He and Beltz turned toward the questioner, who had come around the rear corner of one of the buildings, with a couple of men trailing him.

"Scranton!" Nick Beltz exclaimed.

"That's right," Big Dave Scranton replied. "What deviltry are you up to this time, Beltz?"

"This is none o' my doin'—" Beltz began.

"Boss," one of the other men said, with a note of excitement in his voice, "that looks like a body layin' there!"

"So it does, Anse," Scranton said. "Beltz, you and Jensen step back so we can see what you've done here."

"What!" Beltz yelped. "We didn't have nothin' to do with this!"

Scranton ignored that and said to his men, "One of you strike a match. We need some light."

One of them stepped forward and scratched a lucifer on the building wall. As the glare revealed Bellamy's ugly corpse, Scranton said, "Is that the man who was missing?"

"How do you know about that?" Chance asked.

"The word started going around town that a sick man might be wandering around, in danger from the cold. Some woman was looking for him, and so was the doctor." Scranton frowned down at Bellamy and said, "It wasn't the cold that killed this man, though."

"Damn sure wasn't," Anse Porter drawled. "Somebody strangled him. You can tell that by looking at him."

Scranton's smile was as cold as the air as he looked at Chance and Beltz and asked, "Which one of you killed him?"

"Wait just a cotton-pickin' minute!" Beltz yelled. "We didn't have nothin' to do with this. We're the ones who found him!"

"How do we know that? When we walked up, you were standing over his body. It's just as likely that you killed him and were discussing what to do with the carcass."

"That's loco! Why, this is the fella who was lookin' for Chance, wantin' to do *him* some harm." Beltz pointed at Bellamy.

Chance tried not to wince. Of all the things Beltz could have said in response to Scranton's theory, that was just about the worst.

Scranton cocked his head a little to the side and said, "Is that so? This man had a grudge against you, Jensen?"

"No point in denying it," Chance said flatly. "If the story hasn't already gotten around town, it won't be long before it does."

Scranton hooked his thumbs in the pockets of his vest and said, "That sounds to me like you had a very good motive for killing him first, then."

Chance shook his head. "That's not the way it happened. He was already dead when I found him."

"You mean when the two of you found him?" Scranton said sharply.

"No, I was here first. Nick came along a minute or so later." Chance could tell that Beltz was about to object to that, even though it was the truth. He held up a hand to stop the old-timer and went on, "That's the way it was. Bellamy was already dead when Nick got here. And he was certainly dead when I found him, too. But not for long. His body wasn't completely cold yet."

Porter said to Scranton, "We've got to do something about this, boss. If there was any law in this town, they'd take over. But since there's not . . ."

"Since there's not," Scranton said, "maintaining law and order is up to honest citizens like us."

That brought a contemptuous snort from Beltz.

Scranton nodded to Porter who stepped back quickly and drew his gun with a fast, slick move.

"Don't reach for an iron, Jensen," Porter warned. "You're gonna have to be locked up until we can get a miners' court together and figure this out."

"Higgins, get Jensen's gun," Scranton ordered.

Panic jumped around inside Chance's guts like a small, trapped animal. He had been in jail before. He and Ace had even been tried, convicted, and sentenced to hang for a crime they hadn't committed. He didn't like any of those feelings.

So when Scranton's man circled wide around him and started

in from behind to reach around and take his gun from the holster, Chance was mightily tempted to fight back. A quick whirl, an elbow to the man's jaw, a grab for his own gun . . .

And in the resulting hail of bullets, there was not only a very good chance he would die, but Chance also felt certain Scranton would make sure at least one stray slug found Nick Beltz, thereby eliminating a problem for him.

With that thought in his mind, Chance forced himself not to move as the man disarmed him. He still didn't know what had happened to Tom Bellamy, but he was a prisoner now and couldn't do anything about it.

His only hope was that Ace would find out what was going on and get him out of this mess.

Chapter 29

With Scranton, Porter, and the other man covering him, and Beltz still complaining, Chance walked out of the alley with his hands raised halfway and held out to the sides, in plain sight. He didn't want to give Scranton any excuse to pull the trigger. For that reason, he was glad when some of the few people on the street this chilly afternoon spotted the little procession and hurried toward them.

When somebody who hated you had a gun on you, it never hurt to have witnesses around.

In response to the questions that were called to him, Scranton said in a loud, clear voice, "There's been a killing. The sick man who went missing is back there in the alley behind that building."

A man asked, "Did he die from what ailed him, or did the cold get him?"

"Neither," Scranton said. "Looks like Jensen here choked him to death."

"That's a lie," Chance said. "I never did any such thing."

As if he hadn't heard him, Scranton went on, "That's why we're going to lock him up. Just trying to figure out where to put him, since we don't have a jail here in town."

"What about the smokehouse down at the butcher shop?"

another man suggested. "It's tight and sturdy, and it don't have any windows."

Scranton nodded. "That's a mighty good idea, Jefferson." He prodded Chance in the back with his gun barrel. "Get moving, Jensen."

In his high-pitched, querulous voice, Nick Beltz said, "This ain't right. Chance never hurt nobody. He sure as hell didn't kill Bellamy."

"How do you know that?" Scranton demanded. "Were *you* there when it happened?"

"Well, no," Beltz replied. "I come along a minute or so later."

Chance hoped that the old-timer would stick to that story. When and if it came out that Bellamy was the original owner of the mine that Beltz now claimed, that would give Beltz a reason to want Bellamy dead, too.

And to be honest, Chance couldn't swear that Beltz hadn't killed him. Despite his age and rotund stature, Beltz was in good enough shape to choke a man to death, especially one who was too sick to put up much of a fight. Beltz could have done it, heard Chance approaching, and scurried away, then pretended to come along a few minutes later. As a theory, it held together.

But as far as Chance knew, Beltz had no idea about Bellamy's connection to the mine. He was glad now that he and Ace hadn't said anything to the old-timer about the deed. Nobody could prove anything against Beltz, and Chance didn't believe he was guilty, anyway.

If he hadn't killed Bellamy, though . . . who had? Who else in Panamint City had a motive?

As far as Chance knew, Myra Malone was the only other person in town acquainted with Bellamy, and if she had choked him to death, she was the world's best actress. She had appeared frantic to help the man.

Chance supposed that, logically speaking, Myra had had the opportunity to kill Bellamy in the time between when she and Chance had parted company on the boardwalk and Chance had discovered the body. But the idea was so far-fetched that Chance couldn't bring himself to put any stock in it.

A few other people knew about Bellamy, too, he reminded himself. Priscilla Lansing and Dr. Allan Drake had seen him at the mission, as had the kids in that choir. The thought of considering any of them suspects was even more ludicrous. And Drake even had an alibi. He had been talking to Chance at just about the same time that someone was strangling Bellamy.

That thought made Chance break stride a little as Scranton and his men continued marching him toward the smokehouse. If he could provide Drake with proof of innocence, then the opposite was true, as well. He wanted to talk to the doctor as soon as possible.

Chance turned his head and said to Scranton, "I need to see Dr. Drake. Is he in that crowd following us?"

A number of interested spectators were trailing them.

"I don't know, and I don't care," Scranton snapped. "You look healthy enough. You don't need the doc."

"I want to talk to him," Chance insisted.

"Shut up and keep moving." Scranton put his free hand on the back of Chance's left shoulder and shoved. That made Chance stumble a little, and again, the thought flashed through his head that he could use the misstep as a distraction and make a break for it.

More than likely, that was exactly what Scranton wanted him to do. Chance wouldn't be able to reach any cover before Scranton and the others opened fire on him, and he didn't think he could dodge that many bullets.

If Chance was dead, Scranton could blame him for Bellamy's murder, and the whole matter would be closed. Was there any reason to think that maybe *Scranton* himself was behind the killing?

Chance dismissed that idea. He didn't know of any connection at all between Scranton and Tom Bellamy. No matter how ruthless Scranton might be, Chance didn't think he would go around and choke people to death at random.

No, he thought as they went along the side of the butcher shop, toward the squat smokehouse made of thick beams. There were no answers to be had.

A moment later, he stumbled into the cold, dark structure and the door closed behind him with a heavy thud. The door had a latch with a heavy pin in it to keep it closed so animals couldn't get inside. That latch didn't open on this side of the door, so effectively, Chance was locked inside.

Scranton ordered Porter to have somebody stand guard here, anyway, and then the sound of voices moved off in the distance as the crowd broke up. The smokehouse was empty at the moment. Barely any light penetrated through the tiny cracks between the beams, since it was built to keep smoke in. Feeling his way along the wall, Chance covered the few feet to one of the back corners and sank to the ground. The chill in him went all the way to the bone.

Deeper even than that, he realized. It went all the way to his soul.

But he was a Jensen, he reminded himself as he fought off despair. Jensens didn't give up, blast it! He would fight this to the end, and his brother would fight alongside him.

As soon as Ace found out about it.

Ace was going to have a few things to say to his brother when Chance got back from town with Nick Beltz. By midafternoon, Ace was convinced that somehow Chance had finagled Beltz into staying in Panamint City longer than necessary just so he wouldn't have to work in the mine today. The three

Steingrim brothers had been hard at it ever since sunrise—or what passed for sunrise on a gloomy, overcast day like today.

Ace had spent most of that time standing guard, although now and then he had pitched in to help move some of the largest rocks. He tried not to feel resentful of his brother, but he was convinced Chance was sitting in a warm room somewhere in town, maybe drinking coffee in the café or even visiting with Priscilla Lansing at the mission.

That thought made Ace's jaw tighten more than anything else.

So as he stood at the head of the trail, looking up the canyon, he was in a definite mood to give Chance a piece of his mind.

That feeling vanished instantly when he spotted two horses and the pack mule coming along the canyon toward the mine. Only one of those horses had a rider; the saddle on Chance's mount was empty. The round, shaggy figure riding Ace's horse and leading the other two animals had to be Nick Beltz.

A feeling of foreboding welled up inside Ace. If Chance had stayed back in Panamint City for some reason, he would have kept his horse with him. The fact that Beltz had brought the horse with him could mean only—

Ace wasn't going to let himself think that. Instead, he ran down the trail to meet the old-timer.

Ace reached the bottom end of the last switchback at the same time Beltz did. Beltz reined in and looked down into Ace's grim, worried face.

"I know what you're thinkin', son," Beltz said quickly, "but he ain't dead. Leastways, he wasn't when I left town."

Ace heaved a sigh of relief, even though Beltz's words were plenty worrisome. He said, "What happened? Where's Chance?"

"Remember a fella name of Bellamy? Evidently, you boys met him back in Los Angeles."

"Tom Bellamy, of course," Ace said. He wondered how

much Beltz knew about Bellamy—and the deed that had brought the Jensen Brothers to Surprise Canyon.

"Well, he showed up in Panamint City," Beltz said, "and had a run-in of some sort with Chance. I don't really know what it was about. Something to do with a poker game, Chance told me, but he didn't really explain."

Ace wondered if Bellamy had found out that the mine wasn't worthless, after all. That might explain why he had come up here.

"That ain't the worst of it, though," Beltz went on. "A while later, this hombre Bellamy turned up missin'. He was mighty sick, too, so the gal who was with him got me and Chance to help her look for him."

"Girl?" Ace repeated. He cast his memory back a couple of weeks. "Was her name Myra? Myra . . . Miller? No, Malone! That's what it was."

Beltz nodded. "One an' the same. Pretty gal, but I reckon she had her hands full takin' care o' that troublemakin' varmint." He sighed. "But she won't no more."

Ace felt a chill go through him that had nothing to do with the weather. He said, "Do you mean . . . ?"

"Yep," Beltz said. "I'm afraid so. That there Bellamy is dead as he can be. Somebody choked the life plumb outta him. Chance is the one who found his body, and Big Dave Scranton's got it in his head that Chance done the killin'."

"No!" Ace cried. "That's not possible."

"I feel the same way, but Scranton and a couple o' his gunnies locked Chance up, anyway. Scranton says he's gonna get a miners' court together and put Chance on trial for murder."

Chapter 30

Inyo County had a coroner, but since there was no law in Panamint City, there was no one to notify him of Tom Bellamy's death—not that he would have wanted to ride all the way up Surprise Canyon in December to hold an inquest.

But Dr. Allan Drake thought there ought to be at least some semblance of an official response, so he asked several of the bystanders to take the corpse back to his office.

"We got to bury him, Doc," one of the men protested. "You can't just leave carcasses layin' around. We don't have a real undertaker, but Joe Wilstach over at the cabinet shop can knock together a coffin pretty easy, and we can put this fella in the ground."

"The weather is certainly cold enough that there's no great rush," Drake argued. "Anyway, I just want to conduct an examination of the deceased and write up my findings, so that if there's ever any legal questions about the matter, I'll have everything documented."

The townsman who had raised the objection rubbed his blunt chin and frowned for a second, then said, "Well, I reckon that'd be all right. Could be we'll have some real law here someday, so it won't hurt to do things proper-like."

Drake nodded in agreement and said, "Thank you."

When the group reached his office with their grisly burden, Drake had them put Bellamy's body on the table in the examination room. It was still cooler in here than in the rest of the house, because Bellamy had left the window open when he climbed out. Drake had closed the pane before he'd gone to help with the search for the missing man, but it would take a while for the warmth to build back up again.

Drake didn't mind. Under these circumstances, cooler was better.

He took off his hat and overcoat and hung them up.

One of the men who had carried Bellamy's body down the street asked, "You need us for anything else, Doc?" The nervous glance he cast toward the corpse as he asked the question showed how uncomfortable he was. The other men were shuffling their feet and looking like they wanted to get out of there, too.

"No, that's all right," Drake told them. "You fellows can go on about your business. But thank you for your help."

"I'd say we were glad to do it, Doc . . . but that ain't strictly true."

A moment later, Drake was alone with the corpse. That didn't bother him. He was relatively young, but he had been a doctor long enough that he had seen plenty of death in his time. He had been called to places where men had died in horrible accidents; he had lost patients of his own after fighting valiantly for them against injury or illness, including some women and children. So his nerves were steady as he approached the mortal remains of Tom Bellamy and began studying them.

He started by loosening the man's collar so he could get a better look at the badly bruised neck. He probed carefully around it with his fingertips.

After a minute or so, there was no doubt in Drake's mind

that the injuries he saw were the cause of death. The windpipe had been crushed, the hyoid bone broken. To inflict such damage required a great deal of force. Someone strong or someone filled with rage—or both—had strangled Bellamy.

Drake glanced at the bulging, staring eyes. That sightless gaze *was* a little grotesque and unsettling. Perhaps he should go ahead and close the eyes, he thought. He reached for them—

A step in the doorway made him gasp, jerk his hand back, and take a step away from the table.

"Take it easy, Doc," said the man who stood there. "You *are* the doctor, aren't you?" He let out a grim chuckle. "If you're not, you'll have some explaining to do about why you're poking around a corpse."

"Yes, I—" Drake's voice squeaked a little, so he stopped, swallowed, and started over. "Yes, I'm Dr. Drake. You appear to be injured."

The man was using his left hand to hold a folded bandanna to his right cheek. Drake saw dark stains on the cloth where blood had soaked through the bandanna.

"That's right," the man replied. "I could use some patching up."

Drake gestured vaguely toward the corpse and said, "We can't do anything in here right now, but I have a second examination and treatment room just down the hall. The first door there on your right."

"Thanks, Doc," the man said. He was fairly well dressed, with white hair under a black hat, although his weathered face didn't really look elderly. As far as Drake recalled, he had never seen the man before.

Drake followed him down the hall to the other room. He instructed the patient to sit on the table in there and said, "Let me take a look."

He reached for the bandanna. The man lowered his hand and allowed Drake to pull it gently away from the wound. The dried blood made the fabric stick for a second. The man's breath hissed between clenched teeth as it tore loose.

"Good heavens," Drake said as he looked at the deep cut on the man's cheek. It was almost horizontal, starting on the front of the man's face and running around to the side at a slightly upward angle. The wound had bled quite a bit, but the edges of it were extremely clean. It had taken a very sharp blade to do something like this.

The man forced a smile, which must have been painful, and said, "Hell of a note when a man cuts himself this bad shaving, isn't it, Doctor?"

For a long moment, Drake didn't reply. Then he said, "Indeed. That's going to require some stitches. I can give you a bit of ether—"

"No, there's no need to knock me out. I can stand it. You just go ahead and do what needs to be done."

"Are you sure? It's going to be quite uncomfortable."

"I said I can stand it," the man snapped. "Go ahead."

Drake swallowed again and nodded. The bleeding appeared to have stopped, although it might start again when he cleaned the wound. But it had to be clean before he sewed it together.

He swabbed the cut with cotton soaked in carbolic acid. The patient paled under his deep tan but didn't make any sound. A little more blood seeped from the wound. Drake blotted it away. Then he got a needle and catgut thread and said, "You'll have to hold very still now."

"I understand. This isn't the first time I've had a sawbones patch me up."

No, Drake thought, he would have been willing to bet that it wasn't.

As he worked, his actions were automatic to a certain extent. Even though he concentrated on what he was doing, a part of his brain was free to wander, and it went down disturbing trails.

Tom Bellamy had taken a scalpel with him when he left here, and the cut on this man's face was exactly the sort of wound a scalpel could have inflicted if someone had stabbed wildly at him with it. During a fight, for example. And the terrible pain that had resulted from such an injury could easily have been enough to drive a man into a rage.

A *killing* rage, in which he clamped his fingers around his enemy's neck before he squeezed . . . and squeezed . . . and squeezed. . . .

Drake paused in what he was doing when he realized he was barely controlling the tremble that threatened to take over his fingers.

The man's eyes flicked toward him. He said from the corner of his mouth, without moving his lips, "Something wrong, Doc?"

"No. No, nothing." Drake steeled himself and went back to work. "Just checking my progress so far."

"Good. Wouldn't want anything to get you shaky."

"No, of course not. I'll be done here in just a few more moments."

The wound required an even dozen stitches to close it properly. As Drake studied his work after tying off the final stitch, he was impressed by what a nice, tight job he had done, especially under the circumstances. He had no idea who this man was, but he was absolutely confident he had choked Tom Bellamy to death.

"There," he said as he stepped back. He dropped the needle and the rest of the thread into a basin on a side table. "I'll need to cover that with a clean dressing. You'll want to change that at least a couple of times a day. Actually, it would be best if you came by here and let me do that, so I can check on the wound and make sure it's healing properly." Drake paused. "You *are* going to be around Panamint City for a while, aren't you?"

"That depends. How long do you think it'll take for this to heal up?"

"It should be in fairly good shape in a week or so. We probably should wait a couple of weeks before I remove the stitches, though."

The man nodded. "All right. I'll see what I can do. Finish up now."

He was accustomed to giving orders, Drake thought.

"Of course."

A few minutes later, he had a dressing tied in place. The bandage went under the man's chin and looped up over his head. With a tight-lipped smile, the man said, "I must look like I've got a toothache."

"I suppose," Drake said. "You haven't asked me yet how bad a scar this wound is going to leave. Most people would be worried about that, especially since it's on the face."

The man shook his head. "I've never been vain about my looks. I know I'm not a very handsome fella to start with. And it's not like I don't have plenty of other scars already. Not many places on this body that *doesn't* have scars."

"Well, I'll take your word for that." Drake picked up a rag and began wiping his hands. "I think two dollars is a fair price for what I've done."

"Oh, that's more than fair, and I intend to see that you get what's coming to you."

Something about the way the man phrased that made Drake's guts clench. He glanced around. There wasn't anything in this room he could use for a weapon except the needle, and it wouldn't amount to much. He started edging in that direction, anyway.

"We might as well quit dancing around it, Doc," the man said. "You know who I am."

"I most certainly do not," Drake insisted with a shake of his head. "I've never seen you before, sir."

"I don't mean you know my name." The man gestured toward the bandage on his face. "I mean you know what caused this . . . and who gave it to me."

Drake continued shaking his head, but the man ignored him.

"I knew I'd be taking a chance, coming to get you to tend to it, but I didn't want to bleed to death or have it fester, either. I figured I could watch you while you worked, and I'd know the truth. I'm pretty good at judging folks, Doc. You tumbled to it pretty quick, but you tried to keep me from realizing that. Too bad you couldn't quite pull it off."

Drake swallowed hard and said, "If . . . if you leave here right now, I won't say anything about it to anyone. I don't know your name, and I'm . . . very bad with faces. By tomorrow, I'll have forgotten what you look like."

The man leaned his head toward the wall separating this room from the one where Tom Bellamy's corpse lay. "What about that fella in there?"

"What about him?" Drake asked harshly. "I don't know him. I never saw *him* before today, either, and he means nothing to me. From what I gather, he wasn't an individual of sterling character."

"That's the truth!" The man shook his head. "You know, I kind of like you, Doc. You're a bit of a stuffed shirt, but I think you're a decent enough hombre, deep down."

"Please," Drake begged.

"Sorry," the man said as he drew his gun from its holster.

He wouldn't risk a shot here in the middle of town, Drake thought wildly. The doctor made a frantic jump for the door.

He was lighter than this deadly stranger, probably more nimble. If he could get outside and shout for help—

But the man was quicker than Drake expected. Something smashed against the back of his head. He saw the floor coming up toward him swiftly, but he didn't feel it hit him in the face, because he was already out cold by then.

Chapter 31

Jared Foxx opened the rear door of the Silver Slipper Saloon and slipped inside. His coat collar was turned up and his hat pulled down to keep anybody from getting a good look at his face. He leaned a shoulder against the unattended piano and looked around the smoky room.

Anse Porter stood at the bar, sipping a beer as he talked idly with the bartender. Foxx knew that Porter was Big Dave Scranton's right-hand man, so he waited until the cadaverous gunman glanced in his direction, and then lifted a hand to get Porter's attention.

With a puzzled frown on his gaunt face, Porter carried his beer over to where Foxx stood.

"I need to talk to your boss," Foxx said without preamble.

Porter regarded him curiously, but without any friendship in his eyes. They might be allies at the moment, but that didn't mean they had to like each other.

"What about?" Porter asked.

Foxx shook his head. "That's between Scranton and me."

Porter took another sip of his beer and said, "That's not the way it works." He frowned slightly and nodded toward the bandage on Foxx's cheek. "What the hell happened to you?"

"That's what I want to talk to Scranton about," Foxx allowed. "I can just walk up there and announce myself, you know."

Porter's eyes narrowed. "I'm not so sure about that."

"I am." Foxx leaned his head toward the front of the room, where Kimbrough, who had drifted into the saloon a moment after he did, lounged against the end of the bar, with his right hand hovering only an inch or so above the butt of his gun.

Porter laughed and asked, "You really think that fella can beat me?"

"He's ready to draw. You're not. I reckon that'd give him just enough of an advantage."

For a second, Foxx thought that Porter was going to answer that challenge and reach for his gun. But then the man laughed again and said, using the alias Foxx had given them earlier, "Oh, hell, take it easy, Foster. I just don't like being pushed around, that's all. But you're working for the boss now, and he'd be upset if gunplay broke out in here, so I'll take you up there."

"I'm working *with* Scranton, not *for* him."

"Call it whatever the hell you want. Big Dave's still the boss around here and always will be."

Foxx didn't argue the point. It didn't matter enough, under the circumstances.

"You still didn't say what happened to your face."

"I cut myself shaving," Foxx said, the same obvious lie he had told Dr. Allan Drake a short time earlier.

Porter shrugged, jerked his head toward the stairs, and said, "Come on."

When Porter rapped on the door of Scranton's suite, the man called harshly through the panel, "Who is it?"

"Me, boss," Porter replied. He turned the knob and opened the door part of the way. "Foster wants to see you again."

"What now?" Scranton demanded, the irritation plain to hear in his voice. "Bring him in."

Porter swung the door back all the way. Foxx went into the sitting room. Scranton stood in front of the window. Evidently, he'd been looking out at the gray afternoon, which was darkening even more as the day went on. He had turned away from the glass when he answered the knock on the door.

Foxx didn't see the attractive blonde who'd been in here with Scranton earlier. Maybe she was in the bedroom. That was where Foxx would keep her, if she was his.

Maybe when this was over, and he'd gotten all the use he could out of Scranton . . .

"What do you want?"

"I heard about how you locked up Chance Jensen for killing that fella Bellamy," Foxx said.

"That's right." Scranton's mouth twisted. "We'll have a trial in the morning. I expect to see Jensen hanging from a tree by noon."

"That would be just fine with me," Foxx said, "because Jensen didn't actually kill Bellamy. I did."

Porter had lingered in the doorway. Foxx heard the gunman's sharp intake of breath at that confession. Scranton reacted, too. His eyes narrowed as he studied Foxx.

"I believe you," Scranton said, "but I'm not sure why you'd admit that."

"Because I need your help." Foxx gestured toward the dressing on his face. "Bellamy cut me pretty bad before I finished him off. I'd been following him around, waiting for a good chance at him, but I didn't know he was armed with a scalpel he took from the doc's office. Little varmint took me by surprise, and not for the first time." Foxx's voice hardened. "But he'll never do it again."

"I still don't understand. I can't give you any medical attention. Anyway, you look like you've already been to the doctor."

"Yeah, I have," Foxx said, nodding. "And it didn't take him

any time at all to figure out how I got this cut. He knew Bellamy did it . . . and he knew I killed Bellamy."

"Whatever you want from me, spit it out, man," Scranton snapped.

"All right. I've got Drake hog-tied and wrapped up in a blanket in the alley behind this place. Two of my men are watching him. We're going to sneak him in here, and you're going to keep him prisoner without anybody else knowing about it."

Scranton stared in obvious amazement at Foxx. After a moment, he asked, "Why in blazes don't you just cut his throat, take the body up in the mountains, and drop it in a ravine somewhere?"

"Because he might still come in handy. I've seen wounds go bad, Scranton. I don't want anything happening to this one. Drake stays here so he can keep an eye on this cut and make sure it heals like it's supposed to. Once it has . . ." Foxx shrugged. "Well, then I won't have any real use for him anymore. But by then, I expect Chance Jensen will have been hanged, and the two of us will have dealt with his brother, that old-timer, and those Scandinavians Beltz has working for him."

Scranton hooked his thumbs in his vest and paced back and forth. He said, "When I agreed to throw in with you, Foster, I didn't think you'd act so quickly . . . or so rashly."

"There was nothing rash about it. As soon as I found out that Bellamy was still alive, I knew I was going to kill him myself, preferably with my bare hands. He deserved to die." Foxx let out a bleak chuckle. "In a way, he died twice, since my men beat him bad enough back in Los Angeles that he *should* have died. As far as I'm concerned, he had it coming."

Scranton stopped pacing and said, "All right, what's done is done. Anse, go down and see about bringing the doctor up the back stairs. Stash him in one of the empty rooms up here. I want a man guarding him at all times." He looked at Foxx again. "Foster, I'm not sure you're worth all this trouble, but since you've involved me in it, I suppose it makes sense to help you. That's probably exactly what you were hoping would happen."

"We're helping each other by not fighting over that mine," Foxx pointed out.

"Speaking of the mine . . . if Jensen goes on trial tomorrow, I'm sure his brother will be here in town. Beltz may well be, too. That seems like the perfect time for our combined forces to move in and take over the mine. Those dwarfish louts will put up a fight, but they won't be any match for our men."

"Good idea," Foxx said, nodding. "Fate's given us a chance to get this over with, and we need to take advantage of it."

"We will. Now, when you leave, go down the rear stairs. There's no point in calling attention to that bandage on your face. We have a nice, neat little frame around Chance Jensen, and we don't want anything to cast any doubt on it."

Scranton turned toward the window again. Foxx bristled a little at the man's dismissive attitude, but he told himself he could put up with it—for now. Sooner or later, though, he would come to a reckoning with *all* his enemies.

"Look," Scranton said without turning around. "I think it's starting to snow."

Even though normally there still would have been an hour or so of daylight left by the time Ace approached Panamint City on horseback, today it was almost as dark as night already. Not only that, but he felt cold, wet touches on his face, where the swirling, intermittent snowflakes landed. So far, not enough of the stuff had fallen to put even a dusting on the ground, but it was falling, and there was no telling when it would end or how much would come down before then.

A lot of lights burned in the settlement, creating an inviting yellow glow. Normally, Ace would have been looking forward to getting inside, out of the biting wind, but right now he barely felt the cold. All he could think about was his brother being locked up and facing a hangman's rope for something he hadn't done.

Ace didn't believe for a second that Chance had killed Tom Bellamy. Chance would have defended himself, of course, and shot Bellamy to protect his own life or that of someone else, but to choke the man to death . . . and while he was sick, on top of that . . . No, that was utterly impossible. Ace knew that.

The trick would be proving it to everyone else in Panamint City.

Nick Beltz had stayed at the mine, unwilling to leave the Steingrim brothers there alone, but he had told Ace everything he knew about what had happened in town today. It was enough of a shock that Bellamy had shown up here, along with Myra Malone. The fast-moving series of events after that was dizzying.

Ace brought his horse to a stop in front of the mission. He looped the reins around the hitch rail and stepped up onto the boardwalk. Through the windows, he saw that tables were set up inside, and people were gathered around them, eating. Children, mostly, although a number of adults were present, too. Maybe the parents of some of those kids.

Priscilla Lansing moved around the room, stopping here and there to talk to some of the people. She was smiling, but Ace thought she looked a little concerned, too. He wondered if something else was wrong that he didn't know about yet.

One way to find out, he told himself. He opened the door and went in.

A lot of eyes turned to look at him as he hurriedly closed the door behind him to keep too much of the cold air from getting in. He took his hat off, smiled and nodded as he said, "Evening, folks."

Priscilla came toward him, still smiling, too, but now he was sure something was wrong. He could see it in her eyes. Maybe she was just worried about Chance.

"Mr. Jensen," she said. "Ace. I'm so sorry."

Alarm welled up inside Ace. Had something *else* happened that he didn't know about? Sometimes prisoners were taken out and lynched. . . .

"Is Chance all right?" he asked. "They didn't—"

Her eyes widened. "Oh, no," she said. "He's fine, as far as I know. Cold and miserable, being locked up in that smokehouse, I'm sure, but nothing else has happened since then. Except . . ."

"What is it?"

"Dr. Drake seems to be missing."

Chance frowned in surprise. "The doctor . . . gone?"

"No one knows where he is," Priscilla said. "Someone went to his office a short time ago, looking for him because of a stomachache, and he . . . he wasn't there. But the . . . corpse . . . still was. Allan's medical bag was gone, too."

"Well, that probably explains it," Ace said. "He was called out to help somebody."

Priscilla shook her head. "Not here in town. When I heard about it, I went around asking everyone I could find. No one has sent for him or seen him. And his horse is still in the livery stable."

"He's got to be around somewhere." Ace couldn't bring himself to worry as much about Allan Drake as he did about Chance. He went on, "I was wondering if you could show me where Bellamy was found. Somebody's got to investigate his killing and prove that Chance is innocent. I don't reckon anybody here in Panamint City is likely to do that."

"Probably not, since there's no lawman." Without turning, Priscilla gestured toward the tables behind her. "But I can't leave now. I provide these meals for the people who don't have enough . . . or anything, in some cases. I'd be happy to help you when everyone is finished."

"Of course," Ace said, even though the delay grated on his nerves. But he was asking for Priscilla's help, so he had to respect her wishes. "I'll come back in a little while. Right now, I guess I'll go check on Chance, if you can tell me where they've got him locked up."

Chapter 32

A man sat on a three-legged stool in front of the smoke-house door with a rifle across his knees. A lantern sat on the ground beside him and cast a circle of dim, flickering light. He came to his feet and moved the rifle to point in Ace's general direction as the older-by-a-few-minutes Jensen brother approached along the side of the butcher shop.

"Who's that?" the guard asked suspiciously.

"Ace Jensen," Ace replied. "That's my brother who's locked up in there."

Chance must have heard Ace's voice, because he cried out in a voice muffled by the thick walls, "Ace! Ace, is that you?"

The guard looked nervous. "You better not have come to bust him out," he warned. "I'll shoot, damn it, and that'll bring a bunch of other fellas on the run—"

"I'm not here to break him out," Ace interrupted. "I just want to talk to him, that's all."

"I dunno. Nobody told me I could let him have any visitors."

"They didn't tell you that you *couldn't*, either, did they?" Ace asked.

"Well . . . no, I don't reckon so."

From inside the smokehouse, Chance said, "My brother's

not an outlaw. He's an honest man. If he says he just wants to talk to me, that's all he's going to do."

"All right, all right," the guard muttered. "But I'm gonna stand right here, just to make sure you don't try anything."

"Maybe you could move back a few steps and give us a little privacy," Ace suggested. "You could still see me and stop me if I did anything you didn't like."

"Yeah, I suppose," the man said grudgingly. "Fine. Go ahead and talk. Just don't try anything funny." He hefted the rifle. "I'll drill you if you do."

"Thank you," Ace said. He waited until the man had moved back about twenty feet, then put his mouth close to the tiny crack around the door and asked quietly, "Chance, can you hear me all right?"

"Yeah." Chance's voice sounded strong, but Ace could detect an undercurrent of unease in it. "Ace, you've got to get me out of this. Scranton insists that I killed Tom Bellamy, and he's going to put me on trial for it. I figure he's influential enough around here to get what he wants . . . which is me found guilty and strung up to a tree."

"You're probably right about that. About what Scranton wants, I mean. He's had a grudge against us ever since the day we got here. But I'm not going to let that happen, Chance. You know that."

"If he succeeds in getting rid of me, he'll be coming after you next, along with Nick and the Steingrim boys."

"More than likely," Ace agreed. "So tell me everything that happened. Every detail you can remember."

Chance did so, telling his brother the story through the little gap around the door. Ace interrupted now and then to ask a question or clarify a point. By the time ten minutes had passed, he thought he had a pretty clear picture in his head of the day's events.

What he didn't have was any idea who might have killed

Tom Bellamy. It was as baffling a mystery to him as it was to Chance.

The guard moved closer and said, "I reckon that's about enough. You two have been palaverin' for a while now."

Ace looked over his shoulder and said, "My brother's life is on the line. I'm just trying to figure out a way to help him."

"He shouldn't have choked that fella to death. I saw the body, mister. It was an ugly death." The guard paused. "Sorta like hangin', I guess. That's pretty bad, too."

"It's all right, Ace," Chance said. "I've already told you everything I know about what happened. Now it's up to you to uncover the truth."

"I will," Ace promised.

"But . . . if you don't . . ." Chance's voice dropped so that only Ace could hear him. "I hope you'll be able to get me out of here. I don't want to hang. I'd rather be on the run than that."

"Yeah," Ace said. "Me too."

With the guard still watching him suspiciously, Ace pulled his hat down tighter on his head and walked away from the smokehouse. Maybe the evening meal at the mission was over by now, he thought.

That turned out to be the case. A couple of women were helping Priscilla clean the tables and wash the dishes when Ace got there. They told Priscilla to go on, saying that they would finish up, and she bundled herself in a heavy coat and a fur cap.

Even under these desperate circumstances, Ace couldn't help but notice how pretty she looked as they left the mission. Priscilla brought a lantern with her.

"No sign of the doctor yet?" Ace asked as they walked through the chilly darkness and the gently falling snow.

"Not that I know of," she replied. "Some of the towns-people have promised to let me know right away if they hear anything." She sighed. "Poor Allan has been a good friend to me ever since we both got here about the same time. I . . . I think he'd like to be more than that, but I don't believe that will ever happen."

Carefully, Ace said, "You don't, eh?"

Priscilla smiled. "I came to Panamint City to help people, not to find a husband."

"How did you settle on Panamint City? I don't want to seem too nosy, but I really don't know much of anything about you."

Except how pretty you are, Ace thought.

"Oh, I don't like to talk about myself . . ."

"I wouldn't mind hearing it."

"All right," Priscilla agreed after a few seconds. "My father was a prospector. He led a mule all over the Sierra Nevadas and had just about given up on ever striking it rich . . . when he finally did. He had left my mother and me in San Francisco. She grew to hate him because he pursued his dream instead of settling down and taking care of us. I can understand . . . in a way . . . how she felt. But I don't think she ever tried to understand how *he* felt, not one bit."

A slightly bitter tone edged into her voice as she continued, "When he came back and built a big house on Nob Hill, then everything was all right, as far as she was concerned. But I don't believe he was ever as happy as he'd hoped to be. He always knew how she truly felt about him.

"But that didn't stop him from caring about other people. He told me about all the times he'd been cold and hungry and alone, and he set aside some money so he could help people who were going through the same thing, especially the ones who chased gold and silver and didn't want to give up on their dreams. He was able to do some of that before he . . . died . . . and after he was gone, I discovered he had left money to me to do that same thing. So you see, I can't let him down. I looked around for a place where I could do the most good and found Panamint City."

"I'd say Panamint City is lucky that you did," Ace told her. "That's a nice story. What about your mother? Is she still alive?"

"Oh, yes. Sitting in that mansion in San Francisco. She got what she wanted. She has plenty of money, and she doesn't have to put up with my father anymore." With a sharpness that told Ace she was done talking about it, she added, "We need to turn here and go down this alley. Chance found Mr. Bellamy's body behind this building."

Ace put out a hand to stop her. "Hold on a minute. I want to light that lantern."

"All right, but the body was *behind* the building."

"That's where it ended up," Ace said. He reached inside his coat and took out a match.

"I see what you mean," Priscilla said as he struck the lucifer and lit the lantern while she held it.

Then he took it from her and held it high in his left hand as they started along the alley. Occasional snowflakes swirled down through the light or landed on the hot glass chimney and hissed out of existence.

There wasn't much to see: a stack of crates, some trash, scuffed footprints, which didn't mean anything, because a big crowd had come through here earlier in the day, after Tom Bellamy's body was discovered.

About halfway along the alley, though, Ace paused and moved the lantern so that its light washed over the building's wall.

"What's that?" he murmured.

"What?" Priscilla asked. She leaned closer and squinted at the building, where the light was shining. "You mean those spots?"

The rough-hewn planks of which the building was constructed hadn't been painted. The elements had weathered them to a grayish color. Stretched across one of them in a mostly horizontal pattern was a series of small dark brown spots. It looked almost as if a painter had taken a brush heavy with paint and snapped it toward the wall with a flick of his wrist, resulting in those stains.

"Hold the lantern, if you don't mind," Ace said.

"Of course." Priscilla took it from him. "Like this?"

"That's good." Ace took his hat off and leaned toward the spots, getting so close that his nose was almost pressed against them. He studied them for a long moment, then reached up and pressed the tip of his index finger against one of them. Some of the stuff stuck to his skin. He rubbed it between his thumb and finger, then licked it.

"What are you *doing*?" Priscilla asked, sounding a little repulsed by his action.

Ace straightened. "That's blood," he said. "Somebody was hurt here, and blood sprayed across the wall. It happened today, too. The stains are almost completely dry, but they're still just a little tacky."

"But Mr. Bellamy was choked to death, if that's what you're thinking. He wasn't shot or stabbed."

"According to what Chance told me, Bellamy stole a scalpel from Dr. Drake's office when he left there."

Priscilla's eyes widened. "That's right, he did. I heard about it."

"So if somebody grabbed him here in this alley, and he fought back, his attacker could have gotten cut, maybe badly enough that some of the blood splattered on the wall while they were fighting." Ace's voice grew more excited as his racing thoughts came together. "Then the killer got the upper hand and either strangled Bellamy here or dragged him around behind the building and did it. Has anybody said anything about finding that scalpel?"

"Not that I know of."

"Then the killer took it with him," Ace said. "It would have had blood on it, and he didn't want people to think that Bellamy had wounded whoever had jumped him. Because that would have led suspicion *away* from Chance."

Priscilla shook her head. "Assuming you're right about those stains, the killer couldn't have known that it would be Chance who found the body. So taking the scalpel wouldn't have been a deliberate attempt to throw suspicion on him."

"You're right. He just didn't want folks to know that Bellamy had wounded his attacker. That would have pointed the finger at *him*."

"That makes sense," Priscilla said. "But I'm not sure how much help it's going to be. What are you going to do? Examine every man in Panamint City and look for one with a bad cut?"

"If I have to in order to save Chance from a hanging, I will," Ace vowed. Something else occurred to him, and he blurted it out without thinking. "A cut that bad probably needed medical attention."

Priscilla gasped. "But that means he would have gone to see Allan and . . . and . . ."

"Don't get ahead of yourself," Ace told her.

She clutched his arm. "But he's missing, and if a killer came to see him . . ."

"We'll find him, Priscilla. I give you my word on that."

Ace just hoped that when they found Dr. Allan Drake—and the man who had left those bloodstains on the wall—it wouldn't be too late.

Chapter 33

Dr. Allan Drake didn't know where he was, but he was alive, which was more than he'd expected when that white-haired man clouted him on the head. He couldn't see anything, because a cloth of some sort was tied over his eyes, and he couldn't cry out, because of the gag stuffed uncomfortably in his mouth and lashed in place. His arms had been pulled painfully behind his back, and his wrists were tied together. His ankles were bound, as well.

For a while, an overpowering musty odor had surrounded him, bad enough that several times he'd felt as if he was about to pass out again. He had managed to cling to consciousness, however, and eventually, after a considerable amount of being jolted around, he had been dumped unceremoniously wherever he was now. He couldn't move, but he was glad the air was fresher, at least.

So he lay there an unknowable time, trying to gather his wits and recover some of his strength.

He jerked back when he felt an unexpected soft touch on his face.

"Don't be afraid," an equally soft voice said. "I'm not going to hurt you."

Deft fingers tugged at the blindfold. It came away from his

eyes, and even though the lamplight in the room wasn't that bright, Drake had been in darkness for so long that it struck his vision like a blow and made him wince.

Something moved between him and the light, taking away the glare. Drake forced his eyes open again. The person leaning over him was in silhouette, so he couldn't make out the details of her face. He could tell she was a woman, though. Blond hair made a gleaming halo around her head.

"You're all right," she told him.

Drake made noises through the gag.

"I'm afraid I can't take that away," the woman said. "You might start yelling, and we can't have that. Dave said it was all right to take off the blindfold, though."

Dave? Did she mean Big Dave Scranton? Drake knew the man, of course, had even spoken to him a few times, although Scranton had never come to see him on a medical matter. And now that he thought about it, Drake recalled that Scranton had a woman who lived above the saloon with him . . . an attractive blonde. . . .

This woman certainly fit that description, he thought, now that his eyes had begun to adjust and he could see better. She was very pretty. The silk dressing gown she wore indicated that she was at home here. He had to be in one of the rooms above the Silver Slipper, Drake realized.

Did that mean he was Scranton's prisoner? Scranton wasn't the man who had knocked him out. The man who, Drake was convinced, had killed Tom Bellamy.

But perhaps they were working together. That would explain a lot.

The woman turned her head and said to someone, "There's no reason he has to just lie here on the floor like a dog, is there? Can't you at least let him sit in a chair?"

A man moved forward into Drake's line of sight. The doctor recognized him, too. He worked for Scranton. That was more confirmation, as if Drake needed it, of where he was and who was holding him prisoner.

"I don't suppose it would hurt anything," the man said. He turned and gestured. "Pick him up and put him in that chair."

"You'll need to untie his hands," the woman said. "If you don't, he's going to be very uncomfortable."

The lean gunman grunted. "The boss didn't tell me to keep him comfortable, just to make sure he didn't get away."

"Well, then, you can tie him to the chair," the woman argued.

The man thought about it and then shrugged. "Sure, why not?"

"Thank you, Anse," she told him with a smile, which seemed to make him feel good. More than likely, a woman who looked like this blonde could get any man to do just about anything by smiling at him.

Two men came over to Drake and lifted him onto his bound feet. He would have fallen right back down if they hadn't been there to hold his arms. Once he was upright, he saw that he was in a comfortably furnished bedroom. The men half dragged, half carried him over to a wing chair and lowered him onto the seat. One man bent him forward so the other could reach behind Drake with a knife and cut the ropes around his wrists.

Before he could even think about trying to do anything, they jerked his arms around in front of him and used the same rope to bind him again. Then they took a coiled rope from where it sat on a dresser and wound it around his torso and the back of the chair, making sure he couldn't escape. When that rope was tied in place somewhere behind him, he was completely helpless again.

The gunman who was in charge said to the blonde, "If the boss finds out about this and doesn't like it, I'm going to tell him it was your idea."

"Don't worry about that, Anse," she said. "The doctor can't get away, and as long as he doesn't, it'll be fine." She turned toward Drake and went on, "I'm sorry you're having to go through this, Doctor, but it shouldn't be for long. Once Dave has everything arranged the way he wants it, we'll be able to let you go."

Drake made muffled noises through the gag and blinked back frightened tears. He was smart enough to have figured out something already. By letting him see their faces . . . and mentioning Scranton by name . . . that was all he needed to know to be certain that he would never leave the Silver Slipper alive.

The snow was falling harder by the time Ace got back to the mission with Priscilla Lansing. White patches were starting to collect in the street and on the boardwalks.

"Are you going back out to Mr. Beltz's mine?" Priscilla asked when they stopped in front of the mission doors.

"No, I reckon not," Ace replied. "I'm not sure what else I can do tonight, but I want to be close to Chance. Then, first thing in the morning, I can start looking for the man Bellamy wounded with that scalpel."

"He'll probably be trying to stay out of sight."

"More than likely, but I'll root him out, one way or another," Ace said. "As for tonight, I'll put my horse in the stable and then see about a hotel room."

"If nothing is available . . . there's an extra room here."

That was a mighty tempting offer, Ace thought, but with everything else that was going on, accepting it might not be the best idea. He smiled and said, "If I can't get a room at the hotel, the liveryman probably won't mind if I sleep in the hayloft. Won't be the first time I've done something like that, I can tell you."

Priscilla held the lantern's bail in her left hand. She rested the fingers of her right on Ace's forearm. Even through gloves and a thick coat, the touch sent a tingle through him.

"If you need anything, don't hesitate to ask. To . . . to help clear Chance's name, I mean."

"Of course," Ace said with a nod. He smiled again and turned away, although it required an effort to walk off and leave her there.

He didn't have to sleep in the hayloft. A room was available at the hotel. The clerk looked a little askance at him, knowing he was the brother of the man who was locked up in the smokehouse, charged with murder. But he took Ace's money, anyway, and passed over a room key.

The room was cold, but that wasn't what made it difficult for Ace to doze off. Worrying about his brother's fate was responsible for that.

Along with a few memories of how pretty Priscilla Lansing's face had been, rosy-cheeked with cold underneath that fur cap on her raven hair.

The snow came down all night, but there wasn't much wind, and the white stuff didn't pile up in deep drifts. A layer a couple of inches thick covered the ground and the roofs in Panamint City by the next morning. Flakes still fell steadily, slowly but surely adding to that depth.

The hotel didn't have a dining room, so Ace ate breakfast in a café a few doors away. The talk in there was all about the trial that was supposed to take place later in the morning. Some of the customers fell silent when they realized who Ace was, but the temptation to gossip was too strong. The conversation soon resumed, and by listening to it while he ate flapjacks and bacon and drank coffee, Ace learned that Big Dave Scranton had sent riders out the previous afternoon to all the claims in Surprise Canyon, summoning anyone who could attend to a miners' court.

Ace was just about to finish his coffee when Scranton himself swaggered into the café, followed by the gaunt gunman who always seemed to be shadowing him. Their eyes met across the room. For a second, Scranton looked angry, but then a smug smile spread across his face as he came toward Ace.

"I'm not surprised to see you, Jensen," he said when he stopped beside the table. "I suppose you're here for your brother's trial. And that you'll stay around for the hanging."

Keeping a tight rein on his temper, Ace said, "There may be a trial, but there won't be any hanging. Chance isn't guilty."

"That's not the way it looked to me. And when you stop and think about it, my men and I are the only ones who can give direct testimony about finding your brother standing over that poor man's brutally murdered corpse."

"You didn't see Chance kill him," Ace shot back. "No one did. Because it didn't happen."

Scranton shrugged and said, "That'll be up to the court to decide, won't it?" When Ace didn't reply, he went on, "I suppose you plan on speaking for him?"

"Are there no lawyers in Panamint City?"

The gunman laughed and said, "We don't let 'em in. We've got *some* standards, even in a boomtown."

"Then I'll be defending Chance, I suppose. If it comes to that."

"Oh, it'll come to that," Scranton said.

"Maybe. Maybe not. That depends on what I find when I take a look around this morning."

Scranton's brows drew down. "When you take a look around?" he repeated. "What in blazes do you mean by that, Jensen?"

"Maybe I know something that's going to lead me right to the man who really killed Bellamy," Ace said as he got to his feet and laid a coin on the table to pay for his breakfast. He pulled on his coat, set his hat on his head, and added with a nod, "I'll see you later, Scranton."

"Wait a minute," the man snapped as Ace started to walk away. "Where's Beltz this morning? Isn't he coming in for the trial?"

"I wouldn't know," Ace replied honestly. "He's probably out at the mine. I hope he stays there and doesn't waste his time coming into town."

Scranton scowled at him. Ace could still feel the hostile stare on his face as he left the café.

Saying what he had to Scranton about having a clue to Bellamy's killer had been a bluff. He had no real reason to believe that Scranton was involved in the murder . . . but Scranton had his dirty fingers in just about everything else that went on around here. There was a slim chance that if he did know something, Ace's bluff might spook him into taking some action that would expose his connection.

It was a mighty slim chance indeed, but it was about the only card Ace had to play.

Chapter 34

"He knows something," Scranton barked at Jared Foxx a short time later. "That damned Jensen whelp has something that points right back to you."

Foxx shook his head. "He can't. I didn't leave any kind of trail, we've got the doc stashed safely here, and neither of those Jensens even knows I exist!"

"I don't care. He's found out something dangerous to our plans."

"He's bluffing," Foxx insisted. "That's all. But if you're worried . . . hell, let's go ahead and make our move against Beltz this morning. We'll go out there and grab that mine, and after that it won't matter what happens."

Scranton chewed on the cigar in his mouth as he considered Foxx's suggestion. Finally, he said, "I can't come with you. I have to be here for the trial. It was my idea, after all. Anyway, I can't be mixed up in something like that."

Foxx laughed. "Because you want most folks around here to believe that you still have a thin sliver of honesty to you, I reckon. Well, if that's what's important to you, Scranton, fine. All I care about is the silver."

"But Anse Porter will go with you to represent my interests," Scranton said quickly. "More of my men will go, too. So don't think you can double-cross me."

"Why, the thought never entered my mind, Dave," Foxx lied.

"And this way," Scranton went on, "you'll be safely out of town, just in case Jensen *does* have some sort of evidence that points to you."

"If he does," Foxx said, his face and voice suddenly grim, "I expect you to get rid of it . . . and him . . . partner."

"Of course," Scranton replied.

Foxx wished he could believe the man, but he didn't.

Not for a second.

"Ace! There you are."

Ace paused on the boardwalk and turned to see Myra Malone hurrying toward him. The saloon girl was muffled in her heavy coat and had the hood pulled up over her head. A few flakes of snow clung to the thick brown hair that had escaped from the hood. The snow was coming down heavier now, and the wind had picked up a little, indications that the real storm was just getting started.

"I've been looking for you," Myra said as she came up to him. "Is it true? Are they really going to put Chance on trial for murder this morning?"

"It looks like it," Ace replied. "Some of the miners have come in from their claims, and the townspeople are all stirring about it, too." A bitter, cynical note entered his voice. "A murder trial will sure break up the monotony around here. And it's not even Christmas yet."

Myra shook her head and said, "I just don't believe it. Chance wouldn't do such a thing. I . . . I don't really know him that well . . . either of you . . . but I'm sure he was trying to help locate Tom yesterday afternoon, even after all the trouble Tom caused for him."

"That's right. That's exactly what Chance would do."

"Then we have to find a way to prove he's innocent."

"I'm trying," Ace said, "but there's not much to go on."

He recounted the story of how he and Priscilla Lansing had found stains from the drops of blood that had splattered on the building wall in the alley. As he laid out his theory about how Tom Bellamy had fought back against his attacker and had cut him with the scalpel he'd taken from Dr. Drake's office, he considered it again from every angle himself and came to the conclusion that he still believed it was valid.

Myra nodded, too, and said, "That must be what happened. It's the only thing that makes sense."

"Dr. Drake is missing, too," Ace told her. "I think the killer must have gone to him for medical attention after being wounded."

Myra lifted a hand to her mouth and looked horrified. "And then whoever it was killed him, too? That poor man!"

"We don't know that the doctor's dead. Nobody's been able to find him, that's all. I've been looking for somebody who's bandaged up or showing some other signs of being hurt, but so far . . . no luck."

"And you're running out of time."

"Yes," Ace said. "Although it's really *Chance* who's running out of time."

Out at the mine, over breakfast, Nick Beltz told Folke, Baldur, and Haldor, "I hate to leave you boys out here by yourselves, but I reckon I'd best ride into town and see if there's anything I can do to help Chance. Scranton's bound and determined to put him on trial . . . and I'm sure Scranton don't figure on it endin' well for our friend."

"*Ja*, you must go," Haldor said. "We will be fine."

Folke and Baldur echoed that sentiment. Baldur thumped a

giant fist down on the table inside the tent and said, "If any-one bothers us, we will throw rocks down on them like Odin and the gods throwing rocks from Asgard to Midgard!"

"You know, that ain't a bad idea," Beltz said. "Put some big rocks there at the top of the trail, and if anybody gives you trouble, roll 'em right down the hill." He listened to the wind blowing outside. The tent's canvas sides popped under the force. "I just hope this little snowstorm don't turn into a bliz-zard. There's places in this canyon where the snow don't have to drift very deep before you can't get through."

With that worry still in his head, a short time later he put his saddle on Mehitabel. The mule was sure footed and, like most mules, not prone to getting excited or spooked. If he was going out in bad weather, he wanted to be on a nice steady mount.

With his rifle tucked under his arm, Beltz faced the Stein-grim brothers at the top of the trail. He was bundled in the buffalo coat and had the tasseled fur cap pulled down tight on his head. The brothers, on the other hand, were dressed in their usual overalls and flannel shirts, seeming impervious to the cold. The wind whipped around their beards and long hair.

"This ain't no weather to be workin'," Beltz told them, rais-ing his high-pitched voice to be heard over the wind. "But I reckon you fellas might just as soon be in the tunnel than sit-tin' in the tent. One of you better keep an eye out, though. I can't imagine Big Dave sendin' his boys out here to cause trouble on a day like this, but you never know!"

"We will line up the rocks first, before anything else," Hal-dor said. "Do not worry, Nicholas. We will protect the mine."

"I know you will. I'm sure obliged to you boys. I'll make it back before nightfall, if it's possible. If it ain't, I'll see you as soon as I can!"

With that, he lifted a gloved hand in farewell, shoved the Winchester into the saddle scabbard, and swung up on Mehitabel's back. He had to bang his boot heels against the mule's flanks a couple of times to get her going.

It didn't take long for Beltz to disappear into the swirling clouds of snowflakes as he rode down the trail toward the valley floor.

Jared Foxx didn't know what was worse, the bone-chilling cold, the curtains of snow, or the throbbing pain in his face where that damned Tom Bellamy had cut him.

Earlier that morning, Dr. Allan Drake had been brought into the room where Foxx was staying out of sight on the second floor of the Silver Slipper. Drake's hands had been tied in front of him, but his feet had been free so he could walk. A gag had been tied into his mouth.

The gunman Anse Porter had gripped Drake's upper right arm. Another man had followed with a drawn revolver. Foxx stood in the middle of the room to meet them.

Drake's eyes widened in fear when he saw Foxx. That told Foxx the doctor recognized him as the patient he'd treated the previous day.

"All right, Doc," Porter said. "I'm gonna take that gag out of your mouth so you can talk, because there may be things you need to say to Foster here. But if you start yelling or try anything else funny, you'll regret it. We aim to keep you alive . . . but it's not absolutely necessary."

Foxx wasn't so sure about that. The cut had started hurting during the night. By now it was maddeningly painful, a fresh jolt every time his heart beat.

Porter untied the rolled-up bandanna that kept the gag in Drake's mouth. He pried Drake's jaws open and pulled out the wadded-up cloth, making a disgusted face as he did so.

Drake tried to lick his lips, then husked, "I . . . I need . . . something to drink."

Earlier, Kimbrough had brought some breakfast upstairs for Foxx, including a cup of coffee. A little was left in the cup, so Foxx motioned toward it and told Porter, "Give him that."

Drake gulped at the cold coffee. There were only a couple of swallows, but that was enough to make him able to talk more clearly.

"Why am I here?" he asked.

"I think you can figure that out, Doc," Foxx told him. "You said it yourself. I need you to change this dressing and take a look at the cut."

"If I'm doing that, you should untie my hands."

Porter said, "You can handle it the way you are. Now get busy."

Drake looked too afraid to argue. He moved closer to Foxx, reached up with both hands, and carefully untied the bandage holding on the dressing. His fingers trembled a little as he did so.

The wound had seeped again, even with the stitches holding it together, and the dressing stuck momentarily. Foxx's jaw tightened as Drake pulled the cloth loose.

"I was afraid of this," Drake said.

"Afraid of what?" Foxx demanded.

"Too much time has passed without me cleaning out the wound. Some infection has set in underneath the surface. That's what's making it red and sore looking around the stitches."

"Well, do something about it, damn it!"

"I'll clean the wound again, but I don't know if there's anything I can do about the infection under the skin. It'll have to heal up on its own."

"But it will, right?"

Drake shrugged. "It's impossible to say how bad it is. It may go away on its own in a day or two, or it may spread. I would suggest that if it's still bothering you tomorrow, it might be a good idea to remove the stitches, spread the wound open, and try to clean it again."

"Start over, you mean!"

"It's a drastic measure—"

"All because you didn't do a good enough job the first time, damn you!"

Foxx's right fist came up in a backhand that cracked across the doctor's face. The blow knocked Drake to the side. He fell to one knee and might have sprawled on the floor if Porter hadn't reached down quickly and grabbed his arm.

"That's enough, Foster," Porter said. "You're the one who wanted the doc's help. Let him do what he can."

"All right," Foxx growled. "Get on with it . . . you damned quack."

Now the cut was bandaged again, but it still hurt like the devil, and Foxx was ready to take his anger over that pain out on someone.

Luckily, he would soon get the chance to do just that, once he, Kimbrough, Bracken, Stevens, Anse Porter, and the half-dozen other men Scranton had sent along reached the mine. *Foxx's* mine . . . as he would teach the fools who had dared to try to steal it from him. Tom Bellamy had already gotten what was coming to him. Soon that old man, Beltz, and his three helpers would—

"Who the hell's that?" Porter suddenly exclaimed from where he rode beside Foxx. A bulky figure on horseback—no, on *mule*back—had just loomed up out of the snowfall about twenty yards away, which was as far as anybody could see in this white maelstrom.

The man reined in as sharply as Foxx, Porter, and the others did. A high-pitched yelp of surprise came from him, and that was enough to tell Porter who he was.

"It's Beltz!" Porter cried as he reached under his coat for his revolver. "Don't let him get back to the others and warn them!"

Chapter 35

Nick Beltz's heart felt like it was trying to claw its way up his throat and jump out of his mouth as he hauled on the reins to turn Mehitabel around. What with the snow and all, he hadn't gotten a good look at the men who had appeared in the canyon in front of him, but that yell about not letting him get away proved they didn't wish him well.

"Go, Mehitabel, go!" he called to the mule as he banged his heels against her sides. She could be balky now and then, and this wasn't a good time for that.

She must have sensed the urgency of the situation or heard it in his voice, however, because she lowered her head, lunged forward, and broke into a gallop with the speed and nimbleness of a quarter horse.

Beltz leaned over the mule's neck and urged her on. By nature, he wasn't the sort of man to run from trouble. He would much rather stand his ground and fight.

But he was smart enough to know that he couldn't take on ten-to-one odds and have any chance of winning. Especially when those ten were hired guns working for Big Dave Scranton, and he was convinced that was what he had run into.

The rugged terrain of Surprise Canyon worked against him. Mehitabel couldn't muster up as much speed as she would have been able to do on flat, level ground. But the twists and turns made it more difficult for the pursuers who thundered after him, too.

His only real chance, though, was to get back to the mine before the men trying to kill him caught up to him, as they inevitably would. He hadn't come that far up the canyon when he ran into them, so Beltz believed he might make it.

Either way, he was going to warn the Steingrim brothers. He had realized already that the men chasing him weren't trying to shoot him out of the saddle. The fact that they were holding their fire had to mean they didn't want a lot of gunshots echoing through the canyon, alerting anyone who heard them that some sort of trouble was going on. They wanted to take Folke, Baldur, and Haldor by surprise.

Beltz wasn't going to let that happen. He reached forward and grasped the Winchester's stock where it stuck up from the saddle boot. He pulled the weapon free, then, guiding the mule with his knees, tried to lever a round into the rifle's chamber.

His hands were too clumsy in the thick gloves he wore. Muttering a few blistering curses under his breath, he held the Winchester in his left hand and lifted his right to his mouth. He clamped his teeth on the glove's middle finger and pulled it off his hand, then turned his head and spat it aside. Now he could get his fingers in the rifle's lever and trigger guard. He hoped it wasn't cold enough for his skin to stick to the metal.

Beltz fired three shots into the air as fast as he could work the lever, which was a little stiff and stubborn because of the cold. The loud reports didn't bother Mehitabel, and again, Beltz was glad he had chosen to ride the mule, which continued to run with a strong, steady stride, slowing only to handle the rough spots in the canyon floor. He let a few seconds go by, then fired three more warning shots.

That left nine rounds in the Winchester. Beltz considered twisting around in the saddle enough to throw them back along the canyon toward his pursuers, but he realized he would be firing blindly and the chances of him actually hitting anything were mighty slim.

Better to save those bullets until he could put them to better use, he told himself.

He leaned to the left and used the rifle in his right hand to balance himself as Mehitabel pounded around a bend in the canyon. Because of the snow, he couldn't see more than twenty or thirty yards ahead of him, but he knew this canyon like the back of his hand and didn't need to be able to see farther than that to know where he was. Up ahead was the bottom of the switchback trail leading up to the notch where the mine was located.

"Ho, you Steingrims!" he bellowed as he raced onward. "It's me! Folke! Baldur! Haldor! Trouble's comin'!"

Guns suddenly blasted behind him. Beltz yelped as he felt the wind-rip of a bullet flying past his head. Scranton's men must have figured that since he had already raised the alarm, there was no reason for them to hold their fire anymore. The shots thundered and echoed in the canyon.

"Hey, up there, you dang Scandihoovians! Don't shoot! It's me!"

Mehitabel never faltered as she started up the trail, but Beltz knew the mule had to be getting tired. She was big and strong, but she wasn't accustomed to running at a flat-out pace like she had been doing.

"Just a little farther, Mehitabel," he told her. "Just a little farther."

They reached the first switchback, and Mehitabel slowed for the turn and then lunged ahead again. From where he was, Beltz looked back up the canyon and saw bright orange flashes winking through the snow. Bullets struck the canyon wall and threw gouts of dirt and rock chips into the air all around him. It was a plumb miracle he hadn't been hit so far, he thought. A miracle, and all that snow making it difficult to aim.

The next switchback meant they were halfway to the top. Beltz felt something tug on his cap. That was a bullet, he realized. He'd just come within an inch or two of getting his brains blown out. He grimaced as he urged the mule on. Those varmints were getting too close for comfort with their slugs!

The sound of a furious yell came from above him, cutting through the wind. Beltz looked up and saw Haldor Steingrim standing at the top of the trail. Haldor's arms were above his head as his giant hands gripped a rock that must have weighed forty or fifty pounds.

With another angry yell, Haldor *threw* the blasted thing like a normal man would have thrown a rock a fraction of that size. It sailed out through the snow and then began plummeting at an angle toward the canyon floor, easily clearing the trail on which Beltz rode.

Beltz didn't see where the rock landed, but he heard sudden shouts of fear and surprise from down below. When he looked up again, he saw that Folke and Baldur had joined their older brother, and they hefted rocks that they added to the bombardment.

Like Odin and the old gods throwing stones from Asgard, Beltz thought, with a grin on his round face. He rode on, surging closer and closer to the top.

From the corner of his eye, Jared Foxx barely caught a glimpse of something flying through the air before he heard a terrible crunching impact somewhere close behind him and to the right. He jerked his head in that direction and saw one of Scranton's men toppling out of the saddle. Something about him *looked* wrong, and a split second later, Foxx figured out what it was.

The gunman's head was crushed and didn't really appear human anymore.

An instant later, something struck one of the horses and knocked it, screaming, off its hooves. The rider went down, too, although Foxx couldn't tell if the man had been hit by whatever it was.

"Look out!" Anse Porter shouted. "They're shooting cannons at us!"

No, not cannons, Foxx thought. He saw another of the dark objects plummet through the snow and slam into the ground. Those were rocks. Big, heavy rocks. He'd heard about how strong the Steingrim brothers were, and here was proof of it. You didn't need a cannon when you had men capable of throwing projectiles like that.

Foxx hauled back on the reins and wheeled his mount. He waved his arm and yelled, "Back! Get back! Head for the other side of the canyon!"

No matter how strong the Steingrim brothers were, there was a limit to how far they could pitch those rocks. They couldn't reach very far from this side of the canyon.

Bullets, on the other hand, could cover that distance easily.

Despite knowing that, Foxx had to admit that as long as the Steingrims were up there and had plenty of "ammunition," they could put up a very effective defense of the trail. What should have been a very easy raid, if they had taken the defenders by surprise, was now ruined. Foxx and his allies would have to lay siege to the mine.

Or at least, that was what they had to *appear* to do, he thought as he rode out of reach of the rock missiles. If some of his force settled down behind cover and kept the defenders busy ducking rifle fire, others of the gunmen might be able to creep up the trail under cover of the snow.

Scranton's men had tried that before, but Beltz and the Steingrims, with help from Ace and Chance Jensen, had repelled the attack. They hadn't had a near blizzard to keep the defenders from seeing what they were doing, though.

It was just a matter of time, Foxx told himself as he dismounted in a cluster of boulders on the other side of the canyon and pulled his Winchester from its saddle boot. He and the others would take care of this obstacle.

Big Dave Scranton just needed to do his part back in Panamint City.

The best place in town to hold a trial, the only building large enough to accommodate the crowd that had begun to gather, was the old Odd Fellows hall—now the Panamint City Mission.

"Absolutely not," Priscilla Lansing declared, folding her arms sternly as Scranton and several of the town leaders faced her. "I won't allow such a travesty of justice to take place here. Chance Jensen is innocent."

"Then I'd think you would welcome a trial to prove that," Scranton told her. "What better way to establish his innocence than to have a court declare him not guilty?"

Priscilla frowned. She didn't know why Scranton was so determined that Chance had killed Tom Bellamy, but she was convinced he intended to see the young man convicted and hanged. However, the argument he was making just sounded reasonable to the other citizens. Several of them muttered in agreement.

She wished Ace were here. She had seen him earlier, going around town with Myra Malone, no doubt searching for some clue to clear his brother's name.

"Who's going to be in charge of this trial?" she asked, stalling as much as anything else.

Thaddeus Revere, the owner of one of the general stores, stepped forward and said, "I will be. I was a justice of the peace for a while back in Pennsylvania, before I came West, so

I know how to conduct such a proceeding. Everything will be legal and aboveboard, Miss Lansing, I assure you."

"Will there be a jury?"

"Most definitely," Revere said.

"What about counsel for the defense?"

"No lawyers in Panamint City," Scranton growled. "Jensen's brother said he'd speak for him." He hooked his thumbs in his vest. "And I'll handle the prosecution."

"How can you do that? You're one of the witnesses!"

Revere said, "Well, in a situation such as this, you have to expect that there'll be a few slight irregularities. But everything will be done as close to the book as we can."

Priscilla studied the lean, goateed storekeeper. He depended on Scranton for a lot of his business, so she had her doubts about his impartiality . . . but he seemed to be about the best available option, and all she could do was hope that he wouldn't allow Chance to be railroaded.

"All right," she said. "I suppose you can have your trial. But not until Ace gets here."

"I'll send someone to find him right now," Revere said.

While he did that, Scranton went to the door and told everyone waiting outside to come in. The snow was heavy enough, and the wind was gusting hard enough, that some of the white flakes flew into the hall as the eager spectators trooped in. That gave Priscilla a chill, and she hugged herself.

At least, she hoped it was just the weather that caused the chill . . . and not the feeling of foreboding that something terrible was about to happen here in this mission she had worked so hard to establish.

Chapter 36

Ace and Myra had split up the town between them and visited every business and residence, asking questions about a man who had a bad cut or some other freshly bandaged injury. Everyone they had talked to had denied any knowledge of such a thing. No one had admitted seeing any sign of Dr. Allan Drake, either.

While Ace had searched for something—anything—that might clear his brother's name, he had been unable to stop thinking about how Chance was locked up in that smokehouse. Early that morning, Ace had gone there to check on him. As before, the man on guard duty hadn't wanted to let them speak at first, but he had relented eventually.

"Chance?" Ace called through the crack around the door. "Chance, are you in there?"

He knew it was a foolish question the second the words came out of his mouth.

Even under the circumstances, Chance didn't let an opportunity to rib his brother get past him. Just on the other side of the heavy door, he said, "No. I got skinny enough to slide through that crack, then sprouted wings and flew away."

"Well, you sound like you're still in good spirits, anyway."

"As good as a fellow can be who's half-starved, half-frozen, and practically halfway up the steps to the gallows," Chance replied. "No, wait, they don't have a gallows here, do they? It's not like that other time when we almost got strung up. They'll just throw a rope over a tree limb here in the Panamints."

"That's not going to happen," Ace vowed. "Priscilla and Myra and I are doing everything we can to find out the truth."

"You're spending your time with *both* of them? Aren't you getting a little greedy there, Ace?"

"It's not like that," Ace said, although in truth he wouldn't mind getting to know Priscilla Lansing a little better. Or even a lot better. That would have to wait until this mess was cleared up, though.

As for Myra Malone, she was grieving over Tom Bellamy's death, although as far as Ace could see, the man had never deserved such sympathy and sorrow. In fact, he'd seemed to be a pretty shady hombre. But there was no accounting for what someone's heart told them to feel.

"Well, however you do it, I hope you can find something to prove I didn't kill Bellamy," Chance went on. "Time's running short. When the guards changed, I heard them talking about how Scranton's going to make sure that trial happens this morning."

"I know." Ace glanced around at the thickly falling snow. "There may be a blizzard building up. I'm sure he wants to get things finished before the weather turns too bad."

"And by *get things finished*, you mean me being found guilty and hauled up to dance on air."

Ace didn't want to think about that possibility, so he turned to the guard and demanded, "Isn't my brother going to get any breakfast? He needs some hot food and coffee."

"He'll get it," the man said. "After the trial. Those are Mr. Scranton's orders."

Chance heard that through the door and commented, "I

guess Scranton's trying to save a little money, eh? He figures I won't *need* any breakfast after the trial."

Ace might have argued with the guard, but he knew he didn't have any time to waste. Having confirmed that Chance was all right for the time being, he told his brother, "I'll see you later. And when I do, this whole thing will be over."

"One way or another," Chance responded. Ace heard a hollow note of despair in his brother's voice, even though he knew Chance was trying to keep that feeling under control.

Now he felt some of that same despair as he rendezvoused with Myra in front of the hotel. He knew as soon as he saw her face, even before she started shaking her head, that she hadn't had any more luck than he had.

"It's no use, Ace," she said. "Either Scranton has everybody in town afraid to talk or else there really *isn't* somebody running around with a bad cut from that scalpel Tom had with him." She flung her gloved hands out to the sides. "We've looked *everywhere*."

Ace stared up and down Panamint City's main street, fighting the feeling of helplessness that threatened to overcome him. He saw people still crowding into the mission building, where Chance's trial would be held. Myra's words echoed in his head.

We've looked everywhere.

Well, no, Ace thought suddenly as his gaze moved along the front of the buildings to the Silver Slipper. They hadn't.

They hadn't been up on the saloon's second floor. That was Big Dave Scranton's private sanctum . . . and even though Ace didn't know the reason behind it, he had a strong suspicion that Scranton was tied in somehow with whoever had killed Bellamy.

"I'm a damned fool," he said with uncharacteristic vehemence.

Myra frowned at him. "Why in the world would you say that?"

"Because I am. For some reason, Scranton wants Chance found guilty, right?"

"It certainly seems that way."

"So he wouldn't want any witnesses or anything else that could clear Chance's name to be found, would he?"

"No, I don't suppose he—" Myra stopped short and stared at Ace for a second. Then she turned and looked toward the Silver Slipper, too. "The saloon! He could hide the killer upstairs in the saloon. We haven't been up there. But . . . that would make him guilty of being a . . . What do they call it?"

"An accessory," Ace said. "I think that's the legal term. An accessory to murder. From what you've seen of Scranton, would you put that past him?"

"No," Myra said, shaking her head. "No, I don't think I would."

"That means I have to get up there and take a look around."

"If Scranton is hiding something—or someone—up there, he's bound to have guards, Ace. And I don't think any of them would hesitate to shoot you."

"No, I don't reckon they would, either." He rubbed his chin in thought. "But I still have to do it. Let's see if there's a set of stairs in the back."

They crossed the street in the snow and went through one of the alleys to reach the rear of the buildings, including the Silver Slipper. Pausing at the back corner of one of the buildings, Ace looked along the way and counted them to make sure he was standing precisely behind the saloon. It did have some back stairs, which ended at a small landing on the second floor.

And a man with a shotgun tucked under his arm stood on that landing, huddled in a heavy coat, with his hat pulled down low. He looked cold and miserable, standing there in the snow like that, but clearly, the thought of not following Big Dave Scranton's orders bothered him worse than the icy wind and the swirling flakes.

"Let me deal with him," Myra said quietly as she leaned out to gaze past Ace's shoulder.

"How are you going to do that?"

"Don't underestimate me," she said with a bleak laugh.

A worried frown creased Ace's forehead. "I don't want you getting hurt."

"I've handled things a lot worse than this, Ace. Trust me."

He didn't seem to have much choice in the matter, so he nodded and said, "All right, go ahead. Just be careful."

"And you be ready to move when you need to." With that, she headed along the back alley toward the stairs.

The guard up on the landing didn't seem to notice her until she started up the stairs toward him. Then he straightened from his weary stance, shifted the shotgun into both hands, and stood watching warily.

Ace stayed where he was, pressed against the wall. He heard the guard call out when Myra was halfway up the stairs, "Hold it right there, lady. Who are you, and what the hell do you want?"

The snow muffled the words a little, but Ace could still make them out. Myra replied, "Mr. Scranton sent me. He said I was supposed to go up to the second floor and keep the fella up there company . . . if you know what I mean."

That was smart of her, Ace thought. Not only was she distracting the guard, but she was also fishing for information at the same time.

The guard was still suspicious, though. He said, "I don't know you. If the boss was gonna do something like that, why didn't he send one of the regular girls?"

"Maybe because I can do things the regular girls can't . . . or won't. And maybe that's what the man likes."

The guard grunted. "Yeah, could be, I guess."

That was enough confirmation for Ace. He was confident now that Scranton had somebody stashed up there and didn't want anyone to know about it. As far as Ace could figure, there was only one reason Scranton would be doing that.

"So how about letting me come on up?" Myra said.

"I dunno," the guard said, clinging to his reluctance. "I wish the boss or Anse or somebody would have told me it was all right."

"Well, then, go and ask them," Myra suggested. To do that, the man would have to leave the landing. "I can even go with you." She paused. "Or . . . I could come on up there and show you what sort of things I can do."

Ace could tell by the stiff way the guard stood that he was warring with himself. Lust and curiosity won over caution. He said, "All right, come on up." He laughed. "You're gonna have to do some convincin', though."

"I can do that," Myra said, her voice full of sensual promise. She went up the stairs.

"I reckon we can step inside, where it's warmer," the guard said when she reached the top.

"No need for that. I can keep you warm, even in weather like this." Myra moved closer to him. "I can make you downright hot, in fact." She put her hands on his chest and moved a little toward the door, enticing him to turn along with her, until she had her back to the door and his back to the flimsy railing around the landing. She murmured something Ace couldn't make out, leaned closer, and started to move down the guard's body. She was close enough that he couldn't keep the shotgun between them. He set it aside, leaning it in the corner where the railing was attached to the building.

As soon as he let go of the weapon, Myra lowered her shoulder, rammed it into his midsection, and drove with her feet, shoving him against the railing as hard as she could.

The man barely had time to begin a startled yell before his

feet slipped in the snow that had collected on the landing and he fell against the railing. It gave way, just as Myra must have expected it to, and the guard fell backward toward the snowy ground some ten feet below.

Ace was already moving while the guard was still in midair. The man crashed down on his back. The snow might have cushioned the impact slightly, but it didn't do anything to blunt the force of the hard right fist that Ace swung as he leaned over the man. The punch drove the guard's head to the side. He sprawled there, unmoving, with his arms and legs flung out.

Ace didn't want to take the time to tie the man up. Instead, he grabbed the stair railing, swung around it, and went up two steps at a time toward Myra, who waited for him at the top, with the shotgun now in her hands.

"Do you think anybody inside heard him yell or the sound of that railing breaking?" she asked breathlessly.

"We'll hope not," Ace said as he took the shotgun from her, "but either way, I'm going in."

Chapter 37

Chance was sitting in the rear corner of the smokehouse again, trying not to give in to despair, when he heard the latch being lifted outside.

He came to his feet, but before he could take a step, a rifle and two revolvers were pointing at him through the door, which had been jerked open.

One of the gunmen who held a rock-steady Colt said, "Come on outta there, Jensen, and don't try anything. Time for you to have your day in court."

Chance looked past the three men and saw that the snow was still coming down hard, billowing clouds of it tossed this way and that by the wind.

He lifted his hands to elbow height and made sure they were in plain sight as he walked outside. The three men backed off to cover him.

"Now, don't get itchy trigger fingers, boys," Chance told them. "I'm not going to give you an excuse to shoot me." He nodded toward the crowd gathered in the street, evidently to watch him being escorted to his trial. "And I don't think you can pretend that I was trying to escape when there are that many witnesses."

"Shut your smart mouth," growled the one doing the talking. He motioned with the barrel of his gun. "Let's go."

Chance started walking through the snow. One man led the way, while the other two fell in behind him.

One of them said, "I wouldn't be so cocky if I was you, Jensen. You're fixin' to be tried for murder, you know. If you're found guilty, you won't never see Christmas again. Your neck'll be stretched before the day's out."

"That's not going to happen," Chance said. "My brother will clear my name."

He wished he felt as confident as he tried to sound.

On the other hand, he reminded himself, Ace had never let him down. One way or another, the Jensen brothers always looked out for each other.

The crowd parted. Chance's captors marched him to the mission. He had known that the trial was going to take place there, but despite that, it still seemed odd to have such a grim proceeding in a building that now housed an effort to bring comfort to the poorer citizens of Panamint City.

If he *was* found guilty and sentenced to death, he hoped that wouldn't cast a pall on the good things Priscilla Lansing was trying to do here.

More bystanders were waiting on the boardwalk in front of the mission. Snowstorm or no snowstorm, a murder trial didn't take place here every day. Not only did the folks in town want to find out what was going to happen, but so did many of the miners from Surprise Canyon.

"Make room!" Anse Porter called to them as he stepped up on the boardwalk. The glare that the gun-wolf cast toward them, plus the threat of the Colt in his hand, made the members of the crowd step back hurriedly.

The man with the rifle poked Chance in the back with the barrel as the one in the lead opened the double doors leading into the mission.

"Get in there," the man ordered in a snarl.

"I'm going, I'm going," Chance said.

For a second he wondered if he could dart into the crowd and get away. But he discarded the idea an instant after it occurred to him. If he did that, he was certain Scranton's men would open fire immediately, and innocent folks were bound to get hurt, maybe even killed.

Chance wasn't going to have that on his conscience. He would rather run the risk of standing trial and relying on Ace to clear his name.

That likelihood seemed a little more remote as he stepped into the big room, looked around hopefully, but didn't see his brother anywhere.

As many chairs and benches as possible had been brought into the hall, and every seat was full. Spectators stood two-deep along both side walls and four-deep at the back of the room. An almost deafening hubbub filled the air, along with warmth from the two big potbellied stoves and the multitude of mostly unwashed humans packed into the room.

At the front were three tables, two side by side and one facing them, and off to the right, in an open area, twelve chairs waited for the members of the jury to be selected. Big Dave Scranton sat at one of the side-by-side tables. The other, no doubt for the defense, was empty.

That was where Ace should have been, Chance thought.

"Come on," the leader of the guards said, gesturing with his Colt again. "Get up there, Jensen."

He pointed at the empty table to the left, where there were two chairs.

Chance went to one of them. Before he could sit down, Priscilla appeared from the crowd and rested her hand on the back of the other chair.

"Have you seen Ace?" he asked her quietly.

"Not for a while," Priscilla answered with a worried expression on her face. "I know he was out looking for evidence to prove you didn't kill that man. I . . . I suppose he must still be looking."

"Let's hope he finds it soon," Chance muttered as Scranton got to his feet. "It looks like Big Dave is ready to get this show on the road."

"And it appears that I'm the closest thing you have to a defense lawyer," Priscilla said.

Ace grasped the doorknob and tried to turn it. The knob didn't turn.

"Blast it!" he said under his breath. "The door's locked."

Myra leaned closer to him. "What did you say? With the wind blowing like this, I couldn't hear you."

"I said the door's locked. But maybe the wind's making enough racket that nobody inside will hear if I bust it open."

He held the knob tightly, placed his shoulder against the door, then lifted and pushed at the same time. Instead of crashing into the panel, he put steady, inexorable pressure on it.

After a minute or so, he felt it begin to yield. Then, with a fairly quiet splintering of wood from the jamb, it came loose and swung back. Ace's grip on the knob kept the door from banging against the inside wall.

He swung the shotgun up quickly and pointed it along the empty corridor.

He told Myra, "Stay out here."

"Not on your life," she said. "I've come this far. I'm going to see this through to the end."

Ace didn't waste time arguing with her. He just said, "Stay behind me as much as you can, then."

Without glancing back to see if she was doing as she was

told, he advanced into the corridor, keeping the shotgun raised and ready to fire.

He was approaching the first of the closed doors that lined the corridor when it suddenly opened with no warning and a man stepped out. Ace didn't recognize him, but the man's wolfish look, rough clothes, and beard-stubbled face identified him as one of Scranton's hired guns.

The man was surprised to see Ace and didn't react instantly. That gave Ace enough time to leap forward and lift the shotgun. He slammed the weapon's butt plate against the man's head and drove him off his feet. The man landed on the carpet runner in a limp heap.

The stroke had been swift and instinctive on Ace's part. He knew that a shotgun blast would rouse everyone in the saloon, and he didn't want that until he'd had a chance to search the rooms on the second floor.

He hoped the dull thud of the shotgun's stock against the gunman's head hadn't caught anyone's attention. He didn't have any idea how many people were even up here on the second floor. By now, the trial would be getting underway. Most of Scranton's people might be there.

"Nobody else in here," Myra reported quietly. She had moved rapidly to check the room from which the gunman had emerged.

Ace nodded without saying anything. He looked down at the man he had walloped, who appeared to be out cold. They would just have to hope that was the case.

Myra went to the door across the corridor. Ace stood ready with the shotgun while Myra grasped the knob and turned it. She shoved the door open. Ace took a fast step in and swung the weapon's twin barrels from side to side.

The room was furnished with a bed, wardrobe, small table, and chair but was empty of human occupants.

That was true of the next pair, as well. Myra went to the third door on the right. She and Ace were getting a routine down by now. He jerked his head in a nod to tell her he was ready, and she flung the door open.

On the far side of the room, tied to an armchair and gagged, was Dr. Allan Drake.

The doctor appeared to be unharmed. Ace was relieved to see him, but the fact that Scranton was holding him prisoner was proof of Scranton's involvement in whatever was going on. Ace lowered the shotgun and hurried into the room as Drake made urgent noises through the gag in his mouth.

Ace figured the doctor was imploring him to set him free, but as he stepped in and got a better look at Drake's face, he realized the muffled noises weren't a plea for help.

They were a warning.

Boot leather scuffed on the floor behind Ace and to his right. He tried to twist in that direction and bring the shotgun up, but he was too late. The man who had been hidden behind the door leaped at him and slashed a gun at his head.

Ace managed to avoid the full force of the blow. The gun barrel hit his hat brim and then struck his right shoulder with enough of an impact to make that arm go numb. Nerveless fingers slipped off the shotgun. It clattered to the floor at Ace's feet and tripped him. He fought to keep his balance, but as he jerked backward to avoid the gunman's second attempt to pistol-whip him, he fell heavily to the rug.

The man could have blasted him then, but instead he aimed a kick at Ace's face. Maybe Scranton had given him orders to take any intruders alive. Whatever the reason, Ace had just enough time to fling his hands up and grab the man's boot as it came toward his face. He heaved and sent the man reeling away from him.

Not knowing how many more of Scranton's men were in

the saloon, Ace still didn't want a gunfight if it could be avoided. He rolled, used that momentum to help him come up on his feet, and lunged forward.

The gunman hadn't fallen, because he had run into the wall instead. He bounced off, but before he could set himself or raise the gun he still held, Ace's right fist smashed into his face and knocked him against the wall again.

Ace crowded in. With his left hand, he grabbed the gun and wrapped his fingers around the cylinder tightly so that it couldn't turn and fire.

At the same time, Ace struck again with his right, driving a punch into the man's solar plexus. That bent him forward enough for Ace to raise his hand and bring it down in a chopping blow to the back of his neck. The man collapsed face-down on the floor.

Ace pulled the gun from his hand. The guard was too stunned to resist. Ace slammed the butt against his head to make sure he wouldn't wake up too soon and cause more trouble.

When Ace straightened and turned, he saw that Myra had rushed into the room and was standing beside the chair as she tried to untie the cords holding the gag in Dr. Drake's mouth. Ace tucked the gun he had taken from the guard behind his belt and reached into his pocket for his clasp knife. He opened it and started sawing on the ropes holding Drake in the chair.

Those ropes hadn't fallen away yet when Myra got the gag loose. She pulled it out of Drake's mouth and tossed it aside. He groaned. Having that wadded-up ball of cloth wedged between his jaws must have made them sore.

But he was able to rasp, "Look . . . look out!"

"What—" Ace began, not knowing what Drake was trying to warn them about.

Then he had no doubt, because he heard the metallic ratcheting of a gun being cocked in the doorway. He jerked his head in that direction and saw a very attractive blond woman in a dressing gown standing there, looking at them coldly over the barrel of the revolver she held.

Chapter 38

A door at the back of the mission's main room opened. Thaddeus Revere, wearing a gray tweed suit, came out. One of Scranton's men, serving as the bailiff, called, "Everybody pipe down and stand up."

Revere commented dryly, "You're supposed to say, 'All rise,' Lester, but that'll do, I suppose."

The hubbub quieted, replaced by a shuffling of feet and chair legs as the spectators who weren't already standing did so. Revere went to the judge's table, sat down, and took a small gavel from his pocket.

"A souvenir of my time as a justice of the peace," he said by way of explaining why he owned a gavel. He rapped it on the table and went on, "Everyone can be seated. Those who have a place to sit, that is." He looked around the room. "I see we have a good crowd on hand today. I don't blame you. With the weather like it is, it's better to be inside."

Scranton had sat down when the others in the room had, but he popped right back up again.

"Your Honor, I'd like to make an opening statement," he said, hooking his thumbs in his vest pockets so that he looked as pompous as he sounded.

"Before we seat the jury?" Revere asked with a frown.

"Oh." Scranton nodded. "Yes, I suppose that would be better." He turned and started pointing to men in the crowd. "You, and you, and you—"

Priscilla stood up and said, "Mr. Revere, this isn't right. The defendant should have a say in who's on the jury, too, shouldn't he?"

"You're supposed to say that you object, young lady." Revere scowled at her. "Anyway, since when are females practicing law? That's a man's job, isn't it?"

"I'm the only one here to speak up for Mr. Jensen, sir."

Revere considered for a moment, then said, "I suppose it's all right. As I mentioned before, in a situation such as this, there are bound to be a few irregularities. How about I let Mr. Scranton pick six of the jury, and you can pick the other six?"

"Your Honor, now I object," Scranton said quickly. "Miss Lansing hasn't been around Panamint City as long as I have. She doesn't know all these men. She might pick someone who's not completely honest and forthright." He smirked at Priscilla. "We want this to be a fair trial, don't we?"

"You mean I might pick someone who doesn't work for you or who isn't indebted to you in some way?" Priscilla shot back at him.

Chance smiled and had to hold in a chuckle. Priscilla was a fighter, and anybody who underestimated her might be in for a surprise.

"I take your point, Mr. Scranton," Revere said, "but as you mentioned, we want this trial to be fair, and I understand what Miss Lansing is getting at, as well. My ruling stands."

Scranton glared but nodded. "I'll finish picking my six, then," he said with a sullen note in his voice.

"Proceed," Revere said.

It didn't take long to select the twelve members of the jury. Scranton resumed his seat, apparently satisfied. Priscilla sat down next to Chance again and quietly told him that she'd picked six men she believed to be honest, and as far as she knew, Scranton didn't wield any influence over them.

"So we have at least a possibility of a tie vote, since there's no real evidence against you except the testimony of Scranton and his men."

"Unless you count the fact that I was the only one in town who'd had trouble with Bellamy," Chance pointed out. "Some people might think I'm the only one who had any reason to kill him."

"That we know of."

Chance shrugged. Priscilla was right, but that slight element of doubt might not be enough to save him. In a real court, it could have been, but this trial might play pretty fast and loose with such legal niceties.

Scranton rose to his feet again and said, "Your Honor, *now* I'd like to make an opening statement."

Revere waved his hand. "Go right ahead."

"As you know, since coming to Panamint City, I've done everything in my power to make it a better community for everyone who lives here."

Chance saw Priscilla roll her eyes a little at that.

"That includes establishing an atmosphere of law and order, even though at the current time we don't have any official representatives of such among us. We cannot allow heinous crimes to go unpunished—"

Priscilla came to her feet and said, "Heinous crimes such as intimidation, harassment, and the mysterious disappearances of men who refuse to sell their claims to you after they discover silver, Mr. Scranton?"

He turned sharply toward her and glared. "This is *my* statement, Miss Lansing," he snapped. "I'm sure you'll have a chance to make some remarks of your own. And for the record, I resent the implications of what you just said, as well as your earlier veiled insults."

"My apologies," Priscilla murmured, not sounding the least bit sincere.

"As I was saying," Scranton went on, "we cannot allow such heinous crimes *as murder* to go unpunished, and such a murder . . . a particularly brutal murder . . . took place in our community just yesterday afternoon." He turned and pointed at Chance. "This man, Chance Jensen, savagely choked the life from another man, a recently arrived visitor to Panamint City named Tom Bellamy. With my own testimony, I will prove this to be true, since I discovered Jensen practically in the act of strangling Mr. Bellamy."

Priscilla stood up again, but before she could say anything, Revere raised a hand to stop her.

"You'll have your chance, Miss Lansing," he said. "Let Mr. Scranton finish, so we can get on with this. We sure don't want to wind up with all of us snowed in here!"

"Step back away from the doctor, both of you," the blonde ordered as she brandished the cocked revolver.

Ace judged the distance and the angle and figured he could throw the knife in his hand before she could pull the trigger. But on top of the fact that he didn't want to try to kill a woman, he knew it would be a miracle if she didn't get a shot off, even if he made a perfect throw. With the gun already pointing in the general direction of Myra and Dr. Drake, there was too great a chance that one of them would be hit.

So for now, he did as she ordered, and moved back a step. Myra did likewise.

"Drop that knife," the blonde went on.

"Sure," Ace said. "Just take it easy, ma'am. Don't get nervous."

A cool smile curved her lips. "Don't worry about that, cowboy. I'm not the least bit nervous."

She didn't look or sound like it, Ace had to admit. He

tossed the knife onto the bed. He could reach it easier and faster there than on the floor, if he had to make a dive for it.

"Who are you?" Myra asked.

The blonde didn't answer, but Drake did.

"She's Scranton's woman. Her name is Natalie Fairchild."

"I'm nobody's woman but my own," Natalie said. "Dave may believe he owns me, but right now it's convenient for me to let him think so. And I always do what's convenient for me . . . and what pays the best."

"So you think he's going to pay you off for capturing us?" Myra asked. "That's only what he'd expect of you. He won't think it's anything special."

Natalie scowled. "You don't know what you're talking about."

"Believe me, honey, I do. Men always expect us to do what they want. You should know that, since I've got a feeling you and I are in the same line of work."

"I'm not a—"

Myra didn't let her finish. A contemptuous smile curved her lips as she interrupted, "It sure looks to me like you are."

With a snarl twisting her lips, Natalie advanced into the room and swung the gun more toward Myra, who stopped smiling and backed away, as if frightened. Ace realized the move took the gun even more away from him and Drake, and knew that was Myra's intention.

"Shut up," Natalie said. "I don't have to keep you alive, you know. I could shoot you both. Dave wouldn't care."

Drake said, "But then you'd have to shoot me, too, Miss Fairchild, since I would know you'd committed murder. And that fellow Foster doesn't want me dead, since I'm taking care of the wound Tom Bellamy gave him with my scalpel when Foster killed him. And since he and Scranton are working together to take over that mine—"

The words tumbled quickly out of his mouth. Drake was

trying to give them as much information as he could while he had the opportunity, Ace realized.

Natalie knew that, too, and whirled toward him, thrusting out the gun and saying, "Shut up—"

Ace was already moving as she turned. He knew he wouldn't get a better chance than this. He lashed out. The side of his right hand came down on Natalie's wrist and drove her hand toward the floor. The gun blasted, but the bullet went into the planks between Drake's feet, making him jerk away from it so violently that the chair in which he was tied tipped over backward.

At the same time, Myra tackled the blonde from behind. Natalie cried out as the impact knocked her off her feet. Both of them sprawled on the floor as Ace moved quickly out of the way. He kicked the gun out of Natalie's hand.

Myra grabbed Natalie's hair and tried to slam her face against the floor, but Natalie was able to buck upward and throw Myra off. They rolled over, slapping and grabbing and clawing at each other, neither seeming able to get the upper hand.

Ace set the chair up and asked Drake, "Are you all right, Doctor?"

"I . . . I think so," he replied. "That shot didn't hit me, thank goodness."

Ace snatched the open knife off the bed and started cutting the ropes again. He kept an eye on the battle between Myra and Natalie as he did so. As long as Myra kept the blonde occupied, he could work on freeing Drake. He didn't want Myra getting hurt, though, so he was ready to step in if he needed to.

It didn't look like that was going to be necessary. Myra knelt on top of her opponent. She got her left hand on Natalie's chin and dug her fingers into the flesh in a tight, painful grip. She cracked her other hand back and forth across the other woman's face. Natalie appeared to be half-stunned, with all the fight running out of her like water.

But that was just a ruse. Natalie's knee came up suddenly and stabbed into Myra's belly. Myra bent around the pain. Natalie grabbed her hair and hauled her to the side. She rolled on top and tried to shift her grip to Myra's throat.

Myra recovered enough to shoot a punch straight up that caught Natalie on the chin. The blow rocked the blonde's head back. Myra chopped another punch to her face. Natalie really was stunned this time as Myra pushed her aside and scrambled to her feet. Myra's hair hung loose in thick brown wings around her face.

She was panting and breathless, but she set her feet and swung as Natalie tried to get up. Myra's fist crashed into Natalie's jaw and stretched her out on the floor. The dressing gown flew up as she landed, revealing sleek, bare legs.

That sight might have been more interesting under other circumstances. As it was, Ace glanced to see that Myra was all right and Natalie was out cold, then went back to cutting the ropes holding Dr. Drake in the chair.

As the last of them fell away, Ace grasped Drake's arm and lifted him to his feet.

"Easy," Drake said. "I've been tied up for so long I can barely feel my legs."

"You'd better get some feeling back into them pretty quickly, Doctor," Ace said. "We have to get down to the mission so you can testify that Chance is innocent. Scranton is down there, trying to convict him of murder and hang him."

Myra pushed her hair back out of her face and said, "But someone else killed Tom, right? That's what you just said. Someone called Foster?"

"That's the name I've heard. I don't know if it's his real name or not."

"Who in blazes is he?" Ace wanted to know. The delay

chafed at him, but Drake was working his legs and stamping his feet on the floor, trying to get the circulation restored in them, so Ace figured he might as well find out as much as he could while they waited.

"I'm not sure," the doctor replied. "I've just heard bits and pieces of conversations . . . Foster and Bellamy were partners, I believe, so now he believes that mine should belong to him. Scranton wants it, too, of course. If you ask me . . . they're co-operating now, but I suspect each of them plans to betray the other once they've killed Nick Beltz and his friends." Drake drew in a breath. "That's what Foster, Anse Porter, and a number of other gunmen have gone to do."

A chill gripped Ace. "You mean—"

"By now," Drake said, "they may have slaughtered everyone out there at that mine."

Chapter 39

The snow hadn't gotten any worse—but it sure hadn't let up any, either. Maybe you couldn't quite call it a blizzard, Nick Beltz thought, but only because the wind wasn't blowing hard enough for that. If it picked up just a little more . . .

A bullet whined off the rock where Beltz was crouched. Because of the snow, he couldn't see any gunsmoke drifting up from the other side of the canyon, and it was just pure luck whenever he caught a glimpse of a muzzle flash.

Instead, Beltz aimed by the sound of the enemies' shots, which was only a little better than firing blind.

He squeezed the trigger of the old buffalo rifle, though, and felt the satisfying kick against his shoulder as the weapon boomed. He wanted to keep those boys over there thinking . . . as well as ducking.

"Nicholas!" Folke Steingrim called from another boulder along the rim, where he had taken cover. "I am almost out of bullets!"

"As am I!" Baldur shouted from the other direction.

"And me!" Haldor added from beyond Baldur.

The brothers were using Winchesters. The heavy rifles looked like toys in their huge hands, and they weren't the greatest shots in the world, but under the circumstances, accuracy was impossible, anyway. They were all relying on luck to guide their shots.

"There's another box o' cartridges in my tent," Beltz told them. "Hold the fort, boys, and I'll fetch 'em!"

"Fort?" Baldur echoed. "We have no fort!"

"It might be better if we did," Folke said. "Or a castle."

"No! A mead hall!"

Beltz didn't wait around to explain to them. He turned and, crouching as low as he could, ran back toward the tents, weaving from side to side so as not to tempt fate.

The snow was almost a foot deep. It scattered wildly around his boots as he ran. His feet were cold, but he had more important things to worry about right now. He thought he heard a bullet fly past him, not far away, but he wasn't sure. He wasn't hit, so right now that was all that mattered.

He reached his tent and ducked inside. The snow wasn't as deep, but the wind had blown quite a bit in. The ammunition was in an old trunk. Beltz threw the lid open and bent down to grab the box of .44 cartridges.

As he straightened, he heard a flurry of gunfire from the Steingrim brothers, as well as some roaring shouts. Something was going on. Something bad, more than likely.

Beltz shoved the box of cartridges under his buffalo coat and burst out of the tent to run back toward his friends.

Chance leaned over toward Priscilla and said into her ear, "Things aren't looking good, are they?"

She bit her bottom lip for a second before answering, "Unfortunately, the men I picked for the jury don't really know you that well. No one in Panamint City does. And the story Scranton and his men told was convincing. I'll have to give them that much. If I didn't know better, I'd say he actually believes that you killed Bellamy."

"Maybe he does. Sure, getting rid of me serves his purposes, but he might believe I'm guilty and is eager to take advantage of that."

"Can you think of *anyone* whose testimony might be able to help you?"

Chance shook his head. "Nobody else was around when I found Bellamy's body, just like I told the jury. Scranton may not have set it up deliberately, but everything worked out just perfect for him, anyway."

At the judge's table, Thaddeus Revere asked, "Do you want to call any more witnesses, Miss Lansing?"

Priscilla glanced again at Chance, then sighed. She stood up and said, "No, Your Honor. Mr. Jensen has told the court what really happened yesterday. That is our defense."

"Very well," Revere said. "Mr. Scranton, I expect you want to sum up—"

The doors at the back of the room opened, letting in cold air and wind-blown snow, and the shock of it caused several of the spectators to exclaim. Like everybody else in the room, Chance turned his head to look and see what the disturbance was. The crowd split apart back there. . . .

And Chance's heart slugged harder when he saw Ace, Myra, and Dr. Allan Drake step through the opening and start toward the front of the room.

"Hold on!" Ace said. "We've got another witness here!"

Scranton's response was instant. He shouted at his men, "Stop them!"

Four of the gun-wolves sprang forward, clawing at the holstered Colts on their hips. A shoot-out in this packed room would result in a lot of innocent people getting hurt, some fatally. Chance leaped out of his chair and did the only thing he could think of that might be able to stop such a catastrophe, or at least postpone it.

He took two swift steps and then left his feet in a diving tackle aimed at Big Dave Scranton.

Scranton was already reaching for a gun under his own coat

when Chance slammed into him. The collision drove Scranton backward onto the table. Chance's momentum carried him forward and landed him on top of Scranton.

He got hold of Scranton's wrist just as that hand emerged, holding a pistol. He shoved it aside as Scranton pulled the trigger. The bullet whistled off to the side and smacked into the wall. The next instant Chance had his hand wrapped around the gun and was wrenching it free of Scranton's grip.

The sharp crack of the shot made the spectators yell in alarm. Some of them dived for the floor, while others scrambled for the doors, trying to get out.

Ace stepped in front of Myra and Drake and swept out two guns, his own and the one he had taken away from the guard in the room where Drake had been held prisoner.

But anybody else could start shooting, however. Chance heaved up from the table, with his left arm clamped around Scranton's throat and the gun he had just taken away pressed to Scranton's head.

"Hold it!" he shouted at Scranton's men. "Leave those guns where they are, or I'll put a bullet in your boss's head!"

Instead, Scranton spat curses and ordered, "Kill them! Kill those damned Jensens!"

"That won't do you any good, Scranton," Dr. Drake said quickly, his normally mild voice loud and clear in the room, where the crowd had been stunned into silence. "The truth's going to come out. Chance Jensen is innocent, and you've been holding me prisoner while you help the real killer!"

Looking pale and shocked as he stood behind the table at the front of the room, Thaddeus Revere said, "I . . . I reckon we'd better hear the doctor's testimony."

"N-no!" Scranton forced out past Chance's grip on his throat. "He . . . he's lying! The doctor . . . is lying—"

"It's the truth," Drake insisted. "Let me come up there, and I'll explain the whole thing."

"There's not a lot of time," Ace said. He still held the two guns and kept watching Scranton's men warily in case any of them decided to make a play. "That fella Foster and some of Scranton's men have gone down the canyon to murder Nick Beltz and the Steingrim brothers. We need to go help them, if it's not too late already."

Revere waved for them to come forward. "Let's hear what you have to say, Doc. Everybody but the jury, get out! Jensen, take that gun away from Scranton's head and let go of him. The rest of you men, pouch those irons! This is a court of law, damn it! Scranton, you may not have intended to have any *real* law and order here in Panamint City, but I reckon you've miscalculated."

With obvious reluctance, Chance lowered the gun he had taken away from Scranton. Scranton straightened his coat and glared at Revere.

"I can see that you're right," he said to the former justice of the peace as the spectators rushed out of the building while they had the chance. A murder trial was a novelty, but it wasn't worth dying for if bullets started to fly. "This trial *isn't* going to turn out the way I wanted," Scranton went on. "So I no longer have a choice."

The ominous sound of those words provided a little warning for Ace and Chance. They saw Scranton snatch a second pistol from his pocket, and the man's hired guns saw that, as well, and knew their boss was going for broke. They followed his lead. Their Colts came up and started to spit flame and lead.

Scranton fired, too, aiming his shot at Dr. Allan Drake. An instant before he squeezed the trigger, Ace shouldered the doctor aside with such force that Drake sprawled on the floor between two of the benches, taking Myra down with him, as Ace had hoped. Scranton's bullet whipped past Ace's ear.

He couldn't return Scranton's fire before he was too busy trying to stop the hired gunmen from spraying lead all over the room. He squeezed off his shots swiftly but without rushing them, and each time he pulled the trigger, one of the men spun off his feet, drilled cleanly.

But there were too many of them, and Ace knew it. Their bullets were coming closer and closer. . . .

Suddenly, someone stood beside Ace, fighting shoulder to shoulder with him. Two long-barreled Remington revolvers thrust ahead, and tongues of flame six inches long licked from their muzzles. The gun-thunder was deafening, even in the big, high-ceilinged room.

Ace couldn't afford to take his eyes off his enemies. He and his unexpected ally weaved forward, still firing, their four guns laying down a deadly swath of lead that in a matter of seconds drove all of Scranton's men off their feet and left them in bloody heaps.

Revere had turned over the table and taken cover behind it. The members of the jury had crowded in back there, as well. As the shooting stopped but echoes continued to rumble inside the mission, Ace looked around for Priscilla, anxious to see if she was all right.

A surge of relief went through him when he spotted her huddled behind an overturned bench with Myra and Dr. Drake. He didn't see Chance, though, and that worried him.

"Seems like every time I see you boys, you're in some sort of tight spot you're trying to shoot your way out of," a familiar voice said. Ace turned his head to look the other way, and a shock of recognition went through him.

"Luke," he said.

He and Chance had known for a while now that Luke Jensen was their father, but they still hadn't gotten used to calling him Pa yet. They probably never would.

Like all the Jensens, Luke was tall and broad shouldered. His crisp dark hair under the black Stetson had a slight curl to it. He wore a neatly trimmed mustache, which gave his rugged features a look of distinction, to go with his self-taught but highly educated speech. He wasn't a handsome hombre, but men instinctively liked him and women were drawn to him.

He holstered one of the twin Remington revolvers he carried and started reloading the other one. After a long career as a bounty hunter, Luke did some things without even thinking about them, and one of those was never letting himself get caught with too many empty chambers in his guns.

"How did you—"

"Your letter finally caught up with me, and I went to meet you in Los Angeles," Luke answered. "But you'd already left to come up here. Something about a deed and a silver mine . . . ?" He shrugged. "So I figured I'd follow you and see what you were mixed up in now."

"It's a long story," Ace said. "But I'm sure mighty glad you caught up to us when you did."

Luke slid the reloaded Remington back into its black leather holster and started reloading the other gun. "Where's your brother?"

"That's what I want to know."

Priscilla was back on her feet, and Drake was helping Myra up. As Ace and Luke turned toward Priscilla, she pointed at a door in the front of the room and said, "Chance went out that way. He was chasing Scranton. They traded shots in here, and then Scranton made a run for it."

"We'd better go see if we can help him," Ace said. He finished thumbing fresh rounds into his Colt—the apple didn't fall far from the proverbial tree—and snapped the cylinder closed.

"This Scranton's a bad hombre?" Luke asked as he and Ace started toward the door.

"That's right. He's part of that long story, but for right now, it's enough to say he's a bad hombre."

Ace felt the cold wind blowing in before they reached the

door. Beyond it was a small storage room, and on the other side of the room was a rear door that led outside. He and Luke had just started toward that door when a figure appeared there, coming in out of the thickly falling snow.

"Scranton made it to a horse and got away," Chance said. "I might have winged him. I don't know—"

That was as far as he got before he stumbled and dropped the gun he was holding.

Ace spotted the blood on his shirt and cried, "Chance!" as he leaped forward to try to catch his brother before Chance collapsed.

Chapter 40

"I still don't think this is a good idea," Dr. Allan Drake said as he stepped back from the table on which Chance was sitting at the front of the mission's main room. It had been the defense table during the trial a short time earlier; now it was a medical examination table.

"You said yourself that Scranton's bullet just plowed a little furrow in my arm," Chance said as he slid his bandaged arm back into the bloodstained sleeve of his shirt. "I can get by without the bit of meat it took with it."

"Your arm is going to be very sore—"

"It won't keep me from riding," Chance insisted, "and I don't shoot with my left hand. Although I *can* if I need to. I'm a good shot with my left hand, in fact."

Myra stepped forward from the group gathered around Chance. She began buttoning the shirt for him, since he might have a hard time with that.

"Do you really think Scranton will head for Mr. Beltz's mine? I mean, your mine?" she asked.

Ace said, "Who owns the mine doesn't matter right now. Where else can Scranton go, now that everybody knows he's been working with a killer? And Anse Porter, his right-hand man, went down the canyon with Foster. Scranton probably thinks that if he can grab that mine, he'll be rich enough, and powerful enough, to get away with everything he's done so far."

Luke said, "I don't really know much about what's going on around here, but I can tell you this. Men like this hombre Scranton can never have enough money or enough power. And they'll do whatever it takes to get it, even if it means killing anybody who stands in their way."

"Like Nick and the Steingrim brothers," Chance said as he slid down off the table. "That's why we need to get moving. We should have been heading out there already."

"Not until you got that bullet hole tended to," Ace said sternly. "I wasn't going to have you bleeding to death after all I went through to save you from a hang rope."

"All you went through?" Chance repeated. "Sounded to me like all you did was wander around town, asking questions, until you finally figured out the only place you hadn't looked yet."

"But at least I *did* figure it out. Although to be fair, I think Myra thought of it first—"

"Come on, you two," Luke said. "Let's go save those friends of yours."

Nick Beltz loved snow. Loved the way its pristine whiteness covered up all the ugly in the world when it was freshly fallen. Loved the faint, almost inaudible *shushing* sound it made when it drifted down softly. At moments like that, it seemed as if peace had spread all over the world. It would have been all right with Beltz if he lived somewhere that had snow on the ground all year long.

Today he cussed the snow like it was a balky mule as he ran through it toward the trail leading down into the canyon. He saw dark shapes looming there against the white backdrop, appearing and disappearing as the clouds of flakes closed around them and then opened again for an instant, before cloaking the struggling figures again.

Guns boomed, near enough that the snow didn't muffle the reports, as it had earlier. That meant the enemy was a lot closer. From the glimpse Beltz had gotten, he determined that some of the fighting was hand to hand.

He didn't think any of Scranton's men were big enough to take on the Steingrim brothers, but not even Folke, Baldur, and Haldor were invincible. If enough men piled on them, they would fall. And once they went down, the attack would become even more vicious.

Unfortunately, as Beltz neared the scene of battle, he couldn't open fire, because he couldn't tell who was who. He wasn't going to risk hitting one of his friends. He was going to have to get right in there in the melee with them.

He stumbled a little as he came up behind a man whose height and normal frame told Beltz that he couldn't be one of the Steingrims. The man must have heard the noise Beltz made, or else some instinct had warned him. He whirled around and lashed out with the butt of the Winchester he held.

Instead of getting a crushed skull, Beltz twisted fast enough to take the blow on his shoulder, but it knocked him down. The man swung the rifle toward him, clearly intending to shoot him.

Beltz angled his own Winchester up and pulled the trigger first. The sharply upward-angled slug blew half the man's jaw off and knocked him backward onto the snow, which was splattered red around him.

Huffing and puffing from running, being knocked down, and narrowly escaping death, Beltz rolled onto hands and knees and tried to get up. To his left, somebody yelled a curse. He looked in that direction and saw a man running toward him with a gun stuck out, ready to fire.

Before the man could pull the trigger, a huge, bulky shape appeared behind him. One hand grabbed the man by the back of the neck; the other snagged his belt. The bearded, long-haired Steingrim brother—Beltz couldn't tell which one he was—heaved the gunman off his feet, into the air above his head, and then *threw* him like a rag doll, making him sail off into the snow and out of sight.

But from the length of the man's scream before it ended abruptly, Beltz figured his friend had just tossed the man clear over the trail and out onto the floor of the canyon.

"Much obliged!" Beltz shouted to his rescuer. "What happened out here? Where'd those fellas come from?"

"They crept up the trail like rats! They shot Baldur and Haldor!"

So it was Folke who had come to his aid, Beltz thought. He could see that now.

"Your brothers are dead?"

"I do not know! But I saw them fall!"

Beltz drew in a deep breath and pulled himself up to his greatest height, which was only a little taller than Folke.

"Then I reckon we'll go down fightin', too," he said.

Folke lifted both fists and shook them in the air. "Yes! Tonight we feast with Odin and my brothers in Valhalla!" With that, he lifted his great voice in a shout and ran toward the muzzle flashes that split the storm.

Muttering, "Derned right! Valhalla!" Nick Beltz charged after him.

Ace, Chance, and Luke rode down the canyon as fast as they could, given the weather and the terrain. They actually made pretty good time, but the pace seemed maddeningly slow to Ace.

Especially when they began hearing the faint pops of gunfire up ahead.

"Blast it!" Chance exclaimed. His face was a little haggard from the pain of his wounded arm, but he was staying in the saddle just fine. "They're attacking the mine!"

"We knew that was likely," Ace said. "And it's good that the shooting is still going on. It means Mr. Beltz and the Steingrims are still putting up a fight."

Luke said, "Yes, but from what you told me about the situation, I'm not sure how long they can hold out."

With that grim pronouncement, the three of them continued charging through the canyon toward the sounds of battle.

Across the canyon from the mine, Jared Foxx felt triumph coursing through him as he stood up from behind the rock he'd been using as cover. The shots were getting a lot more sporadic over there. He knew that meant his enemies were almost finished.

It was time for him to take a hand in this directly. He wanted to be in on the finish, if he could.

"I'm going over there," he said to Anse Porter, the only one of the gunmen who remained on this side of the canyon with him. Kimbrough, Bracken, and Stevens had left first, to creep up that switchback trail while the others continued the barrage from the other side of the canyon. The rest of Big Dave Scranton's men had followed a short time later, to serve as reinforcements if needed. From the sound of the shooting over there, all of them were taking part in the fight.

"I'll stay here to provide cover, just in case," Porter said.

Foxx glanced at him suspiciously and then jerked his Colt up to cover the gunman. "And maybe plug me in the back when I start across there, so your boss doesn't have to split anything with me? I don't think so, Porter."

"You're loco, Foster," Porter drawled. "I don't have any orders like that. And I'm not a double-crosser. We're on the same side."

"And we'll stay there, until we're not. But *I'll* say when that is, not you." Foxx motioned with the gun he held. "Come on. You're going first."

"The hell I am."

"Then I'll shoot you down right here." Foxx eared back the hammer of his gun. "By the way, my name's not Foster. It's really Jared Foxx."

It wouldn't hurt anything for Porter to know that. Foxx didn't intend for him to live very long once this was over.

Porter grunted. "Foxx, eh? I've heard of you. Seems to me your line was bank robbery, not silver mining."

"Things change," Foxx said. "Now get moving. We're going over there, and we're going to wipe out the last of those damned claim jumpers."

A bleak laugh came from Porter. "You know, in a bizarre way, you're almost in the right on this. Other than all the killing, of course."

"Move, damn you!"

Porter lifted his rifle. "I'm going."

He turned and loped out into the snow. Foxx hesitated just a second and then ran after him.

He hadn't gone very far before he realized he couldn't see Porter anymore. The man had disappeared into the clouds of snow. Foxx jerked his gun from side to side as panic momentarily welled up inside him. Was Porter waiting in the blizzard to ambush him?

Foxx didn't know, and it was too late for him to do anything other than forge ahead. If he couldn't see Porter, then Porter probably couldn't see him. The gunman would have to get closer to bushwhack him, and if that happened, Foxx would be ready and would get off some shots of his own.

He ran on through the blinding snowfall and hoped that he wasn't going in circles.

Chapter 41

Ace heard a swift rataplan of hoofbeats just before a man on horseback loomed up right in front of him, galloping up the canyon. Yelling a warning to his brother and father, he yanked his horse aside.

The rider charged past them and was there for a second and then gone again, having vanished into the snow.

"Whoa!" Chance exclaimed. "Who was that?"

"I don't know," Ace said as he tightened his grip on the reins. The near collision had spooked his horse a little. "I didn't get a good look at him."

"Well, it doesn't matter," Luke said. "I can still hear shots, so the fight's not over yet."

The three of them rode on. The gunshots were louder now. They were getting close to the mine.

As they swept around a bend, the clouds of snow parted enough for Ace to spot the bottom end of the trail. Horses could make it up those switchbacks, but they had to be led or ridden slowly. Trying to gallop their mounts up the trail under these conditions would be foolhardy, even suicidal.

So as they pounded up to their destination, Ace swung down from the saddle and dropped to the ground before his mount had even stopped moving. They could make better time on foot.

Chance and Luke must have realized the same thing, because they dismounted just as quickly and lunged up the trail right behind Ace.

Even though it took only a minute or so to reach the top, that time seemed a lot longer to Ace. When the three of them got there, they paused.

Bodies littered the ground. Three of them were big enough to belong to the Steingrim brothers, Ace saw with a shock. The brothers had seemed invulnerable, but of course, that wasn't the case. Bullets could bring them down, just like anybody else.

About thirty feet away, at the outer edge of visibility in the blizzard, a man stood with his back to the Jensens. He had lost his hat, and his hair was white as the snow.

That matched the description Dr. Allan Drake had given them of Tom Bellamy's killer. And at the moment, the man seemed to be on the verge of racking up another kill, because he had his gun pointed at Nick Beltz, who stood a few yards in front of him, holding a bullet-drilled arm with his other hand.

Ace, Chance, and Luke held their fire, because with the position the two men were in, any bullets that happened to miss the white-haired man were likely to hit the old-timer.

Anyway, the man was talking instead of shooting.

"Thought you could steal my mine away from me!" he accused. "Everybody keeps trying to steal my mine! First Bellamy, then that damned Jensen whelp, and now you, you old fool!"

"I found this mine," Beltz replied in his querulous, high-pitched voice. "Nobody was workin' it. It was there for the takin'."

"That's a damned lie! It belonged to me first, me and Bellamy! And then he had to go and double-cross me and steal that blasted deed!"

"What are you talkin' about?" Beltz asked. "Are you sayin' you filed on this claim, legal-like?"

"Bellamy did. Then he stole the deed, and Chance Jensen won it from him in a poker game, so I had to come chasing up here after him, only to find you squatting on the place! Well, I got my revenge on Bellamy, Scranton's taking care of Jensen, and I'm going to get rid of you . . . right now!"

The man lifted his gun.

By this point, Beltz had caught sight of the three men coming up quietly behind the white-haired man. Ace waved a hand silently to the side, hoping Beltz would understand what he meant. Whether the old-timer understood or not, time had run out. The white-haired man was about to shoot him.

"Hey!" Chance called. "I'm right here, mister."

The man whirled toward them, and at the same time, Beltz flung himself to the ground, as far to the side as he could. The white-haired man was fast, fast enough that muzzle flame spouted from his gun as he pulled the trigger.

But the three Jensens were faster. Their guns roared an instant earlier, and all three slugs smashed into the man's chest, lifting him off his feet and throwing him backward a good five feet before he came crashing down on his back. Bloodstains spread rapidly and merged to make his shirt front a sodden mess. He twitched a couple of times as he managed to gasp, "Mine . . . mine . . ."

Then the death rattle came from his throat.

Ace pouched his iron and rushed over to Nick Beltz. He reached down to help the old-timer to his feet and asked, "Are you all right, Mr. Beltz?"

"Yeah, except the varmint winged me." Beltz clutched his wounded arm again. "But he woulda killed me if you fellas hadn't showed up." He squinted past Ace. "Who's that older fella with you? I don't recollect seein' him before."

"That's our father, Luke," Ace explained.

"Your pa?"

"Yeah. Looks like we may get to spend Christmas with him, after all. It's a long story."

"But . . . Aw, hell, never mind. What in blazes did that hombre mean about *Chance* really ownin' this mine?"

"That's an even longer story," Ace began, but before he could go on, a shout came from the direction of the canyon.

"*Valhalla!*"

The four of them turned to see three squat but massive figures staggering toward them, arms around each other to hold themselves up.

"The Scandihoovians!" Beltz cried. "You're alive."

"Aye, it will take more than dogs like those to slay us," Haldor declared.

"We are injured, but not mortally," Folke added.

"But for now, we are denied entrance to Valhalla," Baldur said.

"You'll get there soon enough," Beltz said. "Right now, let's get ever'body patched up."

Each of the Steingrim brothers had been shot at least twice, mostly in arms and legs, although Haldor might have a broken rib where a bullet had glanced off it, Luke judged. Due to his long career as a bounty hunter, he had the most experience dealing with bullet wounds under primitive conditions, so he took charge of tending to the injured men as they all gathered around a fire built just inside the mine entrance.

While that was going on, introductions were made, and Ace and Chance filled in Beltz and the Steingrims on everything that had happened in Panamint City.

When Beltz had heard the story, and that information was combined with what the white-haired man had said, the picture was pretty clear. He said to Chance, "I'm sorry I tried to steal your mine out from under you, boy. I sure didn't intend for it to be that way. When I come along and nobody was workin' these diggin's, I figured they were up for grabs. But I reckon the mine and all the silver really belong to you, fair and square."

"We can talk about that later," Chance said. "I want you to know that I don't hold any grudges against you, though, Mr. Beltz. You've been a good friend to us." Chance smiled. "Fair and square."

"Well . . . I'm mighty glad you feel that way. I wouldn't want no hard feelin's between us."

"None at all," Chance assured him.

"You coulda told me about it first off, though."

Ace said, "We wanted to just let things ride for a while, until we got a good handle on the situation. And then all the trouble with Scranton came up almost right away . . ."

"Yeah, we've been a mite busy, all right," Beltz agreed.

When all the wounds had been cleaned and bandaged, Luke looked out at the snow, which was still coming down hard and heavy.

"I think it would be a good idea for that doc in town to have a look at all of you," he said. "None of you seem to be in any real danger right now, but it's best not to take chances with gunshot wounds. Besides, the way that snow's coming down, it won't be too much longer before nobody's going to be able to travel up and down this canyon."

Beltz frowned and asked, "Are you suggestin' that we go off and leave the mine unprotected, after all the trouble we went to, to fight off that bunch o' no-good thieves?"

"Nobody's going to bother the mine in weather like this,"

Ace said. "They won't be able to, because everything's going to be snowed in. Anyway, with that fella Foster, or whatever his name was, dead and Scranton on the run, who's going to cause more trouble?"

"Reckon you could be right," Beltz said grudgingly.

"We'll round up the horses those dead gunmen left behind," Luke said. "The poor critters must be about half-frozen by now. That way you'll all have mounts to ride to town."

Within half an hour, the procession started toward Panamint City, with Beltz leading the way on Mehitabel. Ace and Chance rode beside the Steingrim brothers, keeping an eye on them in case any of them started to sway in their saddles. Luke brought up the rear, keeping an eye on their back trail, although as far as they knew, all their enemies back there were dead, the bodies well on their way to being covered with snow and freezing.

It bothered Ace, however, that they hadn't seen Big Dave Scranton's body in the canyon, and he hadn't forgotten about that rider who had thundered past them on their way to the mine. Those were a couple of loose ends—and loose ends could be dangerous.

The snow had drifted deeply enough in places that the mounts really had to struggle to get through, but they made it and finally began to catch glimpses of lights up ahead through the gloom and the snow. That was the settlement, Ace knew. He was chilled to the bone and would be glad to get out of the storm.

They headed first toward the mission. That was on the way to Dr. Drake's house, and Ace wanted to check on Priscilla. Besides, the lights inside looked warm and inviting.

"I'll take everybody on down to the doc's," Chance said as Ace dismounted in front of the mission.

"He might be in here with Priscilla," Ace said.

"Well, if he is, send him on down to the office. Tell him he's got customers waiting."

Ace waved in acknowledgment and went to the door. He opened it and went inside to see a group of men, including Dr. Drake and Thaddeus Revere, standing at the front of the room. They all turned to look as the door opened, and Ace tensed when he saw the upset expressions on their faces.

Priscilla wasn't with them, or anywhere else in the room.

He hurried forward as Drake came to meet him.

"Thank heavens you're back," the doctor said. "What about your brother and father?"

"They're fine," Ace said.

"The men from the mine?"

"Shot up, but not too bad, I hope. They came back to town with us and are heading down to your office so you can tend to them. Doctor, what's wrong? Where's Priscilla?"

"That's what's wrong," Drake said. "Scranton didn't leave town. He must have hidden somewhere. And then that man Porter came back . . ."

Porter had been part of the group that went out to the mine, Ace recalled. That meant he was the rider who'd galloped past him and Chance and Luke, headed this way.

"Did they cause more trouble?" he asked. A jolt of alarm went through him. "Did they hurt Priscilla?"

Drake shook his head and said despairingly, "I don't know. They freed that Fairchild woman from the room where she was being guarded, shot one man, kidnapped Priscilla and Miss Malone, and vanished into the storm!"

Chapter 42

The heat from the sun that beat down on Ace, Chance, and Luke was shocking, especially considering what the weather had been like where they were less than twenty-four hours earlier.

"What do you think?" Ace asked his father as Luke dismounted and hunkered on his heels to study the faint marks on the hard ground.

"We've cut into their lead," Luke replied, "but they're still a good ways in front of us."

Chance took his hat off and sleeved sweat from his face. "It's not really that hot," he said. "Why does it *feel* like it is?"

Luke straightened and said, "Because the sun's shining and you're not in the middle of a blizzard anymore."

That comment made all three of them glance toward the mountains to the west. The clouds were still thick up there above the Panamints, but they didn't know if it was still snowing in the settlement at the head of Surprise Canyon. The overcast had broken before they reached the edge of Death Valley, and out here in the broad, arid basin itself, it was a clear morning, with the temperature climbing steadily.

The way the wind had been blowing the night before, there

was no way in the world the men they were pursuing would have left any tracks in the snow. But enough witnesses had seen Scranton, Porter, and Natalie Fairchild ride off with their prisoners, heading east, and besides, if they had gone west, they would have run into Ace, Chance, and the others coming back up the canyon toward town.

Only one trail led down from the pass to the basin, so Ace, Chance, and Luke had weighed the odds and started after the fugitives the day before, following that trail until it got too dark to go on. They had made camp in the lee of a huge rocky upthrust that partially blocked the wind, so the snow hadn't drifted there much. They had found enough dry brush to build a fire and had carefully kept it going all night to keep themselves and their mounts from freezing, taking turns trying to sleep a little, although that hadn't been easy under such adverse conditions.

All three had been glad to see morning arrive so they could push on. The storm had eased some. The snow still fell, but the wind wasn't blowing as hard where they were.

Nick Beltz and the Steingrim brothers had wanted to accompany them, but Dr. Drake had put an end to that idea. All of them were wounded badly enough that the doctor had put his foot down and decreed that they weren't going anywhere. They could have overruled him, of course—there was no physical way he could have stopped them—but Ace and Chance had talked them out of it.

"We'll bring Priscilla and Myra back," Ace had promised. "And Scranton and Porter and Miss Fairchild, too, if they'll cooperate."

"They won't," Luke had predicted with a cynical note in his voice.

Ace figured his father probably was right about that.

But they would deal with it when the time came. Right

now, they were concentrating on catching up, and slowly but surely, they were doing it. Luke was an exceptional tracker, and he had been able to pick up their trail at the edge of the basin, out of the storm at last.

Since then, they had ridden several miles into Death Valley, and the thick coats that had helped keep them alive the night before were now rolled and lashed behind the saddles.

Luke swung up into the saddle again. He said, "Looks like they're heading for Furnace Creek."

"Is there an actual creek there?" Chance asked as they nudged their horses into motion again.

"More like a spring," Luke replied. "I've been through these parts a few times before and have stopped there myself. They say the spring always flows . . . but it's not always above the ground, where you can get to it. In the hottest part of the summer . . ." He shook his head. "Well, I wouldn't try it unless it was a matter of life and death."

"Like this is," Ace said grimly. "Scranton's liable to kill Priscilla and Myra."

Luke said, "Not likely, at least not right away. Not until he's sure nobody's coming after him. He might figure on using them as leverage if a posse catches up to him."

Ace thought about it and said, "I'm not really sure why he's doing this. Yes, he tried to steal that mine and sent men to kill Mr. Beltz and the Steingrim brothers, but he didn't take part in any of those raids himself. And it was Foster who killed Tom Bellamy. Scranton gave him a place to hide, but again, he didn't kill anybody himself or try to kill anybody."

"You know what Nick said about how some of the other miners disappeared when they wouldn't sell out to Scranton," Chance reminded him. "Everything he's done lately might be enough to get the sheriff to come up to Panamint City and look into the situation. If that happened, there's no telling what crimes might turn up that Scranton committed."

"What it comes down to," Luke said, "is that Scranton knows what he's guilty of, and he figures it's bad enough that he needed to light a shuck out of there." He scratched at his jaw. "Kidnapping those two girls . . . well, that's sort of the final nail in the coffin. Scranton knows he'll never be able to stay around these parts anymore, no matter how much money he has." Luke grunted. "And from what you've told me about him, he's arrogant enough that he doesn't like it when anybody stands up to him. That's probably why he took that shot at you, Chance, as much as for any other reason."

"You're probably right. And that fella Porter's just a hired killer. He'll go along with whatever Scranton says."

"What about Miss Fairchild?" Ace mused. "Why would a woman like her come with them into a wilderness like this?"

"She's hitched her wagon to Scranton, just like Porter," Luke said. "She has to believe that's where she'll get the biggest payoff in the long run." He squinted into the distance. "Assuming they get out of Death Valley alive, of course."

The three men pushed their horses as fast as they dared as they continued deeper into the basin. Even at this time of year, none of them wanted to be set afoot out here.

After another hour or so, Ace suddenly reined in and said, "What's that up there?" He pointed at a dark shape lying on the ground several hundred yards ahead of them.

Chance and Luke had come to a stop, as well. Luke took a pair of field glasses from his saddlebags and peered through them for a moment before lowering them and saying, "It's a horse. Looks like it played out and they left it there to die."

"I don't see anybody," Ace said.

"Neither do I," Chance said. "That means a couple of them are riding double. That ought to slow them down some."

Luke nodded. "More than likely. Let's go."

From time to time, they stopped so Luke could dismount

and examine the tracks more closely. The trail was faint, just occasional markings on the hard ground or a shiny spot on a rock where a horseshoe had nicked it, but Luke's instincts were so finely honed that he was able to follow those signs.

They were still closing in on their quarry, he told Ace and Chance. It was just a matter of time, especially since one of the horses in the group they were following now had to carry a double load.

By the middle of the day, some scattered dark shapes were visible very low on the eastern horizon. Luke pointed them out and said, "Those are the clumps of trees and brush at Furnace Creek. They don't amount to much, but it's more than you'll find anywhere else in this valley. Compared to, say, Badwater Basin, it's an oasis. Badwater's the hottest, driest place I've ever been. It's just two steps from hell, if that far."

"I wonder if we'll find them there," Ace said. "They have to rest their horses sometime."

"Could be," Luke said, nodding slowly. "In fact, I'd say there's a good enough chance of it that we need to approach the place carefully. You boys swing wide around it. One of you can go north, and the other south. Then you can come in at angles from the other side."

"What about you?" Chance asked.

"I'll just ride straight up to the place."

"You mean you'll put a big target on your chest," Ace said. "If they're there, they're liable to start shooting as soon as you come into range."

"Well, let's hope they're not very good shots."

"Porter will be," Chance said. "He makes his living with a gun. You're just running the big risk yourself so Ace or I don't have to. Why don't *I* go in from the front, while you and Ace circle around?"

"Because I said otherwise. And I'm your father."

Ace and Chance looked at Luke for a few seconds; then Chance laughed. Ace smiled.

"What's so funny about that?" Luke asked, sounding a little offended.

"We went more than twenty years not even knowing you existed," Chance said, "then a few more without any idea we're related to you. So giving us orders and saying, 'Just because,' doesn't really work with us, *Pa*."

"Well, that's a little progress, I suppose," Luke muttered. "You called me Pa. But I reckon I can't make you do what I say. It's the smart thing, though. I've got a lot more experience riding into tight spots than you boys do."

"He's got a point there," Ace admitted grudgingly.

"Yeah, maybe." Chance's eyes narrowed. "Doesn't mean I have to like it, though."

"There's another good reason I should be the one to ride in there," Luke went on. "Porter's never seen me, and neither has the Fairchild woman. Scranton might have gotten a glimpse of me back in town, but with all the guns going off and the powder smoke in the air at the time, there's at least a chance he won't recognize me. So they *might* take me for just some pilgrim riding in to refill my canteens, in which case they'd let me come on in before they killed me and took my horse to replace the one they lost."

"That's . . . pretty good thinking," Ace said.

Luke smiled and said dryly, "As I mentioned, I have some experience at this."

"All right, we'll go along with it," Chance said.

Ace nodded.

"It's not likely they've spotted us yet, if they're there," Luke went on. "We'll split up here. Since you'll have farther to go, I'll wait here for half an hour before I start on toward

Furnace Creek. When you're around on the other side, move in, but not too close. Stay back unless and until you hear shooting."

"And if we do?" Ace asked.

"That'll be the time for you to come a-runnin', with guns in your hands," Luke said.

Chapter 43

It was amazing how quickly a person could go from too cold to too hot, Myra Malone thought as she sat in the welcome shade of a scrubby tree.

Priscilla Lansing sat close beside her. In a whisper, Priscilla said, "That woman's not watching us. We could try to get to the horses."

Scranton had ordered Natalie Fairchild to stand guard over the captives while he and Porter tended to the horses and filled the canteens at the small spring. Natalie wasn't accustomed to riding such long distances and was sore and exhausted. Myra could tell she was about to collapse.

Unfortunately, that didn't really help her and Priscilla that much. Porter was tireless and tough as whang leather, and Scranton, although softened some by success, was still pretty hard nosed.

Porter was fast with his gun, too. One bit of commotion, and he'd be whirling around and drawing. He could blast Myra and Priscilla off their feet before they made it halfway to the horses.

Scranton probably wouldn't kick about it, either. Sure, he had brought the two prisoners along to use as hostages if he needed to, but he would proceed without them rather than let them get away.

Anyway, sooner or later he would decide they had outlived their usefulness and would kill them. Myra couldn't conceive of the universe treating her any other way. It was just too bad that a decent young woman like Priscilla had to get caught up in this.

Natalie Fairchild leaned against a tree trunk and sighed. Her attractive face was haggard from weariness and strain. She called to the men, "How long are we going to stay here?"

"Not much longer," Scranton replied. "I'm surprised you're in a hurry to get back in the saddle, Natalie."

"I'm not," she snapped. "I just want to get out of this damned desert—"

"Hold on," Anse Porter said suddenly. "Somebody's coming."

The trees were scattered enough that Luke spotted the horses among them without any trouble. As he came closer, he saw people moving around.

They must have seen him, too, but they didn't start shooting right away, so that confirmed his guess. Scranton and Porter wanted to see who he was before they killed him. He rode along at a deliberate pace, slouching a little in the saddle. His head was down, so the brim of his hat partially obscured his face. He wanted to look like a drifting pilgrim, not somebody who had pursued them all the way from Panamint City.

He felt a familiar tenseness inside him. It wasn't fear. He had been too close to death too many times in his life to feel anything other than fatalistic about his own fate.

But usually, whenever he walked or rode into a shooting scrape, somebody else's life was on the line, too. Somebody innocent, like Myra Malone and Priscilla Lansing. Luke didn't know either of the women, other than seeing them briefly in the settlement, but he didn't want anything to happen to them.

And, of course, he wanted Ace and Chance to come through this fracas alive. They had been his friends even before he knew they were his sons. Now his concern for them was even greater.

When he was about fifty yards away from the trees, he reined in and studied the situation. He could still see the horses, but not the men. That meant Scranton and Porter had taken cover behind some of the trees and were watching him warily.

He raised his voice and called, "Hello, the springs! All right to come on in and get some water?"

Under normal circumstances, nobody would refuse that request in Death Valley. Scranton and Porter would want him to think that everything was normal here, so he would ride in without being ready for trouble.

The answer came quickly. "Sure, mister! Come on in!"

Luke nudged his horse into motion again.

As he rode up, his eyes were in constant motion, even though his head was not. He took in the scene almost instantly. Myra and Priscilla were sitting under one of the trees, while a blond woman, who had to be Natalie Fairchild, stood next to them. Her right hand was out of sight in a pocket of the dress she wore, so Luke suspected she was holding a gun.

Myra and Priscilla had to recognize him, but they looked at him without a sign of that on their faces. They must have figured out that he was trying some scheme to rescue them. More than likely, they believed that Ace and Chance were somewhere close by, too.

Luke hoped sincerely that they were, since Scranton and Porter stepped out from behind different trees and pointed rifles at him.

"Who are you, mister?" Scranton demanded harshly.

"Take it easy, friend," Luke drawled. "I don't mean any harm. Just need some water for me and my horse." He glanced at the women. "If I'm intruding on something here, just give me a few minutes at the spring, and then I'll be on my way."

"I don't know about that," Porter said. "That's a good-looking horse you've got there. You may have noticed we're one short."

"Nope," Luke said. "You brought—"

"I know him!" Scranton yelled as the barrel of his rifle tipped up more. "He fought with the Jensens back in town!"

Well, that tore it, Luke thought as he kicked his feet free of the stirrups and dived out of the saddle. The shot Scranton fired ripped through the air where he had been an instant earlier.

Porter was probably the most dangerous of the two, even though Scranton had gotten off the first shot. Luke's Remingtons were in his hands by the time he hit the ground. He rolled as Porter cranked two rounds from the Winchester. The slugs tore up the ground inches away from Luke. He came to a stop on his belly and tilted the long-barreled revolvers up.

Gun-thunder rolled from the Remingtons as Luke pounded half a dozen bullets into Anse Porter's gaunt frame. The slugs rocked Porter back, but in a display of stubborn hate, the gunman stayed on his feet and tried to bring his rifle to bear again. Luke put him down with a final shot to the head.

That left Scranton to deal with. A bullet screamed past Luke's ear. He twisted in that direction, but before he could fire, hoofbeats filled the air and Chance shouted, "Scranton!"

Luke lifted his head and saw his sons charging in from different directions, both with guns in their hands spurting fire. Slugs from the Colt and the Smith & Wesson slammed into Scranton and sent him reeling back. He dropped the rifle, pressed his hands to his chest, and stood there swaying for a second before he toppled over. He didn't move again.

Luke pushed himself up on one knee and looked toward the tree where Myra and Priscilla had been when the shooting started. Priscilla peeked out from behind that tree, where she had taken cover.

A few feet away, Myra knelt on top of an apparently unconscious Natalie Fairchild. Luke grinned. The Fairchild woman already had a bruise starting to show on her jaw. That must have been a pretty sweet punch Myra had landed on her while all hell had been breaking loose elsewhere.

"I don't know what she thought she was doing," Myra said as she pushed back some hair that had fallen over her face. "I already whipped her once, and I was damned sure going to do it again."

"Lady, I don't know you," Luke said as he got to his feet, "but I don't think I'd ever bet against you in a fight."

"Is . . . is it over?" Priscilla asked.

Ace swung down quickly and went to her. As he helped her up, he told her, "Yes, this time it really is." He smiled. "All except for Christmas."

Christmas Eve . . .

The singing that filled the mission hall tonight was one of the sweetest things Ace had ever heard. A lot sweeter than the gunfire that had thundered through here several days earlier.

He sat in the front row with Chance, Luke, Myra, and Dr. Allan Drake. The hall was as full as it had been for Chance's murder trial, but the atmosphere was a lot more festive, although it had grown more solemn as the group of children in the front of the room began singing "O Come, All Ye Faithful."

The song came to an end. Priscilla turned on the bench at the piano and smiled as the audience applauded. She waited until the clapping subsided, then launched into the first notes of "Silent Night."

The clear, beautiful voices of the children and the sentiment of the song made Ace a little misty eyed. He wasn't the only one, he saw as he glanced around. A number of people were discreetly wiping away tears, including Myra.

She saw him looking at her and whispered, "You just hush up, Ace Jensen. I am *not* getting softhearted!"

"Nothing wrong with it if you are," he told her. "A little softheartedness never hurt anybody."

"Yeah, it's softheadedness that does," Chance added.

When the song was finished and the applause had died away again, Priscilla stood up, faced the audience, and said, "That concludes our Christmas celebration—"

"No it don't!" a high-pitched voice called from the back of the hall.

The crowd parted to let Nick Beltz through. He had just come in from outside and was dressed in his buffalo coat and fur cap. He carried a canvas sack in his right hand. Baldur, Folke, and Haldor Steingrim followed him, all still sporting various bandages on their huge, muscular frames.

"I've got somethin' here for the young'uns," Beltz went on as he came up the aisle toward the front of the room. "Since me and these Scandihoovian varmints been sort of laid up, anyway, we passed the time by makin' toys and gimcracks. Got plenty here for all the little sprouts, not just the ones singin' up there. Come an' get 'em!"

That started a stampede of children to the front of the room, where Beltz and the Steingrim brothers opened the sack and spent the next few minutes passing out gifts to all the youngsters. The adults crowded around to watch with joy the glee the children displayed at getting these presents, even though most of them were just small carved figurines. In a place like Panamint City, those were true treasures.

Ace found himself standing beside Priscilla. He slipped his

arm around her shoulders, and she snuggled against him, with a big smile on her face.

"Mr. Beltz is a saint," she murmured.

"Oh, I'm sure Nick would deny that," Ace told her. "In fact, he was planning to sneak in here tonight, after everybody was gone, and leave the toys, so that no one would know who brought them. Chance and I talked him out of it. There's no reason why he shouldn't get credit for doing something good."

"Maybe this will start a tradition."

"Maybe so." Ace paused, then said, "There's a present for you, too, you know."

She turned her head to look up at him in surprise. "For me? I don't need anything."

"Maybe not, but this mission does. And Chance and Nick are going to see that it gets it. Nick was ready to hand over the mine, lock, stock, and barrel, to Chance—"

"That means you'll be staying here," Priscilla said as a smile began to appear on her face again.

It pained Ace to say it, but he wasn't going to lie to her. "Not exactly."

She looked confused again. "What does that mean?"

"Chance doesn't want to run a silver mine, and neither do I. So he and Nick came to an agreement, and Dr. Drake helped them draw up the papers. Nick and the Steingrim brothers will keep on running the mine. Nick gets a third of the profits, and so does Chance. They'll split the wages for Folke, Baldur, and Haldor between them, and Nick will send Chance's share to a bank in Denver."

"I don't understand," Priscilla said. "Do you get the other third?"

Ace shook his head. "Nope. That goes to the mission, to support it from now on."

Her eyes widened. She said, "But that could amount to a fortune!"

"If it is, then you'll never have to worry about running out of the money your father left you. And you'll be able to continue doing good work here for as long as Panamint City is around. Myra told me she's going to stay around and help you, too."

"That's wonderful, and wonderfully generous. I won't deny that. But what are you and Chance going to do?"

"That's just it," Ace said with a smile of his own. "We don't know. We won't know what we're doing, or where we're going, until we get there."

Priscilla regarded him intently for a long moment, then said, "And that's the way the two of you like things, isn't it?"

"It's the way we've always lived," Ace admitted, "and I don't reckon we're ready to give it up just yet. But we'll never forget Panamint City. Might even come back here, one of these days."

"I can't guarantee that everything will be the same as when you left."

"I don't expect that it will be," Ace said, thinking about Dr. Allan Drake. The doc was a mite stuffy at times, but he was a good man, no doubt about that. Priscilla's feelings might warm to him, or they might not. But that would be for them to work out.

The Jensen brothers would be gone by then, answering the siren call of whatever was over the next horizon. . . .

But not just yet. Not just yet. Ace leaned over, brushed his lips against Priscilla's midnight-dark hair, and murmured, "Merry Christmas."

France, December 24, 1917

"Very heartwarming," the major said. "And full of action and excitement, just as you promised. Totally unbelievable, of course."

"Hey, are you saying my dad and uncle lied when they told me and my cousins all about it?"

"Fathers often exaggerate, especially when relating their exploits to their children."

The lieutenant said, "Well, maybe so, but in *my* family, truth's got a habit of being stranger than fiction, as they say."

"Perhaps." The major frowned. "But they spent very little time actually *in* Death Valley."

"Maybe not, but that's where all the trouble finally wrapped up. And they were close by the rest of the time."

"And what happened to the Fairchild woman? You didn't say anything about that."

"They let her go, with the promise that she'd leave town and never come back. She had helped Scranton hide the doctor but hadn't really done anything else. As far as I know, she took the deal, and nobody in those parts ever saw her again."

"Rather chivalrous, considering her behavior."

Before either of them could continue, one of the other pilots, a small redheaded young man, came over and said, "You think the Huns are gonna leave us alone tonight, Major?"

"I certainly hope so, Nippy."

"Me too," the young pilot muttered. "I've heard that both sides on the front call a truce on Christmas Eve."

The major held up a finger. "That happened only one time, early in the war. Neither side has felt generous enough to do such a thing since."

"Well, then, tonight'd be a good time to start up the tradition again, wouldn't it, Major Lufbery?" Nippy said.

"You'd hear no complaints from me if that were to—" the major began. He stopped short as somewhere nearby, a siren wailed through the night.

"Blast it!" the lieutenant exclaimed as he came to his feet. "Tonight, of all nights, the Huns have to fly over here and try to jab a stick in our eyes!"

"We shall jab right back at them," Major Lufbery said as all around the room, the other pilots scrambled to grab their flying jackets and helmets. He reached down to pet Soda, the lion cub, one more time, then stood up and joined the exodus to the aerodrome's field, where the mechanics were already warming up the engines in the ranks of parked Nieuport 28s.

"I'm gonna stick close to you tonight, Deuce," Nippy called to the lieutenant as they hurried after the major. "You're a heck of a flier, and I never saw anybody who can shoot like you."

"It runs in the family," Lieutenant William Jensen, Jr., better known as Deuce, called laughingly over his shoulder as he hurried to do battle with the enemy.